This desert oasis has gone ṭ

(Not the dogs tḥ ...ᵤₛₛ are fine.)

TROUBLE PLAY

Comedian EV Lane thought she'd done it all, but taking on the role of mistress of ceremonies for the Desert Fancy Dog Show may be her most challenging gig yet. The locals are a menagerie of high-strung prima donnas and nervous Nelsons, and she's not talking about the dogs.

When high-stakes competition leads to gruesome murder, she's going to need every telepathic power at her disposal—and every psychic friend she knows—to make this show go on. Pesky police detectives, dangerously attractive investigators, and a menagerie of our favorite Vista de Lirio characters make this mystery the most twisted yet!

TROUBLE PLAY is the third book in the Vista de Lirio series, a paranormal mystery series by Elizabeth Hunter, best-selling author of the Elemental Mysteries, the Glimmer Lake series, and The Irin Chronicles.

Praise for Elizabeth Hunter

A fantastic cosy mystery, full of twists and a little spice.

— SASSAFRACK, GOODREADS

Elizabeth Hunter's books are delicious and addicting, like the best kind of chocolate. She hooked me from the first page, and her stories just keep getting better and better. Paranormal romance fans won't want to miss this exciting author!

— THEA HARRISON, NYT BESTSELLING AUTHOR

Developing compelling and unforgettable characters is a real Hunter strength.... Another amazing novel by a master storyteller!

— RT MAGAZINE

The bottom line: if you're not reading Elizabeth Hunter's novels, you should be!

— A TALE OF MANY BOOK REVIEWS

This book more than lived up to the expectations I had, in fact it blew them out of the water.

— THIS LITERARY LIFE

Trouble Play

A VISTA DE LIRIO MYSTERY

ELIZABETH HUNTER

Trouble Play

ISBN: 978-1-941674-98-7

Paperback edition

Cover Designer: Karen Dimmick/Arcane Covers
Content Editor: Amy Cissell
Line Editor: Anne Victory/Victory Editing
Proofreader: Linda/Victory Editing

For more information, please visit ElizabethHunterWrites.com

Recurve Press, LLC
PO Box 4034
Visalia, CA 93278
USA

For Charlie,
Chidi,
and Simba

Also for Abbie and Regal,
And always and forever,
For Mac, the bestest boy

Note from the author:

No canine, feline, or camelid (real or imagined) was harmed during the writing of this book.

There were, however, countless hours that the author's dogs did not receive either attention, pats, or treats. Please appreciate their sacrifice in the creation of this fictional work.

Chapter One

The camera operator drew nearer, and Evy fixed her smile as Lexi Storm, morning news anchor and fixture of Palm Springs society, opened the live segment.

"It's that time of the year again, dog lovers. The Desert Fancy Kennel Club Dog Show is almost here, and I'm with this year's hosts, local entertainer EV Lane and—all the way from the London, England—Chip Dunklin!" Lexi turned away from the camera and pointed her perfectly white smile at Evy and Chip. "Thanks for being with me this morning, you guys. Evy, great to see you again. Are you excited about this? I'm so excited about this!"

"Happy to be here." Evy turned on her television persona. "I am *so* excited. I'm feeling a little sorry for Chip though." Evy pointed at her cohost. "He's the knowledgeable, serious person who's going to have to correct my mistakes all week. I'm just that lady who loves dogs."

It wasn't the first time Evy had appeared on *Desert Daily*, but it was the first time when she'd been highly medicated. The world around her felt a little muffled, but it was better than the telepathic onslaught she'd been fearing.

Chip chuckled jovially—playing the part of the kindly, seasoned professional—and responded to Evy in a soothing British accent. "I'm sure Evy will be an amazing cohost. I can already tell she's a dog lover, and what's not to love?" He spread his hands and looked around. "In just a few days, the convention center will be full of intense competition, the thrill of victory, and I'm sorry to say, probably a few disappointed howls."

Evy turned to Lexi. "Chip's talking about the owners and handlers of course. The dogs are much better sports."

Both Chip and Lexi laughed, and Evy was grateful she only heard their audible voices and not the rush of garbled dialogue that made up the mental background noise of most people's minds.

For months she'd been learning to live with a form of telepathy that forced other people's thoughts into her head. It was confusing, exhausting, and the only way she'd managed to control it a little bit was with heavy antianxiety medication.

Evy wasn't an insecure person—you couldn't survive in the comedy world if you were insecure—but lately she felt like she'd been battling for her sanity.

"I do think that dog shows attract very strong personalities though, don't they?" Lexi directed her attention at Chip. "And this year the kennel club has made this an open. Chip, as the experienced dog-show professional in the group, what does that mean?"

"That's a great question." Chip turned his beaming smile to the camera. "The president of the Desert Fancy Kennel Club, the visionary Bunny Butterfield Barker, has decided that this year the annual competition should not only celebrate dogs from local and national shows but a select group of international competitors as well."

"Wow!" Lexi said. "How did they qualify?"

Chip continued. "These are all champions in their own respective countries who have been invited by the club to take part in this show."

"That's amazing!" The television host was grinning. "So this is not just a national show anymore but an international one?"

"That's right." Evy popped in. "There are dogs and handlers coming from purebred-dog clubs in Asia, the Middle East, and South America this year. It's really exciting."

"Chip, you've been working in the dog-show world your whole career, isn't that right? Is this a common thing? To have an international show like this?"

"It's a bit unusual in the US, Lexi. Definitely a way to put the Desert Fancy Kennel Club show on the map for international breeders."

Evy might have felt out of her depth in the technical aspects of Dog Show World, but at least she looked good. Her two best friends had helped her pick out her slim black suit. With her chin-length hair recently trimmed and new blunt-cut bangs that emphasized her large eyes, Evy knew she looked striking, which was what she needed with a cohost who looked like he'd been born to wear a tuxedo.

Lexi was still focused on Chip. "And you've been working with dogs your whole life, is that right?"

Chip's warm brown eyes were fixed on Lexi. "My father was a Norwich terrier breeder, and I grew up handling the dogs for local shows. That grew into around ten years of professional handling in the dog-show world. In all those years, I've never seen a competition like this. It's very exciting."

"You've worked with some of the owners and breeders who are participating this week, isn't that correct?" Lexi's eyebrows rose. "Now is that a conflict of interest?"

Chip smiled, and Evy couldn't help but think that Chip and Lexi looked like a matched pair, Lexi with her carefully coiffed hair and Chip with his neat jacket and perfect accent.

If she left, would they notice?

"Luckily, I'm not *judging* this competition," Chip said. "And I have my wonderful cohost to keep me in check." Chip turned to

---

Evy, and his eyes lit up. "I've only just met Miss Lane, but I'm confident this is going to be one of my favorite commenting jobs. It's wonderful to have a cohost who knows so much local color."

Evy nudged his shoulder with her own. "That's polite British-speak for I know all the local gossip." Evy turned to the camera and winked. "Better watch the dog show, *Desert Daily* viewers. You never know what secrets might slip out."

"Now that's a promise!" Lexi laughed. "Evy, I can't wait to listen to you and Chip for the broadcast. When is everything starting?"

Chip answered again. "This is a benched show, so the owners will show up starting on Monday of next week to get their stations set up, the pens situated, and allow the animals to acclimate before the breed judging starts on Tuesday."

Evy added, "We'll have an opening ceremony on Wednesday; then group judging will start on Thursday. Chip and I will be there to be your guides for everything."

"And it will run through the weekend?"

"The Best in Show judging will be on Sunday afternoon," Evy said. "But there are hundreds of wonderful dogs that visitors will be able to visit and observe in the convention hall starting on Tuesday, along with visiting the vendor market, of course."

"Shopping." Lexi's eyes lit up. "I understand there will be over one hundred vendors at the show this year?"

Push the vendor market. That's what Lorain, the show chairwoman, had emphasized. "That's correct," Evy said. "Palm Springs is a shopping town, and this show will have something for everyone. There are vendors catering to two-footers and four-footers at the market."

Lexi kept her brilliant smile fixed on Evy, who grinned back like she'd been caught on hostage video. It felt unnatural and uncontrollable.

"And what about the kids?" Lexi asked. "I'm assuming this is family friendly?"

Evy kept going. "Watching dogs on TV is always fun, but the show organizers have gone out of their way to make this a real family event. There are crafts, activities, games, and a petting area, so please come down and bring the kids. They're going to have a blast."

Chip added, "That's one of the best things about dog shows, Lexi. They really are wonderful entertainment for the entire family."

"Chip, Evy. Thank you so much for joining me today, and I cannot wait for next week." Lexi turned to the camera. "After the break we have the current Best in Show title holder coming to visit us! That's right—Baron, the legendary standard poodle, and the woman herself, Bunny Butterfield Barker, are up next along with one of the international guests this year, Juliet Lomax of London and her adorable miniature schnauzer Jade."

There was a pause, and then a camera operator shouted, "And we're off. One minute thirty, Lex."

Evy felt her gut unclench, and with that moment of relaxation, a flood of background voices managed to slip in.

—*ready for the nine o'clock*—

—*think I'll get a wrap for*—

—*noticed me? She hadn't even looked*—

Nope. The jumbled voices weren't welcome. Evy closed her eyes and clamped down on the mental shields she'd been practicing for months.

"Thanks, guys! You were great." Lexi jumped off her tall chair and hustled to the wings where a young woman was holding a bottle of water and a mirror. "Evy, I expect you to drop some shockers."

Evy laughed, but it sounded brittle to her own ears. "I'll see what I can do."

"That's not the EV Lane I know!"

"What can I say, Lex? They're keeping me on a short leash for this one."

Chip was already off to the side, chatting with an older woman in full show regalia who had a black standard poodle sitting near her feet. Near them stood an elegant woman in a brilliant orange wrap dress who carried a tiny brown dog with curled whiskers in her arms.

Evy guessed that Bunny Barker was the tiny White woman with a silver bob wearing a designer suit. The woman next to her was much taller, Black, and carried herself with a regal air. She had to be the international competitor, Juliet Lomax from the UK.

Evy wandered over and held her hand out to the black poodle. "Hey there."

The poodle ignored her, keeping his eyes fixed on Bunny and Chip, but the small brown dog shook in her owner's arms and barked with righteous ire.

"Jade, no." The tall woman tapped the dog's nose and gave Evy a cutting look. "Please don't stress the animals."

"I'm sorry, I shouldn't have—"

"No, you shouldn't have." Bunny cut her eyes away toward Chip. "Charles, nice to see you. We need to get the dogs on the stage, but I'll talk to you later."

Bunny led the other woman and the two dogs onto the stage where they took their place on a low couch an assistant pointed out to them. The black dog named Baron immediately sat at attention on Bunny's left side while the little brown dog turned in circles, inspecting the area before she settled down.

The broadcast had come back, and a chirpy meteorologist with abundant curls was sharing the weather forecast.

"I used to work for her."

The weather lady? Evy turned to Chip. "Who?"

Chip nodded at the stage.

Evy's eyebrows went up. "The Lomax lady from London?"

"No—Bunny." He smiled. "I worked for Bunny."

"She's not very happy Lorain hired me, you know."

"I'd heard there was some tension." Chip smirked a little.

"Bunny has very fixed opinions, but she's not bad at heart." He nodded at Baron. "I was Bunny and her ex-husband Stewart's handler in the show ring for years. I probably know her dogs better than she does."

Evy didn't know what to say to that. "Well... That one doesn't look neglected."

"Oh no, Baron is the pampered prince. Did you see his collar?"

"I didn't notice." Evy looked back at the dogs. "*Very* sparkly."

Chip leaned closer as the forecast ended and the camera turned back to Lexi, Bunny, the British woman, and the two champion dogs sitting at their feet.

"Those aren't rhinestones," he said. "They're not even crystals."

Evy's eyes went wide. "You can't mean—"

"Twin custom-made Cartier chokers," Chip said. "Platinum with diamonds for her dog Zara and platinum with diamonds and onyx for Baron. I heard someone say her ex-husband spent something like a million dollars for the pair."

Holy shit, that was insane. "Who spends that much money for dog collars?"

"Bunny." Chip looked amused. "They had a custody fight, you know."

"Wouldn't their kids be too old for that?"

"No kids. The custody fight was about the dogs."

Evy's mouth dropped open. "No way."

"They had a huge kennel, but Bunny's ex ended up with most of the younger dogs, and Bunny got the prize. They both agreed that Baron and Zara shouldn't be separated, so she got them both."

And their collars. Evy shook her head. "Lexi was right. These dog shows attract some very strong personalities."

Chip's eyes hadn't left the two dogs on the stage. "You have no idea."

EVY GOT HOME AND CAREFULLY HUNG HER BLACK SUIT in the closet. She only had three designer outfits that fit in with the Palm Springs society crowd, and those pieces had been carefully chosen.

"Aunt Marie?" She slipped into a pair of linen joggers and a cropped tank top. She might have hated having a flat chest when she was younger, but the older she got, the more she loved her lack of boobs. "Marie?"

Evy lived with her aunt, which suited both of them most of the time. They were independent, busy with their own work, and didn't step on each other's toes too often.

She wandered out to the kitchen in Marie's midcentury home and poured herself a glass of iced tea, then rinsed her breakfast dishes from the morning and set them in the strainer to dry. They didn't have a dishwasher, and with just the two of them, it didn't seem that important.

The house was her aunt's and hadn't been updated much since the 1970s. There was still shag carpet and dark wood paneling. The roof needed to be replaced, and the whole place needed an exterior coat of paint.

She didn't pay rent, but the house wasn't hers either. Updates or big projects were always a stress for Evy. How much did she contribute? Was the house going to be hers someday, or would Aunt Marie leave it to another relative? If it wasn't going to be hers, should she really be the one to pay for a new roof?

Evy was forty-four, still lived with her aunt, and didn't own her own home. With real estate the way it was in Palm Springs, she'd probably never be able to afford one.

Her best friends were a real estate mini-mogul, a dentist, and trust fund babies with real estate, vacation homes, and fancy cars. She hung out with rich people without ever having any hope of paying back their generosity.

It wasn't that she couldn't pay the bills. Her pool-cleaning company was humming along at a good pace and made her excellent money, and though her hosting and comedy work had taken a hit when she'd been "blessed" with telepathy, that was picking up again too.

If she could use Geoff...

She glanced at her ventriloquist dummy in the corner of the room. She'd picked up Geoff years ago from a secondhand shop and developed a whole comedy routine where Geoff was a rude old man and she was the zany sidekick who tried to keep him in line. It worked because ventriloquism was a dying art and also because she was a damn good joke writer and performer.

But the revelation two years before that her dummy was literally haunted by the ghost of its former owner had put a damper on her routine. Agents still called to book her and Geoff, but Evy didn't have the heart.

She felt bad about putting Geoff in his box, but she also didn't want to talk to him. He stayed in a corner of the living room, and the only one who acknowledged his existence was Aunt Marie, who was far from fazed by any of her niece's supernatural quirks.

Evy heard keys rattle in the front door, then the familiar sound of her aunt's voice.

"Evelyn?"

"I'm in the kitchen."

The door closed, and Aunt Marie's keys jingled in the tray by the front door. She'd been at the hairdresser that morning.

"Hey, kid." Marie walked through the door and smiled when she saw Evy. "How was the TV thing?"

"Good. How was the hairdresser?" Evy could already see that Aunt Marie had taken a new color challenge.

"Purple." Marie held out a long curl. "What do you think?"

"Looks good with your silver."

"That's what I thought." The old woman reached for a mug

and swirled the dregs of coffee that were left in the glass carafe. "I'm making a new pot. You want some?"

"Too hot."

"It'll cool you off." Marie started making a piping-hot pot of coffee.

Marie was a firm believer that drinking hot things in hot weather would lower your body temperature. Evy wasn't sure if it was true, but she wasn't going to argue with her aunt.

"I'm good with the iced tea. Thanks."

"You'll see when you get older."

Statements like that made Evy feel her age. She was "older," so why did she feel like she was still learning how to adult at her age?

"The British guy seems nice," Evy said. "He used to work for Bunny Barker."

"I'd send my apologies, but it sounds like he escaped."

Evy smiled. "What's so wrong with Bunny?"

"Other than having a stick the size of a saguaro cactus wedged up her backside?" Marie flipped on the coffee maker and turned. Her expression was all amusement. "Nothing."

"Now that's a mental picture." Evy shook her head. "She certainly comes across as a prima donna every time she emails me."

"Is she the one who hired you? Shouldn't she be grateful you agreed to host this craziness?"

"She didn't hire me," Evy said. "She's president of the kennel club, but the board is in charge of putting a chairperson in place to head up the dog show, and apparently the lady who's in charge this year, Lorain Matthews, is Bunny's mortal enemy or something."

"And the mortal enemy is the one who hired you?"

Evy nodded. "Yeah, but Bunny keeps emailing with directions that contradict Lorain's, so you can see how fun that is for me."

"Sounds delicious." Marie's eyes were dancing. "Backstage drama is the best drama. Plus that will be a great place for you to practice."

"Marie, I really don't think it's a good—"

"The medication is an emergency measure, Evelyn." Marie walked over and put her hand on Evy's cheek. "You can't keep taking it forever; it dampens your abilities. The medications hide your gift."

And I'm fine with that.

She didn't say it; Marie would be horrified. Her aunt had always carried a touch of the second sight, and she wished she had more. For her, psychic powers were a gift. They were something to be cultivated and used to protect and guide the people she cared about.

But for Evy?

If she could snap her fingers and never hear another internal voice, she would. For her, telepathy was anything but a gift.

It was a curse, and one that medication had finally allowed her to conquer, at least most of the time. She could be in a crowded restaurant again. She could perform. She could even go on a date without hearing her partner's every thought.

If Marie thought she was giving up that freedom willingly, she was off her rocker.

Chapter Two

Friday morning Evy pulled her giant beast of a Cadillac up to her friend Sergio's house. Sergio had met Evy after she'd done a benefit show years ago for a charity his mother sponsored, and he'd subsequently collected her into his group of quirky friends.

Evy couldn't say she minded. Sergio and his husband, Dean, were two of the nicest people on the planet, and they had twin daughters who would probably take over the world someday plus a hell of an estate in the best neighborhood in Palm Springs, Vista de Lirio.

The streets of the neighborhood were winding and shaded by palms, jacarandas, and wispy paloverde trees. The estates were all surrounded by decorative walls, creating an atmosphere of hidden gardens and private nooks around every corner. It was a place that lent itself to exclusive parties, artists, old money, and—according to her friend Julia—many, many ghosts.

She spotted others in Sergio's friend collection as she walked up the path between the pool house and the main house. There was Julia, resplendent and tan in a flowing blue caftan. Her part-time boyfriend was nowhere in sight, but Mick might be on a movie set since he was a well-known film director.

Opposite Julia sat Genevieve de Winter, Sergio and Dean's next-door neighbor and Evy's personal hero. Genevieve was five feet tall on a generous day, had a salt-and-pepper pixie cut, and always wore large sunglasses that covered half her face. She was an artist of some kind, had been married to five husbands, and lived on an estate guarded by two illegal savannah cats and a three-legged poodle named Gaston.

Genevieve usually had some kind of interesting houseguest staying with her, and this morning was no exception. A regal woman with silver-blond hair sat next to her, sipping on a frothy cocktail and whispering something into Genevieve's ear. Both of the women were joined by dogs—Genevieve's standard poodle at her side, and the silver-haired woman had a long-haired dog seated on her left, the dog's eyes sliding closed as it sat in the sun.

"Evy!" Sergio waved at her from behind the bar. "I'm making Ramos Gin Fizz as the cocktail of the day. Would you like one?"

Evy sat next to Julia. "That sounds amazing."

Julia elbowed her. "Saw you on the show yesterday morning. You looked fantastic."

"Thank you." Evy bowed toward her. "Your fashion advice was stellar, as always."

Genevieve pointed an empty cigarette holder at Evy. "The bangs suit you. Very Louise Brooks. You should always wear your hair that way."

And Genevieve had spoken.

"Thank you." Evy, never one to wait, leaned forward and held her hand out to Genevieve's friend. "Hi, I'm Evy Landa. EV Lane if you're a booking agent."

The woman set her drink down and took Evy's hand in hers. "I'm Marina Montegu Wesley, an old friend of Genevieve's." The woman's crisp British accent took Evy by surprise. "It's very nice to meet you. I'm in town for the dog show next week."

"Oh! I'll see you there. I'm cohosting with Chip Dunklin. We're the presenters for the event."

"Oh lovely." Marina gestured toward the dog at her feet. "You'll get to know Soraya then. I fully expect her to be in the finals this year with her handler Karim. She took first in the hound group last year, and as long as the judges aren't in Bunny's pocket again this year—"

"Marina..." Sergio's voice was amused. "We don't know that she paid them off. Baron is an exceptional dog."

Marina rolled her eyes. "Five years' worth of exceptional? Don't tell me his stack wasn't falling off a bit last year. They gave him Best for sentimental reasons. She was a fool to enter him again this year." She turned to Julia and Evy. "You'll hear nothing but show talk this weekend, I'm afraid."

Julia pointed at Sergio. "We expect it, knowing this one. He's determined that Cleo is going to win this year."

Evy knew that Sergio bred and showed his golden retrievers, but she somehow hadn't realized that he'd be competing at the event she was hosting. "You're showing Cleo? What about Caesar?"

Sergio's smile was sad. "Caesar had his final show last year. He's a champion so many times over I didn't want to push it, and Cleo just lives for the ring. She loves showing off. She was my better bet to beat Bunny this year."

Julia sipped her gin fizz. "You people and your fancy dogs." She glanced at Evy. "Mick is talking about getting another one, but he goes the mutt route. Heck, he's due home tomorrow from Thailand, and I half expect him to have a dog in his suitcase."

"Awww." Evy didn't have any pets, but she loved animals. She was on Mick's team though. The only dogs the Landas had ever had growing up were the kind that wandered into her dad's shop and wouldn't leave. "I think that's so cool. Then he'd have someone to keep him company when he's on location."

"That's the idea since I'm mostly stuck here." Julia's job as a real estate agent didn't afford her much time for long trips, though she was supposed to be cutting back. "So how's Geoff lately? You haven't brought him around much."

Julia was a medium, which meant she could directly communicate with Evy's haunted dummy. "You know I always feel left out of those conversations."

"Bullshit," her friend said. "You're avoiding him."

"I don't need him to read people anymore, so he's kind of..."

"Uncomfortable? Stressful? Intrusive?"

"I just don't need him, all right? I don't need him to be funny. Isn't that a good thing?"

Julia pursed her lips. "It's not a bad thing except that I really do think you miss him. You're not doing as many comedy gigs as you used to, and I think it's because you and Geoff need to work things out."

Genevieve frowned. "Who is Geoff?"

"Geoff is my ventriloquist dummy," Evy said.

"And he's possessed by the spirit of the original owner, a really nice ghost named Geoffrey," Julia added. "He's part of the reason Evy unlocked her telepathy."

"Of course." Genevieve sipped her drink and reached for a croissant.

Marina's eyes were wide. "Excuse me, did you say—"

"I'll explain it later, my dear." Genevieve patted Marina's hand. "Where's Rafe gotten to?"

Marina looked over Evy's shoulder. "He said something about the alpaca, and then I lost him. I think I see him coming up the driveway though."

"Oh?" Julia turned. "Oh look! There's Vivian, Richard, and Henry too."

Evy turned to see her friends walking along the pathway, accompanied by one of the singularly most attractive men she'd ever seen in her life.

"Here he is," Marina said. "Ladies, meet my son, Rafe Wesley Bamford-Howell."

The man approached Evy, his eyes already locked with hers, and Evy could feel the zings of attraction zipping between them. Good Lord, was everyone feeling this way? The man was absolutely magnetic, from his dark, shoulder-length hair to his vivid blue eyes.

He reached out his hand and took Evy's. "For the love of God, call me Rafe."

Accent. Accent alert.

Evy was a sucker for an accent, and Rafe Bamford-Howell had one in spades. It was that kind of easy, cultured, I'm-rich-but-we-don't-talk-about-it English accent that left Evy in a metaphorical puddle on the ground beneath Dean and Sergio's patio table.

Evy had moved on from feeling like the only woman in the world to a lucky bystander when she realized that Rafe flirted with everyone. Her, Julia, Genevieve, Sergio, even Baby Henry. He seemed particularly taken with Baby Henry, but then, all of them were.

"Look at all his hair." Rafe bounced the six-month-old on his knee. "God, I love it. Mum, did I have hair like that?"

"At least that much." Marina's eyes were warm on Rafe and the baby. "But we never lived anywhere that was as hot as Palm Springs." Her eyes turned to Vivian. "Are you going to cut it when summer comes?"

"We'll see." Vivian still had the rosy glow of new motherhood and new love. "I hate to even touch it, but he might be really hot." With Richard at her side, Vivian made single parenting in your forties look fashionable and chic.

Not that Evy was tempted. She had myriad nieces and nephews

to carry on the Landa name, and she had no desire to add to the gene pool.

"Rafe's sister has four small ones," Marina said. "So he's a very practiced uncle."

"They're all in Denver though." Rafe popped a kiss on the top of Henry's fuzzy head. "And I'm in Arizona. I don't get to see them as much as Mum does." His eyes darted to Evy. "What about you, Evy?"

She smiled. "No kids for me, but I'm also wealthy in the auntie department. I work so much I don't even have time for a dog."

Genevieve harrumphed. "Everyone should have time for a dog. Tell your boss not to be such a bitch."

Evy smiled when she saw Rafe's mouth drop open.

"She's only saying that because I work for myself."

He frowned. "I'm not sure that makes it better."

"Fair point."

Rafe bounced Henry from his own knee over to Richard's waiting arms on his left side. "There you go, little man."

Richard turned to Vivian. "I think he'd take a bottle if you have one ready."

"I do."

"And brunch is served." Dean walked out of the kitchen and gestured to the door. "We're keeping everything inside, so make yourself at home and grab a plate."

All the guests filtered into Sergio and Dean's expansive kitchen and took turns filling their plates with quiche, fruit salad, and some of the pastries Julia had brought. Drinks were refilled and chaos reigned until Evy escaped outside, thankful not to be stuck in the crowded house.

While her shields were holding with the help of her new medication, interior spaces with a lot of people were still the hardest place to be. She couldn't help but feel the press of thoughts and the energy of so much thinking without getting a fairly intense headache.

Vivian sidled up to her just as she was heading out the door. "Hey, could you take Richard this plate? He's giving Henry a bottle, so I made him one."

Evy smiled. "You two have been very cozy the past couple of months."

Vivian smiled. "It's good cozy, not smothering cozy." She glanced out the window. "Richard's so enthusiastic about all the little parenting things—it's hard to deny him."

"I think it's sweet," Evy said. "And you can tell that Henry just adores him."

Richard was an old friend of Dean's who'd only discovered he was a father when his grown daughter had shown up and made herself known in her late twenties. He'd missed out on all the younger years, so even though he was in his early sixties, he was absolutely thrilled to participate in all the baby chores with Vivian's new son.

Evy, on the other hand, had spent her childhood taking care of younger siblings and cousins. If she never changed a diaper again, it would be too soon.

She walked out and gave Richard his plate, then sat down, leaving a space for Rafe to join them.

"Vivian said you're hosting the dog show this year," Richard said. "I'm neighbors with Bunny Barker, you know."

"Oh really?"

"Yes, her property juts right up to mine along the hills. I've had a few poodles in my yard over the years."

Evy took a bite of quiche. "They seem like nice dogs though."

"They are, and very well trained. It wasn't a big deal. I enjoyed the visits, though it annoyed Bunny and Stewart any time the dogs went missing, especially Baron."

"He's the champion everyone is talking about winning the dog show, right?"

Richard nodded. "Gorgeous animal but also a beautiful temperament. Bunny breeds him to her female Zara. I think I asked out of curiosity once, and their puppies go for some ridiculous amount like ten thousand dollars apiece. I was floored."

"Ten thousand for a dog?" Evy nearly choked. "Then again, they put Cartier collars on them, so I shouldn't be surprised."

"I just hope he hasn't wandered too far this time."

Evy paused, her fork hovering over her plate. "What do you mean? I saw him yesterday morning at the television studio."

"There were two police cruisers over at the house this morning before we left." Richard frowned. "I'm sure it's nothing, but one of them mentioned Baron was missing. Asked me if they could search my garden. I said yes, of course."

"But you said he does that fairly often? Run away?"

Richard nodded. "Usually only on our street though."

Vivian came to join them. "Are you talking about Baron going missing?"

Richard nodded. "Evy met Baron at the television station yesterday."

"He's so sweet, right?" Vivian set down her plate and reached for Henry, who had finished his bottle. "Baron has that crazy haircut, but you have a feeling he really just wants to roll in the mud."

Evy shook her head. "If he's going to compete, they better find him before Tuesday. All the dogs have to be registered by then. Side note: I know way more about dog shows than I ever expected to. Weird, right?"

Richard smiled. "The owners in the show community are very intense."

"I'm thinking about getting a dog for me and Henry," Vivian said. "The next time Sergio breeds Cleo and Caesar. I've always wanted one, and Sergio's dogs are so amazing."

"Golden retrievers are wonderful dogs," Richard said. "Great with kids."

Evy couldn't stop thinking about Baron, that beautiful ink-black poodle with a small fortune fixed around his neck. Had

Bunny's generosity with her dogs made them a target? It was a horrible prospect but all too likely.

"Poor Baron."

Vivian looked at her. "I'm sure he'll show up. Everyone in the neighborhood knows him, and he's so friendly."

"Unless someone took him," Richard said. "I'm sure the police have to look into that as well."

A dog with a half-million Cartier dog collar around his neck? Who would dare steal that?

Only everybody.

"Bunny must be going out of her mind," Vivian said. "I've only talked to her a few times, but every conversation we have is about her dogs. She lives and breathes for them."

Richard nodded. "She and Stewart had an actual custody fight about Baron and Zara when they split."

"I heard that." Evy shook her head. "Let's hope he shows up soon."

"Poor Bunny," Richard said. "She must be worried sick."

Chapter Three

E vy was sitting in her dressing room, Chip lounging on the couch, when they heard a knock on the door. She looked up from the notebook they'd been using to outline their introductions and commercial breaks.

"Come in!"

Chip sat up and took his feet off the ragged coffee table where he'd propped them. "Hello?"

Evy saw the familiar face of John Marcos, Palm Springs chief of police in her doorway. "Hey. What are you doing here?"

He shrugged and stepped through the door, wearing his typical uniform of khaki pants and a white-collared golf shirt. "I'm a dog lover obviously."

"Okay..." Evy didn't believe him for a minute. She viewed cops the way someone born into a borderline criminal clan would. They were to be avoided, distrusted, and evaded, in that order. The fact that she'd helped John Marcos on more than one murder investigation didn't mean she trusted him, it just meant she distrusted him less than other cops.

Chip stood. "Hello, I'm Chip Dunklin. I'm cohosting with Evy."

"Yep, you're on my list." John took Chip's offered hand and shook it. "I'm actually here to ask you a few questions. The director lady..." He pointed to his ear. "Or whoever she is—the one with the headphones and like three radios—she told me that you'd be writing with Evy."

Chip frowned. "Why am I on a list?"

"I need to ask you a few questions about the dog."

"What dog?"

Evy's heart sank. "Does this mean Baron was stolen?"

Chip's eyes went wide. "Oh my God, something happened to Baron?" He looked at John. "What about Zara? Is Zara okay?"

"Zara?" John frowned.

"Bunny's other poodle," Evy said. "The white female. She had two show dogs, and they both had those crazy expensive collars on them."

"Ah." John nodded. "The other dog is fine. The dog... nanny? I don't know what you'd call someone who watches your dogs."

"Are you talking about Baron's handler?" Chip said. "I used to be Baron and Zara's handler before Bunny and Stewart divorced, and I'd often watch the dogs during the day, especially leading up to a show. The handler lost Baron?"

"Bunny said he'd let Baron out before he left for the day, so she didn't think anything was wrong for a while."

Chip was shaking his head. "So irresponsible for the handler to let him roam outside. I would never have let that happen. He's an intact male and his roaming instincts are very strong, especially if there's a bitch in the neighborhood."

John Marcos was staring at Chip. "Excuse me?"

"Dog bitch." Evy jumped in. "He means a female dog. Literally a female dog."

"Oh."

"Of course," Chip said. "What did you think I—?"

"The estate is fenced, but it backs up to the hills, so it's not out of the question that an animal could have gotten to him, but a standard poodle isn't a Pekinese. It wouldn't make an easy snack for a mountain lion or a coyote the way a cat or a small dog would."

Chip looked ill. "Bunny must be going insane. Baron and Zara are her entire world."

Evy raised her hand. "Listen, I don't want to be crass or uncaring about Baron going missing, but is anyone talking about the fact that this dog had half a million dollars hanging around his neck?"

John smirked. "Yeah," he said. "I have thought about it."

"I mean, I know the dog is valuable but—"

"I don't think you realize how valuable he is." Chip sounded indignant. "Baron is probably the most valuable poodle in the country right now. He's one of the only remaining males from a very prominent breeding program in Germany that can be traced back to the 1700s and the German royal family. He's *irreplaceable*."

"But so is his collar," Evy said. "I don't want to insult Baron, but let's be honest, a lot of people are going to see a dog wearing a Cartier necklace and think 'some people just have too much money.'"

John hadn't taken his eyes off Chip. "Mr. Dunklin, I understand there was bad blood between you and Mrs. Barker after she let you go?"

Chip's mouth was catching flies again. "I beg your pardon."

"Is it true? Did you and Bunny hate each other?"

"Not at all!" Chip's eyes darted around the room from Evy to John to her dressing table and back. "I mean... I-I wasn't happy that she wanted a new handler, but I understood. Stewart had been the one to hire me, and I always got on with the man." He threw up his hands. "But Bunny and I have buried the hatchet, as you say here. She even recommended me for this job."

"I need to ask where you were yesterday morning between six and seven a.m."

"This is outrageous." Chip crossed his arms over his chest. "I came here to lend some legitimacy to your little dog show, and now you're asking me—"

"It's a simple question, Mr. Dunklin." John pointed at Evy. "I'm going to ask her too."

Evy frowned. "Me?"

"Yeah." He looked at his notebook. "I believe Bunny mentioned that you might have been tempted to steal Baron by spending time around people who were—and these were her words—'not Miss Lane's typical social crowd.'"

Evy wanted to snort and laugh at the same time. "Well, at least I know what Bunny really thinks of me now. She's still pissed Lorain hired me." She looked at Chip. "Six in the morning? I was at home sleeping."

John asked, "Can anyone verify that?"

"My aunt Marie was home, but she was sleeping too. I didn't see her before I left for brunch."

John looked at Chip. "You?"

"At my hotel," Chip said through clenched teeth. "Alone. Are we done now?"

"You both essentially told me you don't have alibis for the time the dog went missing," John said. "I guess it goes without saying, but you should not leave town until we get some clarity on this."

Evy spread her hands. "I live here. Where am I going to go?"

"I'll be hosting the dog show, per my contract." Chip's accent had grown stiffer. "Then I will be leaving for London as I had planned. You have no evidence that I had anything to do with this because I didn't."

John nodded slowly. "As I said, Mr. Dunklin, I'm just asking questions right now. Thanks for your cooperation." He looked at Evy. "Miss Lane, I'll see you later."

Why?

She didn't say it out loud, but she didn't have any desire to get involved in this investigation. She felt sorry for the dog, but not enough to put her mental health at risk, which was exactly what John Marcos was going to want.

Stretch her psychic muscles over a missing dog? Nope. Not worth the pain and mental stress.

THE VENDOR MARKET AT THE DESERT FANCY KENNEL Club Dog Show was shaping up to be a microcosm of Palm Canyon Drive. Though none of the vendors could officially set up until Tuesday, they were allowed to bring in supplies and direct the carpenters on-site to customize the booths to their specifications.

While the dogs took center stage in front of the giant curtain, the marketplace was the focus behind. There were satin, designer dog carriers, and rhinestones. So. Many. Rhinestones.

"I guess they know their audience, huh?"

Evy turned to see John Marcos staring at the massive gateway being constructed to highlight the shops.

Evy smiled a little. "We're dealing with an entire community of people with gobs of disposable income, very few children at home, and a pathological need to one-up their neighbors," Evy said. "People spend way too much on dogs."

He sat in a ragged blue chair and kicked his heels up on a sawhorse. "Can't say I disagree. What's your read on Chip Dunklin?"

"Don't have one," Evy said. "At least not the kind you want. We've been writing material together for the show; that's about it."

John frowned. "You haven't gotten anything from..." He pointed to his temple. "Really? Nothing?"

"I take medication for that." She smiled. "It's literally the only thing that keeps me sane."

"I thought your puppet guy helped with that."

"Geoff?" She had to laugh. "No. I used to have to carry Geoff to hear other people. He was like a microphone. Then whatever it was that made me... hear... It's like it grew. Then I heard *everything* all the time." She leaned toward him. "Now I hear *nothing*, and I like it that way. Thank you, drugs."

"You can't just listen in when you want to?"

"Oh right. Maybe I should try that. Like..." She snapped her fingers. "I got it." She held up her hand. "Don't see this, okay? Just don't see it." She flipped him off. "How did that go?"

He rolled his eyes. "Okay, fine. It's like any other sense to you and you can't just turn it off. But isn't there a way of... I don't know, shielding your brain or something?"

"Yeah. It's called high doses of antianxiety pills and lots of meditation."

His lip curled up just a little. "I could use your help on this one, Landa."

"But I don't want to help you, and you can't make me." She flipped through her notebook. "You don't think me or Chip had anything to do with this, do you?"

"You? No. Chip?" He shrugged. "It's early. He could have done it, and the dog would have trusted him. He's a good suspect."

"He's staying in a hotel and flying back to England in a little over a week. You think he's going to smuggle a prize poodle out of the country in a week?"

"You're the one who pointed out that the dog had half a mill around his neck. Maybe Chip doesn't care about the dog."

"Then why take him at all? If Baron knows him, it would have been way easier to just take the collar and leave the dog if you wanted a quick getaway."

"True." He glanced at her. "See? You're good at this. That's why you should help me with this case."

"I can't tell you anything that you can't figure out yourself," Evy said. "I'm not Vivian or Julia. I can't use this *thing* a little bit.

It's like throwing myself into a crowded club where everyone is shouting in my ear." She shook her head. "I've tried meditation, shielding, all that shit. It doesn't work with the telepathy."

"So you're just going to pretend it's not there?"

"Yep." She patted his shoulder. "That is exactly the plan. Come to me if someone's life is actually at stake. I'm not risking my sanity for Bunny's dog and a fancy necklace."

"Are you sure? I understand there's a very handsome reward for finding Baron."

That made Evy pause. "How handsome are we talking about? Henry Cavill undeniably handsome or Benedict Cumberbatch weirdly handsome but nonetheless compelling?"

John frowned. "I don't know how to answer that. It's fifty thousand dollars."

Evy nearly choked. "Fifty thousand United States of America dollars?"

"And that's just for the dog."

"The reward doesn't mention the necklace?"

"Nope." He raised an eyebrow. "Interested yet?"

Yes. No. Definitely maybe? "I'll keep my eye out for anything or anyone here at the show. Why so much for one dog? I realize he was a champion and obviously really special, but—"

"Do you know how much they got for new puppies from Baron and Zara? Seven thousand for a pet and ten to fifteen thousand for a dog that they considered 'show quality.' Sometimes even higher than that if it was an unusual color."

"Good Lord." Evy had said it before and she'd say it again. "Some people just have way too much money."

"The important thing is, fifty thousand is a reasonable investment to get a dog like Baron back. So if I were you, I'd think about what edge I could use to find that pooch." He started to wander away. "And Landa?"

She turned and met his eyes. "Yeah?

"Keep your eye on Chip Dunklin. There's something about him that sets off my radar."

"Sounds like you need to be the department psychic, not me." It wasn't like she wasn't going to keep an eye on Chip anyway. He was her cohost for fuck's sake. "Take care, Chief Marcos."

Chapter Four

Saturday drinks with the girls varied in location, but that night they were meeting at Casa de Lirio, Richard's palatial house, and borrowing the pool and Richard as a bartender. Henry had already gone to sleep, so Vivian was relaxed and lounging in a loose summer dress while Julia and Evy sat on the steps of the pool.

"I'm just saying," Evy said. "If Richard wanted to marry you, it wouldn't be a bad thing."

Something hit Evy on the back of the head. She looked down and fished a waterlogged napkin out of the pool.

"You're starting to sound like my mother. Stop."

Julia only looked amused. "They've only been together for a few months."

"And you've been with Mick for like a year now, and you'll never marry him."

"I don't believe in marriage." Julia stared off into the distance. "It's incredibly beautiful tonight."

Richard's garden hosted a portal that attracted ghosts and spirits. It wasn't always there, but when it appeared, it produced a joyful and peaceful feeling in all three of them, which was one of the reasons Vivian had suggested they meet at Richard's tonight.

"Any ghost activity tonight?"

"No one crossing over that I've seen." Julia's smile was beatific. "Mae and Elton both came from Sergio and Dean's. They're just hanging out and partying with the band."

According to Julia, the Vista de Lirio neighborhood was chock-full of famous ghosts, but she rarely identified them.

"Hey, Evy?" Vivian called from the lounger. "Did John get ahold of you today?"

"I talked to him. Why?"

"I thought you might be able to help him out with the investigation. I don't think Julia or I would be much help, but with your telepathy—"

"Okay, I'm telling you the same thing I told John." She sipped her Paloma for courage. "You all have these nice, manageable gifts that don't make you crazy. If I flip that switch and stop my meds, I will very quickly become a slobbering mess. I cannot control it, and I'm not risking my mental health so that John can retrieve a fancy dog."

Julia said, "You should never have stopped your lessons with Maud."

"Maud wasn't helping," Evy said. "She said it herself. She'd never known anyone with true telepathy like mine, and she didn't know how to limit it without just cutting it off." Evy shrugged. "So we did, it worked, and I can function again. I'm fine with it."

"I guess that's fair," Vivian said. "After all, Bunny is distraught about Baron, but it's not like someone has been murdered. I have a feeling the dog will turn up with that giant reward on the table."

"The giant reward is the only thing I find tempting about the case," Evy said. "Fifty thousand dollars. I might be able to buy a run-down hovel on the edge of town with fifty grand as a down payment."

Julia lifted her sunglasses and frowned at Evy. "You never told me you wanted to move out of Aunt Marie's house."

"I don't really." Evy shrugged. "But you both own your own homes. I'm in my midforties now, and I own nothing other than my car. I feel like I'm... falling behind in life. I don't have a retirement account. I do have a profitable business, but I can't clean pools forever."

"Don't look at it that way," Vivian said. "Trust me, houses are a lot of work too. They're assets, but they cost money to maintain. Renting isn't a bad thing."

"Says the woman who has owned two homes already and is dating a millionaire."

"Okay, fair. But we all know you'd be making better money if you'd go back to performing with Geoff. Not all of this is inevitable."

Julia winced. "I hate to bring it up, but it's true. You know it's true."

Geoff. The ten-pound dummy in the room.

"I'm carving out a Geoff-free niche," Evy said. "Gives me more versatility. It'll be good in the long run, trust me."

"Okay." Vivian sat up and reached for the pitcher of Palomas to refill everyone's drink. "Just know that if you ever needed help or want to practice trying to tame your telepathy, we're here for you."

Evy's eyes drifted to the shadowed roofline of the mansion next to Richard's. While Richard's estate was a sprawling Spanish-style house that seemed to follow the line of the mountains, the mansion next to it jutted into the sky with confectionary arrogance. The Barker estate was a colonial revival house that looked as comfortable in the desert landscape as a duck in wading boots.

Evy stared at the Barker estate and sipped her drink. "Did I tell you what John Marcos told me today?"

"No. Something about Baron?"

"He told me that Bunny suggested he talk to me. That she said spending time with people who—as she put it—were not my typical social crowd might tempt me into dognapping and theft."

Vivian's eyes went wide. "Are you kidding me?"

"Nope."

Julia's mouth dropped open. "Look at the balls on that one. I don't even know what to say to that."

Seeing Julia's and Vivian's shock and disgust over the accusation soothed a part of Evy's ego she didn't know had been wounded. It wasn't that she didn't know her friends were better off than she was, but she'd never thought that made a difference to them. She'd never even thought they'd think about it until Bunny's accusation had weaseled into her brain.

"John knew it was bullshit too, but he said he had to ask."

Vivian's eyes were narrowed on the roof of the Barker estate like Evy's had been. "I have half a mind to march over and give Bunny Barker a piece of my mind."

"I'll never sell her a house," Julia said. "What a snob."

"Can you imagine working for her? That's what I was thinking about earlier," Evy said. "She probably accuses all her employees of stealing."

"Yeah, I bet she's a treat." Vivian stood and brushed off her dress. "I'm going to go over there."

Evy jumped out of the pool. "What? Don't be crazy. Vivian, I still have to work for her. She's the president of the kennel club, and she's the one calling all the shots for my job right now. Can you please—"

"She won't know it's about that." Vivian wore a wicked little smile. "But it just occurred to me that Bunny might have orchestrated all of this. How much you want to bet she's already contacted her insurance company, huh? About the Cartier necklace. Baron was probably insured too."

"That doesn't mean she orchestrated his dognapping," Julia said.

"In my experience, when people go around throwing accusations at others, it usually means they've thought of doing the exact same thing themselves." Vivian started walking toward the front of the house. "I'm going to go read how she's feeling. I'll bring a bottle of wine. You two coming?"

Julia and Evy both exchanged a look. Then Julia shrugged. "We're not going to stop her."

"I guess not."

And that's how Evy found herself wrapped in a sarong and walking through Bunny Barker's garden gate.

THE SOUND OF BARKING HIT THEIR EARS BEFORE THE dog came into sight. A large black poodle with short, sport-clipped hair and a silver-grey muzzle bounded toward them, paused fifteen feet away, and barked until they stopped walking.

"Bunny!" Vivian held up the bottle of wine. "It's Vivian Liu from next door. I just wanted to stop by and say hello."

Bunny walked out the front door and snapped her fingers. The poodle immediately went to her side and sat. "Vivian." Her voice was warm, but her eyes were unreadable. "How lovely of you to stop by. I just got home a few minutes ago." She carefully scanned the group. "And Miss Lane too. How are you?"

"Doing *great*." The third Paloma was starting to kick in, and Evy realized it had probably been a bad idea. It was hard to predict how alcohol would react with her meds, and this time it appeared the drinks were wearing down her shields, not making everything duller than normal.

So... that wasn't good.

"Would you like to join me for a drink?" Bunny sighed. "I have to admit with Baron gone, the house feels empty."

Vivian appeared as shocked as Evy by the invitation, but Julia jumped in. "That would be so nice. Always good to have a drink with neighbors." She walked forward, subtly tugging on Vivian's sleeve. "We'd love to."

"Good." She showed them all into the house. "I have coffee or wine—that's about all I drink since my doctor told me to cut back on gin martinis, though I could dearly use a martini these days. What do doctors know anyway?"

Evy stepped through the door of the house and felt a dull roar in the back of her head, as if she were hearing voices underwater.

"I think your doctor would understand a martini at a time like this." Vivian was loosening up. "I was so upset when I heard about Baron. Henry and I just loved his visits. Bunny, I'm so silly; you've met Julia Brooks, haven't you?"

"We met at the club once," Julia said. "But we didn't really get a chance to visit. I'm so sorry about your dog."

"Thank you." Bunny looked Julia up and down with an inquisitive stare. "You look like a dog person. Havanese?"

"Um..." Julia cocked her head. "No. No dogs right now, but I know someone with a Havanese and I've always thought they were great little dogs."

"I have a dear friend who breeds them. They're excellent for working women, but only if you can take your dog to the office. They don't like being left alone for too long. As long as they're with you though, they've very independent." She looked at Evy. "And you were born to have a greyhound. I can't think of any dog that would suit you better."

"Thanks?" Evy didn't know what to think of Bunny's pronouncements. Did she have her own psychic gift of picking the right dogs for people?

Bunny led them through the house, and Evy struggled to keep her expression even as the roaring grew louder behind her ears. The black poodle brought up the rear.

The voices turned from a dull roar to a watery murmur.

"So Bunny." Vivian was speaking again. "What do the police say? Have they gotten any leads since you announced the reward?

"Oh, hundreds I think." She walked down the central hall and into a large kitchen with granite countertops. A fair-haired poodle with a show cut lifted their head and examined the visitors. Bunny walked over and gave the dog an affectionate pat. "As you might guess from Zara's expression, none of them have been fruitful leads of yet. I'm wondering if the reward was a good idea."

"Did you suggest it or did the police?" Evy forced herself to ask.

Bunny stood straight, and Evy finally got a real look at her face. It wasn't coldness or disinterest like she'd initially thought. Bunny was suffering from bone-deep exhaustion.

"My insurance adjustor suggested the reward. They even offered to cover half the amount."

Bingo. Vivian was right; Bunny had already called her insurance.

"Interesting." Vivian was all ears. "I haven't thought about insuring dogs, but of course you'd have to if you're a professional dog breeder."

"Baron is priceless." The look on Bunny's face was genuinely heartbreaking, and Evy felt a corner of her heart thaw for the woman. "If we don't find him, I don't know if Zara will be able to recover. First she lost all her children—"

"Wait, what?" Julia frowned. "What happened?"

"Oh, Stewart and I had quite the kennel, and of course Baron and Zara were the foundation of it. Well, Baron first, and we have two of his dogs from other bitches before we found Zara. The pups they produced though." Bunny sighed. "Exceptional dogs, every last one of them. Stewart took them all. He left me with Baron, Zara, and Roman here, who is a wonderful companion and guard but clearly not a show dog."

Roman came and sat at Bunny's feet.

Julia asked, "How many dogs did you have?"

"We'd built up a kennel of over a dozen champions, being very careful with our breeding program of course. Stewart took them all. Built some massive indoor complex over in La Quinta." She shook her head. "He'll be at the show this year with Hercules, Baron and Zara's oldest."

Evy closed her eyes and began to filter the inevitable background noise that had crept into her mind. She recognized Julia's and Vivian's head voices. Vivian thought in linear phrases and made the most sense. Julia thought in bubbles, her mind an unpredictable mix of words related to the images and sounds Evy couldn't see. Julia was difficult to read unless she concentrated.

"Miss Lane, are you feeling quite well?"

"Oh, I'm fine." Evy forced a smile. "I imagine you're feeling the same way, just exhausted from the show. It's such a huge production."

"It is, but we're right on the cusp of having a real national presence, don't you think?" Bunny's eyes lit up. "For too long the most highly regarded shows were on the East Coast. Even though every year, more breeding excellence moves west. Giving western breeders the recognition they deserve is so much bigger than my own problems." She drew a ragged breath. "Which is why the show must continue. No matter what happens with Baron."

Snatches of Bunny's thoughts were filtering through the dull roar, and she and Vivian took four wineglasses from the cupboard and made small talk.

...nice women...

...more time for friends...

...mistake. It was such a mistake...

...Zara, forgive me.

Bunny's thoughts were a mix of exhaustion, regret, guilt, sadness. There was definitely information she wasn't sharing with the police.

Evy wanted to run away, but she couldn't without making a scene. She drifted to the back of the kitchen where a breakfast nook looked over the extensive grounds behind the house. The black-and-grey poodle, Roman, who had greeted them on their arrival, came and sat at her feet, staring out the french doors and into the darkness.

A low growl built in his throat just as an unfamiliar voice drifted into her mind.

...oh God...

...dying...

...Sarah...

Evy's heart began to race when she realized what she was hearing. "There's someone in the back."

"What did you say?"

"Who—?"

Without waiting to ask, Evy flung the french doors open, and Roman tore out of the house without looking back. She raced after him, trying to follow the dying thoughts of someone she couldn't see.

Roman barked over and over. Evy ran toward him and saw a dark shadow lying in the grass under a billowing willow.

"Call 911!" Evy yelled. "He's still alive!"

Chapter Five

Once again, Vivian, Evy, and Julia sat in lounge chairs on the pool deck of Casa de Lirio while John Marcos questioned them and patrol cars flashed their lights next door.

He leaned against the patio table and tapped a pen on his notebook. "Why is it always you three?"

"This time it was Bunny." Evy pointed at the Barker house. "We just happened to be there when she found him."

"How is he?" Vivian said. "Did he wake up?"

"No." John fixed the frown on his face. "White guy, midthirties I'm guessing. No ID. No phone or wallet on him. Blunt force trauma all over the body. Someone absolutely whaled on him. We have no idea who he is, so until he wakes up—*if* he wakes up—we're out of luck."

Julia said, "Shouldn't you be thanking Evy?"

He cut his eyes toward Evy. "Did you hear him? I thought you said you turned all that off."

"It turns out three Palomas and enough exhaustion will turn it on again." She curled her lip. "The dog heard him first. Or smelled him, I don't know."

"What did you hear?"

"Nothing clear." Evy tried to think back. "He thought he was dying. Thought about the name Sarah." She shook her head. "That's about it."

"If he was thinking about a wife or girlfriend, there should be someone out there to report him missing. We'll have to wait and see."

"Also, Bunny's hiding stuff from you," Evy said. "I don't think she's involved in this guy's attack, but I'm pretty sure she's hiding something from you."

Vivian nodded. "I felt a huge wave of exhaustion from her, but that was mixed with a lot of guilt. Now the question is, is it guilt because she made Baron a target or was she involved in his disappearance somehow?"

John frowned. "How did she make Baron a target?"

Evy touched her collarbone. "The collar. It was practically a red flashing sign that said 'steal me!'"

Vivian turned to Evy and Julia. "Was Zara wearing her fancy collar?"

Julia frowned. "I didn't notice it."

"If it had been her old collar, you would have," Evy said. "Bunny must have taken it off."

"I say it's an open question," Julia said. "Was the guilt you and Vivian got off Bunny because she was involved in Baron's disappearance or because she'd put that collar on him and made him a target for thieves?"

"There's no way of knowing at this point," John said. "What about Bunny's reaction to the man in her garden?"

"Shock," Vivian said. "Pure shock."

"Any recognition?"

"No," Vivian said. "But we couldn't see his face very well."

John turned to Evy. "You?"

"I wasn't concentrating on Bunny," Evy said. "I was focused on keeping a link to the almost-dead guy's thoughts. I don't know if it helped, but I kept thinking if I could keep a connection until the paramedics came, he'd have a better chance of making it."

"You could be right," he said. "The EMTs said he was right on the edge. It could be feeling you there in his mind helped him focus on staying alive." The police chief walked over and crouched next to Evy. "Tell me again how you're not willing to help me with this case?"

She shook her head. "It was a fluke."

"Your gift saved a man's life tonight," John said. "You told me you weren't going to risk your sanity to find a dog and a necklace. How about finding the guy who beat someone nearly to death?"

"It's not a gift."

"It was tonight."

Evy closed her eyes and tried to block out John Marcos's thoughts as he crouched next to her.

Evy, I know you can hear me.

You can do this. Whatever you need to do to make your telepathy work for you, do it.

Because I need your help.

Baron needs your help.

That nearly dead man needs your help.

She opened her eyes and looked him dead in the eye. "You're not playing fair."

"No, I'm playing to solve this case." He stood. "Come on, Landa. Maybe helping catch a bad guy will cancel out all the bad karma from the Landas who *were* the bad guy."

Aaaaaand her sympathy fled. "Good thing I don't believe in karma, Chief Marcos." She stood and left him standing on the patio with his notebook in his hand.

Evy wasn't taking any chances for Sunday Dinner. She loaded up on her anxiety medication and brought her own virgin cocktails to the party. The last thing she wanted was more unwelcome telepathy while surrounded by fifty to seventy-five of Sergio and Dean's closest family and friends.

Sunday Dinner was a monthly event in Vista de Lirio, and everyone in the neighborhood was welcome. While Evy and Aunt Marie weren't technically in the Vista de Lirio neighborhood, Sergio had collected Evy as one of his people years before, so they had a standing invitation.

"Evy!" Sergio's luscious voice cut through the raucous crowd as Evy left her '80s-era Cadillac in the packed driveway and crossed the lawn toward the pool.

"Sergio!" She ran toward him, a six-pack of virgin Palomas in her right hand. "You're a sight for sore eyes, sexy."

He kissed both her cheeks and slid his arm around her waist. "I heard about the body at Bunny's. What is that about?"

"I know." She forced herself to keep the tone light. "This is the fancy part of town. All attempted murders should take place inside, not behind the garage."

Luckily he was accustomed to her dark humor. "Such a bougie crime."

"Gauche, darling." She laid her head on his shoulder as they walked to the house. "I called Chief Marcos this morning. The victim's still hanging on."

"But no ID?"

She shook her head. "He's hoping someone will report him missing."

"You know, everyone else calls him John. Should I read into you putting up deliberate barriers to friendliness?"

"You can read into it that I don't trust cops. Dirty cops sent my grandfather to jail when my father was a baby, and two of my cousins are serving time they shouldn't be because cops are lazy assholes. Plus he pissed me off last night."

Sergio raised an eyebrow. "I don't need to be told twice, doll. Understood."

"Honestly, the fact that I'm even civil with a cop is enough to make numerous members of the Landa clan write me off entirely, so forgive me if I don't want to make myself buddy-buddy with the guy."

"Fair." Sergio hugged her to his side. "No John tonight. No other law enforcement personnel at all, though it's up in the air what Genevieve's friend's delicious son does for a living. I'm guessing spy or used-car salesman."

Evy rolled her eyes. "I mean, what else could he possibly be?"

She caught a glimpse of the man who'd been a guest at brunch. He was sitting shirtless in the shallow end of the pool, three women surrounding him, while he appeared to be trying to carry on a conversation with Julia's boyfriend, Mick.

"Maybe he's in entertainment." She nodded toward the pool. "Looks like he and Mick are talking."

"Oooh, I love that idea, but he seems too smart for that." Sergio pouted. "I like my idea of a spy better."

Evy snorted. "Okay, Double-O-Dad. Not likely, but okay."

Sergio gasped. "How did you know Double-O-Daddy was Dean's nickname for me?"

"Ew!" She shoved him away playfully. "I said Double-O-Dad. Don't make it gross, Sergio."

He blinked innocently. "Um, do you know me?"

"Speaking of your fatherly inclinations, where are your terrifying offspring tonight?"

"Phones have been confiscated for the evening, so blackmail pictures shouldn't be an issue again." Sergio walked across the patio, dodging two half-naked bathers squirting giant water pistols at each other. "They've moved on from Korean horror films to avant-garde Swedish directors. They said something about Liv Ullmann being their new muse."

"I will never understand your children."

"I don't understand them, so that seems fair."

Evy leaned on the brightly tiled bar and watched Sergio swiftly hide her virgin cocktails, but not before snagging one and pouring it over a glass with ice and garnishing it with a lime.

He handed her the glass and popped a pink-striped straw in the side. "I suppose that's what we get for leaving the job of hiring a nanny to my mother. She found Analu at a graduate film seminar she was teaching one summer in Rio."

"I was a nanny for a while after high school, but I only got paid in loose cigarettes and lotto scratchers, so I gave it up." She sipped at her cocktail, which was hardly anything more than fancy grapefruit soda.

Grrrr. Damn you, telepathy.

Sergio pursed his lips. "And another layer of the EV Lane onion is pulled away. Whatever will we discover next?"

"Undoubtedly something—"

"Who's an onion?"

Evy looked over her shoulder to see Rafe Howell drying off with a vivid blue towel that nearly matched his eyes. He was wearing a pair of swim trunks and not much else.

"Evy," Sergio said without skipping a beat. "She has *layers*."

Evy nodded graciously. "And most of them stink. Thank you."

Rafe chuckled, and it was one of those deep, delicious laughs that crept down your spine and fluttered your lady parts.

Down, girl.

"Rafe, can I get you a drink?" Sergio asked. "Or a refill?"

"How about whatever the lovely Miss Lane is having?" Rafe leaned on the bar next to Evy, angling himself so she felt surrounded but not caged in. The man had skills.

"Sergio's special then, the Three Sisters Paloma." He started cutting the fresh grapefruit and oranges for the drink. "Rafe, we're taking bets on what you do for a living. I say used-car salesman; Evy was betting spy."

Rafe's eyebrows went up. "Spy?"

"I believe both those options were actually Sergio's picks." Evy sipped her drink and enjoyed the lovely buzz that Rafe exuded.

43

Was he walking sexual chemistry like Sergio? Possibly, but that didn't mean she couldn't enjoy it.

"Well, now I must know what your guess is."

Evy narrowed her eyes and took the opportunity to examine Rafe from toes to the ends of his shoulder-length dark hair. He had strong legs that looked like they belonged to an athlete or at least someone who worked out regularly. His hips were narrow and in perfect proportion to his shoulders. He had a slightly visible vee rising just above his waistband, and his stomach was flat without being overly defined. He kept his body fit, but he also enjoyed a beer after work.

She took his hand and examined it front and back. Then she noted the highlights in his hair that appeared to be natural.

"Mmm." He shifted and the corner of his mouth turned up. "I think I like being under your scrutiny."

Good God! That accent was absolutely deadly.

"You're the outdoorsy type. You have an office job, but you'd rather be in the field." She took his hand. "You have old calluses that have worn down and softened."

He leaned closer. "So far you're correct."

"You like working with people; it comes naturally to you. You use your charm in your work."

Something in his eyes flickered. "Do I?"

"Oh yeah." Her voice dropped. "You know how to get what you want."

"I know what I want right now."

Her eyes lit up at the challenge. "You think you do."

Sergio shoved a drink at him. "One Paloma for you, and I'll be leaving now. Pretty sure the back gazebo is empty, if that's helpful information."

Rafe's eyes landed on Evy's lips. "Very helpful. Thanks, Sergio."

Evy sipped her drink, grateful for the medication that allowed her to be right there in the delicious moment of anticipation instead of fighting her way through waves of mental traffic.

"So this gazebo that Sergio was talking about..." He ducked his head, allowed his lips to hover close enough to hers that she could feel the heat and smell the lime juice that stained his mouth.

"Follow me." She turned and walked backward, weaving through the patio chairs and tables, her hips throwing off just a little more sway than she usually sported. "Have you had the grand tour of Sergio and Dean's place?"

"I haven't." He caught up with her and hooked a finger in the front of her jeans. "Are you offering?"

"It's a stunning estate," she said. "It would be a crime not to show you around."

He pulled her closer, set his drink on a table under a spreading pepper tree whose branches dipped low and created a hidden enclave at its base. Lights sparkled in the upper branches, but the cloak of night and the drooping tree hid them from view as Rafe spun Evy around, taking the drink from her fingers and setting it next to his.

"Is this a willow?" he asked.

She felt the curling bark of the pepper tree against her back. "Pepper tree."

"Spicy." He pressed her against the trunk of the tree, leaned down, and trailed soft lips along the line of her jaw.

Evy let her head fall back and reveled in the sensation of Rafe's warm mouth tasting her skin. He kissed along her jaw, teased the skin of her collarbone, and hummed in the back of his throat when her hands stroked down his bare back and teased along his spine.

"It's so sexy feeling your clothes against my chest when I'm practically naked." His voice was a whisper against her neck. "Can I kiss you, Evy?"

"I think you already are."

He froze, gripped his hands on either side of her waist, and lifted his eyes to meet hers. He leaned closer, his lips almost reaching hers, but still waiting.

Still wanting.

"You don't know who I am," he murmured.

"Not yet."

"But you will."

Evy smiled. "Kiss me."

His mouth finally met hers, and Evy didn't *think* that Sergio and Dean had arranged fireworks that night, but if you asked her later, she couldn't be sure.

Chapter Six

Genevieve de Winter kept linen sheets in her guesthouse, and Evy knew that because she woke up on them the next morning. She sat up, wiped a drop of drool from the corner of her mouth, and almost immediately fell back on the pillows.

"Oh God."

"No, just me." Rafe reached over and patted her thigh. "Hello, darling."

Evy blinked and realized he was lying next to her, wearing nothing but a pair of dark boxer briefs. "Wow." She stretched her neck. "Last night was—"

"Wild."

"Phenomenal."

"Surprising."

"I try."

He chuckled, and it was still just as effective as it had been the night before. "You are one of the most ridiculous women I've ever met in my life, and if you don't take that as a compliment, I won't let you leave."

She rubbed her eyes. "Is that a threat, because I don't really understand how that would be a threat."

"It's not really a threat; I just don't want you to leave."

She smiled and rolled toward him. "I had a good time too."

The sex had been acrobatic and fun. They'd fooled around, then went back to the party for a couple of hours, hanging all over each other and generally making a spectacle of themselves, then returned to Rafe's guesthouse for round two.

Evy was too old to consider any sexual encounter a promise; she was all about living and loving in the moment. Rafe was from out of town; a night with him might turn into something great, or it could just be a fabulous memory.

He trailed a finger over her shoulder and along her side. "You said you do need to get to work though. Am I remembering that correctly?"

"Yes, I am not a man of leisure like you appear to be."

He lifted an eyebrow. "Appearances can be deceiving."

"Man of mystery," she whispered. "But you are staying all week with your mom, right?"

"I am." He settled into the sheets and let out a sleepy sigh. "I don't have to be back for work until next week Tuesday, and Genevieve said I was welcome to stay as long as I wanted."

"So is she like an aunt or cousin or something? She and your mom seem close."

"Just a really dear friend. Genevieve de Winter is one of my favorite people in the world for obvious character reasons but also because she was one of the few friends who stuck by my mother when the money went away."

Evy frowned. "What happened?"

"Oh, my father is a criminal." He lifted his eyebrows. "You didn't hear about that part? Hugo Bamford-Howell swindled several hundred people out of their life savings and then fled to Thailand or the Bahamas or somewhere with his mistress. Left my mother in London to deal with the police and the investigation and all that. I was about thirteen or so? She was never charged, but of course we lost everything but our house."

"Oh my God, that's awful."

"Well..." He frowned. "It was and it wasn't. My mother was remarkably good at making the best of things, and she managed to restart her life with help from a few friends—Genevieve being the most notable. And of course, her whole family is quite rich, so..." He smiled. "I got to visit a lot of fancy places growing up—I was just the poor cousin."

"I was also the poor cousin... among a lot of other poor cousins." She smiled. "We were just all poor. I also had a sprinkling of criminals in the family though." She held out her fist, and he bumped it with his own. "So I got ya there."

"That's a relief. A lot of people assume I have money because of the accent."

"Most people in Palm Springs assume I'm a criminal when they hear my last name. It's one of the reasons I changed it professionally."

Rafe sat up and rubbed a hand over his unshaved jaw. "It's strange though, isn't it? When I was young, I used to think that I'd be able to make all that stuff up when I grew up. Coffee?"

Evy glanced at the clock on her phone. "If you can make it very quick."

"I can." He jumped out of bed and walked to the mini bar by the french doors where Evy saw a small automatic espresso machine. "When I was young, I assumed I'd be able to go to school, get a great job, and help my mom. Do all those things so I wouldn't be the poor cousin anymore, right?"

"I know what you mean. I was convinced that growing up poor just gave me a more inspiring origin story when I achieved inevitable fame. I didn't know it meant that I'd have to work twice as hard at everything and still not make as much money." She laughed. "Don't get me wrong; I'm doing okay. Sometimes it just feels like..."

"Swimming upstream?" The coffee machine buzzed and the smell of fresh espresso filled the room.

"Exactly."

"I had the same experience. I graduated with a degree in finance, thought I could go into banking like my father, but I didn't have the connections anymore. Those who recognized the Bamford-Howell name didn't trust it. Those who didn't…" He shrugged. "I was just another lad looking for a job. How do you take your coffee?"

"Black with a little sugar is great."

"Coming at you."

Evy could definitely get used to the sight of a half-naked man in boxers making her coffee in the morning. "So what are you doing tonight?"

Rafe walked over with a cup of coffee. "Your coffee, madam. As for tonight…?" He took a moment, a frown marring his forehead. "Tomorrow breed competitions start, so I will likely be helping my mother and Karim give Soraya a bath and deep condition her hair."

She frowned. "Soraya…?"

"The dog."

"Oh! Right. She's an Afghan hound? Is that right?"

"Correct. Lots of hair maintenance on that one. Sweetest animal in the world though. She's a complete love. My mother has been raising Afghan hounds for over twenty years now, and I think this one is her best yet."

"You're not trying to butter me up for better screen time, are you?"

"I mean, you'll need to do behind-the-scenes features with the Best in Group competitors though." He smiled.

"Oh! I see someone is confident." Evy drank her coffee fast, then handed the cup back to Rafe. "I need to get going."

"Are you sure?" He leaned over and drew her into a deep and

yearning kiss. "I could tell you more about hot-oil treatments and dog pedicures."

She laughed. "As fascinating as that sounds, I need you to consider something." She turned his face to the french doors. "What do you see when you look out there, Rafe?"

"Genevieve's back garden."

"No. That is a minefield. You see, I have to cross Genevieve's garden, then Dean and Sergio's, dodging curious alpacas, teenage twins, and nosy friends to get to my car, which I foolishly left in their driveway last night."

"Ah."

"Exactly." She kissed him again. A little harder. "Wish me luck."

He stood up, saluted her, and said, "Come back alive, Evy. That's all I ask. And maybe park in Genevieve's driveway next time. Shall I send a longing letter by airmail?"

Dammit, why was he so cute?

Evy tweaked his chin, gave him one last kiss, and ran out the door.

AS ANYONE RAISED IN THE CHAOTIC LANDA HOUSEHOLD knew, the best defense was a good offense. Therefore, she was already on the phone with her little cousin Danny by the time she stepped onto Dean and Sergio's lawn.

"Hey, how's the week looking for you so far?"

Danny sounded like he'd been awake for hours. "I'm good, coz! Just finished over at the Matthews place, now I'm heading to Three Palms to get the pools and the spa there."

"Don't forget to check the filter at Three Palms, bud. Remember, those old people like to party."

Danny laughed. "The stories we could tell."

"But we don't." She came up short when a large alpaca stepped into her path. "Hello, Paco."

"Paco?" Danny was still on the phone. "Where are you? I thought you were doing the dog-show job this week."

"I am. Had to leave my car at a friend's house last night, and now I'm dodging their guard alpaca." Evy stepped to the right, and Paco stepped back. She stepped to the left, and he stepped forward.

"Dude, rich people are weird," Danny said. "Hey, I'm almost to Three Palms, so—"

"Call me if you have any issues."

"No worries. I'm needing the extra cash, so I appreciate it. I'll take good care of everyone."

"Thanks, Danny. You're the best. Dammit, Paco!" The ornery camelid had Evy stomping her foot. "I need to cross the lawn!" Instead, she was being herded to the back door of the house. No doubt her shouting had already roused Dean's and Sergio's attention. "You big jerk."

He flared his nostrils and let out a long, high-pitched alarm that sounded like a cross between a teakettle and a police siren.

Evy slapped her hands over her ears. "Gah!"

Paco let out what had to be the sound of an alpaca laughing in his twisted, dark heart; then he jogged off, leaving Evy standing at the edge of the back patio with Dean looking up at her, a cup of coffee halted halfway to his mouth.

"Hey." Evy glared at Paco as he trotted off.

Dean cleared his throat. "Well, I'd say Paco caught you doing the walk of shame, but—"

"We both know I have no shame." She plopped down in the seat next to Dean and reached for a warm scone. "I had coffee but no breakfast."

Of the two men, Dean was infinitely more normal, reserved, and respectful than Sergio, which meant that Evy could probably escape the house with less than a third degree as long as Sergio didn't catch her.

Dean mostly looked amused. "Rafe didn't cook you breakfast?"

"He probably would have, but I need to go home, clean up, and get to the convention center before ten. Dogs are starting to show up today, so we need to get some promo shots and do some online content."

"Huh. That explains why Sergio is already gone with Cleo."

"And Rafe will be helping his mother shampoo a hound with more hair than your entire family put together."

"Did he talk to you about the hot-oil treatments?"

Evy blinked. "Wait, that's a real thing?"

"Oh yes. The hot-oil treatments are real. As are the pedicures, the last-minute dental checks, and the on-call personal groomers." He lowered the newspaper he was reading. "This isn't a dog sporting event slash beauty pageant, Evy. It's *war*."

She stuffed half a scone in her mouth. "You people are crazy."

He shrugged. "The dog-show stuff only takes over my husband's life in short spurts, so I put up with it."

"Did you know that golden retrievers are one of the most consistently popular purebred dogs in the country, but they've never won a major Best in Show prize?"

"Since I am married to a golden retriever breeder who was raised by another golden breeder, I have heard that, yes."

"Maybe more than once," Evy whispered.

"Just a few times." Dean's smile was tight. "Every year is like a grudge match with the poodles."

"And the little smashy-faced toy dogs?"

"Bulldogs." Dean shook his head. "Don't get Sergio started on the unsustainable breeding habits of brachycephalic dogs."

"That sounds like a lecture I don't want." She stuffed the rest of the scone in her mouth and stood. "Okay, am I clear from alpaca confrontation?"

"He's over trying to make Caesar stop following him, but he keeps looking over here," Dean said. "Caesar is depressed right now because Cleo got to sleep in our room last night but he didn't."

Evy gasped. "You monster."

"I know. Go. Now. He's running away from Caesar and he's not looking at you. Escape while you can."

Evy bolted for her car, digging her keys out from her pocket while she leaped over errant wineglasses, a lounger cushion, and a unicycle. She made it just as Paco turned and saw her, but she started her car and flipped the alpaca off while she backed out of the driveway.

Paco was well trained enough not to follow the car out of the gate, but the animal's narrowed eyes and slow chomping told Evy that he was already plotting his revenge.

Chapter Seven

C hip stood in front of the camera, his perfectly pressed suit a deep grey that complemented the blue-grey coat of the Kerry blue terrier that sat in front of the crossed palm trees on the crest of the Desert Fancy Kennel Club seal.

"Come down to the Desert Fancy Dog Show, visit dogs from all over the world, and have a howling good time." Chip's smile didn't falter, but Evy could see the small part of his self-respect die a little with every passing pun.

"Okay, one more set and change positions. Evy, back in the frame."

Lorain Matthews, the show organizer and the woman who had hired Evy after seeing her MC the Desert Prep Booster Club fundraiser, hovered on the edge of the set, watching everything with her clipboard held like a shield in front of her and her phone gripped in the other hand.

Lorain was a nervous woman, but nervous in the way that told Evy a lot was riding on her designer-clad shoulders. She was directing a purebred-dog competition, an agility demonstration, and a trade show, all in one facility. She also had to keep track of all the publicity for the show and the local station that was broadcasting. Added to that, participants were flying in from all over the world and she had a limited amount of time that the convention center belonged to the club.

The woman had to be a wreck.

Evy walked over and checked her shirt in the mirror by the makeup stand. Her suit was black, her tux shirt was forest green, and her eye shadow was sparkling. Chip was the respectability side of the show, she was the local glamour, and she knew how to play her role.

"Right or left side, Keke?"

The assistant director angled her head back and forth a few times. "Chip's left. One step down with your left leg propped up on the stairs."

"You going for a booty shot?" The crew laughed. "Never pegged you for a corgi girl."

Keke smirked. "You call that a booty?"

Evy pointed at her. "You take it back, Martin. The only thing I did get from my family is a sizable ass—they just didn't give me the tits to match."

Chip looked like he was on the verge of expiring. "Please God, tell me you know this director quite well."

"I got arrested for shoplifting with her big sister."

Chip paled. *Recently?*

Evy waved at Keke and got in position, putting her foot one step up and angling her body toward the camera. "It's fine."

"Oh my God, I almost forgot about the shoplifting scandal." Keke was checking the camera angle. "I don't think my parents ever let Shannon hang out with you again. Evy, drape your hand on Chip's shoulder, and Chip, try to loosen up a little bit. Maybe put one hand in a pocket?"

"How's your sister doing?"

"Good." Keke looked at the shot. "She's teaching high school science in Tehachapi now."

"Yeah, that fits. She was always a straight arrow."

"Greg, we have those lines ready?"

The cue card guy got his placards ready and nodded.

"Okay, we're going to grab a bunch of these rapid-fire. Don't pause too much, just go when Greg hits the next one."

Chip cleared his throat. "The Desert Fancy Dog Show! Come for the competition..."

"Stay for the howls," Evy finished, her voice a low purr.

"Next!"

Evy saw the line was marked for her. "Escape the heat and the pup-arazzi at the Desert Fancy Dog Show."

"Wednesday through Sunday at the Palm Springs Convention Center," Chip finished. "Dear God, are they all dog puns?"

"Next!"

It was another line for Evy. "Get ready to raise the *woof* this week with the best and brightest canines in the valley!"

"Watch the Desert Fancy Dog Show on your very own KDEZ, the choice of local news and entertainment."

"One more!"

Chip started this one. "It's fun for the whole family this week at the Desert Fancy Dog Show."

"We're having a ball, so come cheer on your favorite canine competitor!"

"And we're good!" Keke clapped. "That gives us a bunch of promos, and you guys are out of here. There will be a roving reporter wandering around behind the curtain that you might see around, but I won't see you until Wednesday before the big opening and the..." She frowned. "What are they starting with?"

"Hounds," Chip said. "From what I understand, Evy and I will be covering the big intro tomorrow, then we'll go live just before the group judging starts. We'll fill in the background on the breed judging—"

Lorain broke through the crowd that was taking mics off Evy and Chip. "What about the vendor spots? Do we have vendor spots filmed?"

Keke looked annoyed, but she answered anyway. "We already have a crew in back who'll be focused on doing live spots with any areas of interest, and that includes the vendors, yes." She looked back at Evy. "And there will be short clips of the individual breeds to fill with, but let's face it, no one wants to see a dozen beagles who all basically look alike line up to get judged on live TV."

Chip cleared his throat. "Well, obviously they don't all look alike—"

"Close enough," Evy said. "I get you. We'll do fill for the main broadcast with the breed judging highlights" —she looked at Lorain— "and the roving stuff from the reporters behind the curtain for individual interest stories, vendor and groomer highlights, that sort of thing."

Lorain looked slightly relieved, but only slightly. "Okay, that sounds fine."

"And don't forget there will be some back-and-forth during the show with the reporter behind the curtain." Keke started backing away from them as parts of the crew tried to grab her attention. "Her name is Mika Dobashi; you'll meet her tomorrow, or if you see her around, just say hi. She's super friendly, and she has experience in the Japanese dog show and grooming world. She's done some reporting on that for her old station, so that's a nice angle on the international side."

Evy perked up. "Oh cool! Look forward to meeting her."

"This all sounds excellent." Chip waved. "Pleasure working with you, Miss Martin."

"Same." Keke smiled and then nodded toward Evy. "Good luck dealing with that one. I'll be praying for you."

"Hey, I heard that!" Evy protested.

Keke winked at her, then started shouting at her crew to pack up while Evy and Chip grabbed their things and retreated back to the greenroom they'd been assigned.

Chip lowered his messenger bag to the sofa. "Dear God, the dog puns."

Evy burst into laughter. "Right? So many of them."

"Is that going to be all week? Do people in Palm Springs communicate best through pun? That's new." He opened a bottle of water and took a long drink.

"How long has it been?" Evy asked. "I remember you said that you used to work for Bunny, so you must have lived in the valley."

"I did, but I was fired after the divorce finalized. So it's been nearly five years. I was always closer to Stewart than Bunny, so I don't think she trusted me even though I knew Baron and Zara so well." He looked a little sad. "Is there any news about Baron?"

"Sadly, no. I think the police thought that man turning up behind her garage would be a lead but—"

"I heard about that." Chip took another drink. "What on earth happened?"

"No idea. My friend Vivian's boyfriend lives next door to Bunny, and so they know Baron. We went over Saturday night to see how she was doing, and one of her dogs was going crazy. We went out to the back garden and found the guy."

"Horrible. He's alive though, isn't he?"

"He is, but he hasn't woken up. And I guess the longer he goes without waking up, the worse it is, so... not much of a lead about Baron and the necklace."

"It won't feel like the Desert Fancy Dog Show without Baron," Chip said. "Of course, him missing means that his son, Hercules, is practically a shoo-in for Best in Breed and Group. Stewart's handler is top-notch, and that dog has been waiting in the wings for about two years now."

Evy's ears perked up. It was an unfortunate side effect of being nosy as hell.

You are not investigating this case. You are not investigating—

"So Baron was the only dog holding Hercules back?"

Chip nodded. "It sounds crazy, but it's true. In these competitions, being second place in breed gets you absolutely nothing even

59

if you're a better dog than countless others in the ring. You can only move forward if you're number one."

"And Baron always got Best in Breed."

"And... to be fair, in the past couple of years, even I would say it was a questionable call. Hercules was right on his heels, and a lot of it came down to judge's preference. Stewart always claimed that Bunny had an unfair advantage as the president of the club."

"Interesting. But with Baron gone, Hercules will take it?"

"I'm almost positive. He's an incredible dog."

"Hmm." Evy wondered if John Marcos knew about Hercules. Wondered if he knew about Stewart Barker and the rivalry that continued between the former spouses.

And if Bunny's ex-husband thought Baron had a competitive advantage by being the president's dog, did anyone else feel the same way?

EVY WAS WANDERING BACK BEHIND THE GIANT GREEN curtain when she heard the commotion start.

"Don't know why or how they were admitted—"

"Bunny, they paid the fee. They're a well-respected company in the valley. Just because you and they don't get along—"

"Do you realize what they did? To me? To Zara? She was traumatized by those people, Lorain."

"You already practically ran them out of business, Bunny. They don't even have a shop anymore. They have a mobile van and they do trade shows. What more do you want?"

Evy was following her ears and nosiness before she even realized she'd drifted back to Groomer Row.

"This is an amateur mistake." Bunny was standing in front of Lorain and her clipboard, a diamond choker around her neck, her hair a sculpted tower of blond engineering, and her arms crossed over her green Chanel suit. "You should have gotten the blacklist of vendors I always send to Sherilyn. If she didn't pass it on—"

"She did pass it on."

Evy wasn't the only one who took a quick inhale. She looked around and saw that the fight at the Desert Fancy Kennel Club table had gathered quite the crowd. At least two dozen random people had gathered, along with a substantial clutch of groomers on the opposite side of the vendor market identifiable by their aprons, clips, and scissors.

"As far as I could see, Tamara and Kevin Hudson are widely used by our membership and they have great reviews online. They have zero complaints against them with the city business bureau, and they're both licensed and members in good standing with the CPPGA." Lorain might seem a lot smaller than Bunny, but her voice was growing and she wasn't backing down. Her chin came up. "I do not have any reason to keep them off Groomer Row."

Bunny glared at her. "I told you—"

"Bunny, if we blacklisted every groomer you've ever had a problem with, we wouldn't have a single local grooming business; they'd all be people shipped in from LA!"

Someone in the background let out a whoop, and another person attempted to cover a laugh with a cough. Bunny turned, glared, and the area fell silent. She turned back to Lorain.

"I see." Her smile was small and vicious. "It's an interesting approach you've taken to my show this year, Lorain. I'll be curious how things work out for you."

"It's not *your* show, Bunny." Lorain was bright red in the face.

Bunny laughed a little. "Of course it is, Lorain. You're new." Bunny scanned the crowd, and no one said a word. "You'll see."

And with that parting shot, she marched off, her stacked heels clacking on the concrete floors of the convention center hallway.

The collective breath that released from the crowd was broken when Lorain shouted, "Bob, those informational flyers are not going to hang themselves!"

Evy was about to walk away when a small voice spoke from behind her.

"It is though."

Evy turned and saw a broad-shouldered woman with thin blond hair staring at the space where Bunny had departed.

"What?"

"It is her show." She pointed at herself with a pair of shining scissors. "I'm Tamara Hudson. They were arguing about me and my brother Kevin. We have the mobile grooming van you see around town sometimes. Wags and Washes?"

"Oh!" Evy smiled. "You have the green-and-pink truck. It's so cute."

"We used to have a shop right downtown on Palm Canyon Drive. Really nice place not too far from the hospital. Hudson Grooming Company? Our mom was in the business too. She left it to us."

"What happened?" Evy had a sinking suspicion.

"Bunny." Tamara's shoulders slumped. "We'd trimmed her dogs for years, but Zara came in one time and she was just... I don't know, she was oddly aggressive because she didn't come in with Baron. Usually they were always together. Anyway, she snapped at me and I cut her. Complete accident. It happens when you're dealing with dogs, but Bunny flipped out. Said we'd never groom her dogs again. She spread all these rumors about us, especially about Kevin." The woman shrugged. "If you piss off Bunny in the dog world in this town, you're toast. Within a month, we'd lost three-quarters of our customers."

Evy's eyes went wide. "Oh my God, are you serious?"

"Yep. There was no way we could keep going. We sold the place, put a little money away, and bought the mobile unit. Changed our name to try to get a fresh start."

Evy blinked. "I just can't believe that. That seems so cruel. I thought Bunny was on edge because Baron went missing."

"Oh no, she's always like this." Tamara turned and started

walking back to her table along Groomer Row. "This is the first time in three years we've gotten a table here, and it's only because Lorain wants to thumb her nose at Bunny." She shrugged. "Whatever works. We need the exposure."

EVY GOT HOME A LITTLE AFTER SEVEN IN THE EVENING, simultaneously keyed up and burned out from the amount of performing she'd been doing. She hadn't ever taken a job this stressful before, and she was starting to rethink her choices.

Sure, it paid more than all her pool jobs put together, and yes, it put her on the roster of local funny people for hosting work, but good Lord, were all conventions and shows this high drama?

Bunny had buzzed around Chip and Evy all afternoon, clearly upset about her missing dog but also driving them completely up the wall. Keke had changed her mind and pulled them in for five more commercial spots, and they'd had to throw a live spot together at the last minute when Mika happened upon Evy and Chip while she was touring the sheepdog grooming area.

Evy didn't know how much white fluff she'd managed to inhale during the two-minute recording, and she was still trying to erase the image of two grown men throwing down in the middle of a circle of Pomeranians when she heard the tapping on her car window.

"Gas is too expensive for you to idle this long." Julia and Vivian hovered on the other side of the glass. "Come out; Aunt Marie called us."

Evy frowned. "Why?"

Vivian crossed her arms. "Why are we talking to you through your car door?"

"It's just... really comfy in here." Cadillac knew how to make a cushy bench seat in the 1980s. Evy leaned back in her seat. "Like... really comfy." She could nap in her car. She could camp in her car.

Her car was a haven. A plush oasis of American manufacturing excess in a desert of modern, electronic minimalism.

Julia opened the car door, killing the dull quiet inside the vehicle and allowing a whoosh of heated desert air inside.

"Gah!" Evy tried to close it, but the little blonde was stronger than she looked.

"Come inside the house. Do you need help carrying anything?"

"Nope. Left my dignity and all comic self-respect back at the dog show."

Vivian held out a hand. "I thought you said comedians don't have any self-respect."

"That's probably why it was so easy to leave it there." She took Vivian's hand and eased her body out of the car. She was tired enough that she was beginning to hear Vivian and Julia on the psychic plane, and she just couldn't handle that tonight. "Hey, guys—"

"Aunt Marie said you didn't come home last night, and I told her you were probably staying over at Genevieve's place with Rafe."

Evy waved a hand. "That's cool. She knows I'm not a puritan."

"All she asked is what kind of accent Rafe had," Julia added.

She smiled. "Ah, the old broad does know me." She glanced at Vivian. "You missed last night, but I shamelessly flung myself at Genevieve's friend's son."

Vivian perked up. "Oh! The cute one at brunch on Friday? Nice catch. He was *very* handsome."

"And so much fun." Evy felt more and more grounded the closer she got to the house. "He'll be in town all week, but now I'm wondering if I'm going to have the energy to even say hi. These people are exhausting." She opened the front door and escorted all of them inside. "Bunny especially, and she wasn't even showing a dog."

Julia closed her eyes. "I'm imagining Sergio showing Cleo or

Caesar and multiplying that by seven hundred." Her eyes flew open. "Oh my God!"

"Exactly." Evy lowered herself to the couch in the front room and let her body melt. "And Sergio is on the rational side for this crowd."

Vivian said, "You know, I thought it sounded like fun, but now I'm questioning the little bit I know about dog shows."

"These people—forgive the pun, but they've been drilled into me today—are a different breed." Evy kicked her shoes off and put her feet on the coffee table. "Do you know there are debates about whether some of these people dye their dog's fur?"

Vivian blinked. "Dye the... They dye their fur?"

"They're obviously not supposed to, and then there's a whole chalk thing I don't understand, so many rumors about different groomers, something about mascara? And don't even get me started on the ear-cropping debate."

Julia perched her backside on the edge of the old recliner. "This sounds worse than the beauty pageants I got dragged to when I was little."

Vivian cocked her head. "You know, that fits. I can see that."

"I didn't enjoy it. Trust me. My sister did, and I was along for the ride."

Vivian looked at Evy in her melted state and put a hand on her shoulder. "What do you need? Wine? Water? Coffee doesn't sound like a good idea. Herbal tea?"

"I really want a glass of wine, but I'm about ready to start hearing all your mental judgment about my life choices, so I'll have to pass." She lifted Vivian's hand and kissed it. "Just water would be amazing. No ice."

"About that." Julia slid her butt into the recliner and kicked her feet up.

"About what? Water?"

"No, about your telepathy."

65

Evy blinked. "What about it?" It was almost time for her evening pill, and she was ready for it.

"Vivian and I were talking—"

"With Aunt Marie and Maud! It's not just us." Vivian returned with a glass of water and a bottle of ibuprofen. "Take a couple and your feet will thank you."

"Oh, good call." Evy sat up and opened the bottle. "Okay, what about my telepathy? I told you guys, the anxiety medication—"

"Is for anxiety." Vivian gave her a stern look. "But you don't have anxiety, you have telepathy, and it's past time for you to figure out a way to live with it."

Evy took the ibuprofen and swallowed the water before she answered. "I know you two have come to grips with these... so-called psychic gifts that the universe gave us, but I'm not sure you realize—"

"It's shit." Julia stopped her. "I cannot even imagine what it's like to hear people's thoughts. Ghosts are... intrusive, uncontrollable, sometimes pretty scary. But I wouldn't trade seeing them for telepathy. Not ever."

"And being an empath is challenging in ways I never expected, especially now with my parents and Henry being so close all the time." Vivian sat across from Evy. "But I know that it's manageable, and I have learned to deal with the flow of feelings. It's nothing like thoughts."

Evy let out a bitter laugh. "Either one of you would have been so much better at dealing with this, you know?"

Julia frowned. "No, I don't know."

"You both are so... together." Evy cleared her throat. "You have houses and careers and retirement accounts. You pay your taxes on time, and you have file folders with important documents that you probably don't lose at least twice a year."

Vivian sighed. "Evy—"

"And I have a room in my aunt's house, a car that's almost as old as I am, and a pool-cleaning company my uncle left to me when he wanted to retire." Evy blinked hard. "I'm forty-two and I barely feel like an adult most days. And now I have this thing that could so easily control my life if I let it slip out even a little." She swallowed. "I don't want to deal with it." She nodded. "*Not* dealing with it is letting me at least pretend I'm normal for a while."

"But learning to live with it might make you the person you're meant to be," Vivian said. "There has to be a way to make the telepathy work for you, Evy. You're stressed all the time. We both see it. And your comedy is such a huge part of your life. You love being on stage, but you have to limit what you do because of the telepathy."

"And how do you—?"

"Wait," Julia said. "Just wait and hear us out. We have an idea, and it's Maud-approved."

"We have a theory," Vivian said. "And it has to do with Geoffrey."

Evy froze; then her eyes traveled across the room to where her former partner in crime, the haunted dummy with the impeccable fashion sense, sat in his corner.

Geoff was the dummy's name, so Julia had named the ghost Geoffrey for clarity.

"What about Geoffrey?"

"You know he's here, right?" Julia glanced across the room. "He's being incredibly polite and very quiet, but he's here."

"You told me he stayed by the dummy."

"Yeah, in the front room. It's kind of... his space, and come on, that only seems fair."

"Fair? Fair is me not having a haunted dummy that ruined my career trajectory."

"It's not Geoffrey's fault that you didn't know his dummy was haunted."

"Why on earth would I ever think that?" Evy asked. "What normal comedian ever assumes their dummy could be haunted?"

Vivian narrowed her eyes. "I mean, you don't ever wonder with dolls?"

Evy felt a chill shiver down her spine. "Well, I didn't before, but now I will, thanks."

"I assume everything is haunted these days," Julia said. "Of course, I can actually see the ghosts, so I know."

"So I should just assume there are ghosts everywhere?"

Julia pursed her lips. "Well..."

"You know," Vivian jumped in, "I was raised Buddhist, but I've been studying Hinduism and Shintoism lately to broaden my perspective about energy and psychic power." Her voice was forcefully upbeat. "In Shinto tradition, everything carries its own kami, like a spirit or energy, that belongs to that thing."

Evy frowned. "That's really interesting, but what does that have to do with Geoff?"

"Maybe instead of thinking that Geoff is *haunted*—which feels negative—think about Geoff having a kami. His spirit is tied to this object that was very important to him and brought him incredible joy. It brought you joy too."

Evy felt herself begin to soften. If she thought about it that way, it felt a little less intrusive. It probably seemed stupid to outsiders who didn't practice ventriloquism, but Geoff had felt like a buddy. A friend.

So maybe his ghost wasn't as creepy as she'd been feeling. Maybe Geoffrey was... a friend of a friend. A kami who was part of Geoff.

It still might take some getting used to.

Evy looked at Julia, then at Vivian, two women she would have never been friends with when she was twenty-five and stupid. She would have judged Julia as a superficial airhead. She would have rolled her eyes at Vivian for being too serious or judgmental.

But these women had stuck with her when she tried to write

them off and push them away. They'd seen through the bravado when she was struggling, and they hadn't ignored her problems even when she'd done her best to ignore them herself.

They were girlfriends. The real kind. It had taken until her forties to find them, so she wasn't going to be stupid enough to ignore them now.

"Okay, so what's your theory?"

Chapter Eight

T he dummy was staring at her, and Evy was taking deep breaths. She'd skipped her anxiety medication for the moment, and Vivian and Julia's thoughts were starting to poke at her mind.

"Okay, so he's out. Should I be holding him?"

"Not unless you want to." Julia took a deep breath. "Geoffrey, go ahead and join us now."

Evy felt something like a pop in her mind, and then it sounded like Julia's thoughts were coming from the back of a tunnel.

What does my voice sound like right now?

Evy turned to Julia in shock for a second, then closed her eyes and tried to focus. "It's very clear. Kind of hollow sounding, like if you were talking through a cone or something. But really clear."

She didn't hear Vivian at all, which was odd. Usually she heard a mix of voices that blended into a kind of pervasive white noise.

"Okay, that's good news for our theory." Julia turned to her right. "Geoffrey, if I could get you to stay here in the room with us but move to the corner, that would be great."

Immediately, Julia's inner voice was muted, nearly silent, and the room went dead.

"Oh wow." Evy blinked. "What is happening?"

Vivian leaned forward and took Evy's hand, but she still didn't hear Vivian's voice. "Initially you had to be holding Geoff for the telepathy to work."

"Yeah, the good old days."

"But then it started to get louder and louder."

"Yes."

"But here's the thing," Julia said. "The ability for the telepathy must have always been there. Something about Geoffrey being tied to Geoff and, of course, whatever weird curse your aunt put on us when she was half drugged up for her dental work meant that ability was unlocked."

Evy whispered, "Literally the worst day of my life."

"But." Julia raised a finger. "What if the key to controlling your telepathy is Geoffrey?" She turned to Geoffrey. "Can you head over and stand... uh, be next to Vivian for a minute?"

Evy felt a change in the air; then she could hear Vivian's thoughts just like she'd heard Julia's before.

We think the ghost acts like a microphone. Vivian's sensible voice entered her mind. *He focuses the thoughts so you don't hear everyone at once, just whoever Geoffrey is focusing on—*

"Oh my God!" Evy stood up and spun from Julia to Vivian. "That was so clear, it was like you were talking in my ear." She shook her head. "How is this...? I mean, what does this mean for... I don't know! Does this mean I need Geoff's ghost with me everywhere?" She had tears in her eyes. "I'm going to just be haunted by a ghost until I die because that's the only way I'll be able to function in life?"

Evy felt like laughing and screaming at the same time. How was the solution so simple and yet so... horrifying?

"Evy." Julia stood and took her by the shoulders. "I want you to think about before. I want you to think about before we knew any of this was out there. Before we knew ghosts were real, before we knew psychic powers weren't just a phone scam, before we knew any of this stuff, okay?"

Evy took a deep breath, blinked back the tears that were starting to form, and let out her breath slowly. "Okay."

The good old days. The good old ignorant days of bliss.

"Geoffrey was still there. You not knowing about him didn't mean he wasn't there. Just like the ghosts at Sergio and Dean's place have always been there, just like you will probably haunt your Caddie when you die because it's your favorite thing in the world and you'll love going on road trips with whoever inherits that land shark from you when you croak."

Evy choked out a laugh. "I do love that car."

Julia slowly pushed Evy back down to her sofa and sat across from her, next to Geoff the puppet. "The energy, the power, the kami—like what Vivian said—it's not bad. I'm not saying all spirits are good, because we know they aren't. We know some are bad, but *not this one.* This spirit is with you. He's your biggest fan, Evy. He wants to see you succeed."

Vivian put her hand on Evy's arm and squeezed it. "And as weird as it may seem, when he's near me, I can feel his emotional energy, and what Julia is saying is the truth. He's excited and happy. Very positive emotions."

"That's definitely true. He can talk to me, and he's..." Julia turned to the side. "Are you sure?" She looked at Evy. "Geoffrey would like to speak to you directly with me translating, but he wants to make sure that's okay with you."

Oh fuck, this was communing with the spirits on a much more direct level. She'd had an easier time thinking of Geoffrey as a nameless, faceless energy. Him speaking directly made him feel like a person again.

Then again, maybe she should think of him more like a guardian angel or invisible assistant if he could help control her telepathy. That would be fucking magical. She nodded. "Okay.

Can you tell me where he is? It feels weird to talk to someone and not look at them."

"He's going to sit on the other side of the dummy for now, okay? So right next to Dummy Geoff."

Evy turned and stared at the space next to Geoff the puppet. "Hey, Geoffrey. First off, I'm sorry for putting Geoff in the closet so much. It's kind of hard to feel like a really independent person and then suddenly realize that you're not alone and you haven't been alone for a long time. I'm having a hard time with it."

Julia spoke, but the words definitely had a different cadence. "That is completely understandable, and I am terribly sorry that my existence came as such a shock." Julia paused. "I hope you know that what your friends are saying is true." She paused again. "You haven't known me for long, but I have watched your career and your comedy progress with such pride." Julia smiled and her eyes got a little teary. "You bring laughter to so many people, many of whom do not expect to find it at the end of their lives, yet you bring them happiness. That is a tremendous gift."

Evy smiled a little. "Yeah, Geoff's a hit at the retirement homes for sure."

Julia spoke again. "Retirement homes may not be the venue you imagined when you thought of a career in entertainment, but laughter can save lives, Evelyn. Laughter *has* saved lives."

She nodded. "So what do we do with us, Geoffrey? Do you really think you can help me with the telepathy?"

"You have always had a keen insight into reading people, and I think that's why the telepathy manifested in you. But I can feel people's thoughts, feel where they are directing their mental energy; it's hard to explain."

Evy frowned. "It sounds like it."

"If I stay close to you, I think I can keep it away or direct it, as you direct me. You'll have to keep Geoff with you, of course, but I think we should try. You're really not yourself on all the pills, my dear." Julia blinked. "You're really not. That's me, by the way, not Geoffrey. Sorry, I interrupted."

Vivian spoke. "So Geoffrey, you can feel the mental energy around Evy the way I feel emotional energy from people?"

"He said he can," Julia said again. "He can't hear what people are thinking, but he can feel if their thoughts are leaking out. Not all thoughts do?"

Evy shook her head. "No, thoughts are a really weird combination of actual words, images, and kind of... bubbles of awareness that we don't even name or think of. It's not linear or even verbal for most people."

"And it's all blended with emotions that color everything," Vivian said. "Thoughts and emotions go hand in hand."

Evy took a deep breath and slowly let it out. "Here's the deal. Let's give this a try, but maybe after this big dog show, okay? I mean, yes, there's a missing dog and someone got beat up pretty badly, but so far no one is dead. For now I don't really want to rock the boat. After I get done with this job, Geoffrey and I can start experimenting with the telepathy, only under less stressful conditions."

Julia said, "Geoffrey says that seems very sensible to him, and he's fully on board."

"Great." Evy let out a long breath. "And for now... let's just let Geoff live on the front couch." She nodded. "Is that cool with everyone?"

"I'm fine with it," Vivian said. "But I don't live here."

"I think that just having him around the house is a great start to the experiment," Julia said.

"And I can't think that Aunt Marie will have a problem with it. She knows all about Geoff and Geoffrey." Evy reached over and straightened Geoff's miniature bow tie. "It'll be nice to hang with you again, bud."

EVY WOKE TO THE SOUND OF A TEXT MESSAGE BUZZING her phone. Since no one who knew her texted before nine in the morning, she was tempted to ignore it but figured it might have something to do with the dog show, so she picked it up.

Meet me for a proper breakfast this time?

The name was listed as Rocket Man and the picture showed a half-naked Rafe singing karaoke at Sunday Dinner.

Evy smiled in spite of the hour. She texted back. *Fancy brunch place or greasy diner?*

Greasy diner if you please.

So polite, Rocket Man.

Dear God, is that how I'm listed in your phone?

Meet me at John's on Palm Canyon Drive in 30.

She tossed her phone across the bed and decided that he could respond or not, but she was already thinking about John's veggie omelet and hash browns, so she was definitely going there for breakfast.

She stretched out her back, mentally thanked Vivian for suggesting the ibuprofen for her feet, and glanced at the clock. Seven forty-five? Ugh. Had she just figured out Rafe's fatal weakness? Was he a... morning person?

Unacceptable. Still, since she'd collapsed in bed before midnight, Evy couldn't complain. She'd had more than enough sleep and not enough dinner. She jumped in the shower, washed her hair, then tied a bandanna around it, threw on her favorite band shirt and a pair of ripped jeans with flip-flops.

John's was not a place to dress up and she'd have to redo all her hair and makeup when she got to the show, so she didn't feel like bothering. She swiped on her favorite tinted sunscreen and mentally thanked her mother for good cheekbones.

By the time she reached John's, her stomach was growling. She wanted a veggie omelet, but she also wanted chocolate chip pancakes, french toast, avocado toast, and maybe an oversize almond croissant from the bakery across the street.

Rafe was leaning against the low stucco wall outside the restaurant, looking at his phone and frowning.

"Hey, stranger."

He looked up, and a slow smile grew across his face like a sunrise. It was ridiculously dreamy, and Evy mentally pinched herself when her heart gave a little flutter.

"You've arrived." He pushed against the wall and walked to her. "Good morning."

He met her with a kiss that told Evy he'd been thinking about it for a while.

"Mmm." She licked her lips and smiled. "That was nice, but this girl is hungry. You?"

She led him inside the restaurant and got in line behind the duo of construction workers who were waiting to order.

"I'm absolutely starving." Rafe hooked his finger with hers. "I forget how little old women eat," Rafe said. "I think Genevieve served an artichoke and a small salad for dinner last night. I was desperate for a steak at midnight."

Evy pursed her lips. "Well, this is Palm Springs. If you wanted a steak at midnight, you could probably find one."

"I was worn out from dog-hair maintenance." He shook his head. "Dear God, I'm glad this isn't my job every year."

"No?" She grinned. "So you and your sister trade off dog-show-assistant duties?"

"You laugh, but we do. This year is actually the first time that my sister isn't the one handling Soraya, so I think that has my mother a bit nervous. Her new handler, Karim, came highly recommended, but he's not bonded to the dog like my sister is."

"I can already tell that probably makes a difference, because all the dogs I saw yesterday looked incredibly beautiful. I don't know how the judges decide how one is better than another." She nodded at the menu over the counter. "Make sure you know what you want."

"I see tri-tip and eggs and I'm sold. You?"

She stepped up and ordered her veggie omelet with a side of avocado, then let Rafe give his order. Two coffees later, and they were sitting at a comfortable booth near the windows.

"So you were asking about how the judges decide," Rafe said. "And it really comes down to the most minor things. Soraya is showing this morning, and Mum won't want to go until right before because she knows she'll make the dog nervous and even that could throw off their chances."

"Wow."

"Dogs are very intuitive."

"Do you have one?"

"I do, yes." Rafe grinned. "His name is Harvey, and he's one of Soraya's brothers. Well past breeding age, so Mum was looking for a nice place for him to retire and..." Rafe pulled out his phone. "Well, he's a complete couch potato and a bit of a doofus, but I love him."

He showed her a picture of a large, floppy-coated dog that looked like a cross between a wolfhound and a sloth. He was draped over a leather couch with his legs splayed at various angles.

Evy's heart fell absolutely at this dog's feet. "I love his goofy face! His hair is so short."

"Well, shortish. It's short for an Afghan, but it's still quite shaggy. I live in Northern Arizona, so it's not as hot as here, but I just can't keep up with the brushing."

"He looks like a complete doofus, not a bit of one."

Rafe smiled. "That's probably correct." He rubbed his eyes and yawned. "My neighbors are watching him while I'm here. I figured another dog visitor this week was probably not a great idea."

Evy leaned forward and propped her chin on her folded hands. "I'm so tempted to ask what you do for a living, but now I'm kind of invested in the mystery."

He smiled. "It's really not that interesting. I'm afraid anything other than a spy is going to be a disappointment after so much buildup."

"Are you employed in any illegal capacity? Getaway driver? Mob boss consigliere? Corporate tax strategist?"

He grinned. "No, but thanks for suggesting consigliere and not just a random knuckle breaker."

"Oh Rafe, you don't have the calluses for a knuckle breaker." She shook her head sadly. "It's pretty clear there's a home office at your house somewhere."

He smiled. "I have a printer/copier/fax machine."

"Oh my God, you have a fax machine?"

"It's a multifunctional machine; don't judge me."

She whispered, "Too late."

He smiled and the corners of his eyes crinkled.

Adorable. Dangerously adorable.

A brusque waitress delivered their food, and Evy fell on it with the ravenous enthusiasm of a teenage football player. She wasn't worried about seeming ladylike, not when Rafe didn't say a word for five minutes straight. By the time they resurfaced from stuffing their faces, half of both their plates were gone.

"Fuck me, I was hungry." Rafe took another gulp of coffee. "And I don't even have a good excuse for it since you didn't come over last night." He raised an eyebrow. "Can I reserve any time tonight from your busy, busy schedule?"

Evy smiled. "Let's see how the dogs treat me today, shall we?"

He raised his coffee. "To the dogs."

"To the dogs."

Chapter Nine

B ut by the time Evy actually managed to make it to the greenroom, she was fairly sure that sexy times with Rafe were going to be off the table that night.

"Evy, did you get the memo about—"

"Evy, did you receive the promo shots for your publicist? You have a publicist, right?"

"Did you just touch my dog's coat? She's already been brushed and we're in the ring in ten minutes!"

"Hey uh... host lady! Yeah, you. Do you know where Chip is? He's supposed to be doing a spot with my dog."

"Evy, I think you stepped in some poo."

It was the poo that nearly sent her over the edge. She supposed it was inevitable with this many canines in one place, and with seven hundred dog owners who literally did not believe their dog's shit stank, it was the job of the janitorial staff to run around the hall with pooper scoopers, trying to keep things sanitary. For the most part, they did an amazing job.

She was cleaning off her black loafer when Chip walked in.

"Ah. I see you had to walk through the toy group area." He looked as tired as she did. Maybe more.

"I think about three people stopped me, asking for you to do spots with their dogs."

He collapsed in his chair. "Not going to happen. All competitor spots have been assigned already, and it was Bunny's choice. She and Lorain were bickering about it, and I'm sure she raised some ire with her picks, but she's the president of the club and she has final say."

Evy smiled. "Does Bunny live to piss people off? I'm getting that feeling."

"Don't even ask about how the professional groomers around here feel about her. She hires someone to drive all the way from LA once a month for her dogs now."

"Holy shit, I heard from one lady who Bunny ran out of business, but what did she do to the rest of them?"

"She's angered pretty much all of them over minor things at this point, but the Hudson siblings were one of the most egregious cases I heard about. The whole grooming community was up in arms about it. She truly had it out for those people, and I don't understand why."

"Wow." Evy shook her head. "Dog people are kind of crazy, Chip."

He smiled politely. "I can't openly agree with you, of course, because I *am* dog people."

"I did notice they don't want me doing any of those winner highlights with the dogs and the handlers."

"Well..." Chip stammered. "It's that it's more of a... technical kind of—"

"Relax!" She smiled. "I'm not offended, I'm relieved. I know I'm here to provide some comic relief, not know details about how much white is allowed on a certain breed's tail."

"I've been informed by my publicist that you are doing all the heavy lifting in the photographs, so you've definitely got the upper hand there." Chip spun in his seat and took a spray bottle to his face. "My agent wouldn't say it directly, but I know I'm showing my years. Bunny made a few snide comments too."

"Oh, I've just got lucky genes." Evy knew she looked like she was maybe in her early thirties, and she had her mother to thank for that. "You're a *very* handsome guy, Chip. And with the accent, that jawline, and the hair, you can even get away with wrinkles and call them *distinguished*."

He smiled and looked back in the mirror. "You're very kind."

"Seriously, I'm surprised that Bunny even let you in the ring to show Baron. I'd think she'd be worried you'd show the dog up. No pun intended."

He chuckled. "You know, there is debate about whether the appearance of the handler affects judging."

"Oh, I'm sure."

"Some people are convinced that the plainest handler in the frumpiest clothes is the best idea because it highlights the dog."

"So those oversized suits aren't just worn to hide dog toys and liver treats?"

Chip smiled. "Not exclusively."

"Thank God there's a reason for them. But let's not beat around the fire hydrant—I have some seen some very attractive handlers out there, particularly men."

Chip nodded. "It's getting more and more superficial every year. I think some people say why not have a beautiful person showing a beautiful dog, you know? It can't hurt."

Evy was about to respond when she heard shouting in the hallway. Her eyes went wide, and she turned to Chip. "What—?"

"Shhhh." He frowned and looked at the door. "That's Bunny."

Voices drifted in past the door.

"...don't see what you're doing. My dog is missing, and neither you nor the insurance investigator seem to be doing anything except asking about his collar!"

Evy jumped up and went to the door so she could hear better.

"Bunny, with all due respect, the collar is easier to track and more valuable."

John Marcos was using his "soothing voice." Evy had experience with that voice. She leaned her hip against the wall of the greenroom and got comfortable.

"Baron is priceless, Chief Marcos! *Priceless.*"

John continued, "But I'm sure if we find the person who took Baron—"

"And who was that man behind my house? Do I need to hire guards? Is Zara in danger? I'm telling you, that man looks familiar to me. I've seen him before."

Chip whispered loudly. "Who is she talking to? A detective?"

"It's John Marcos," Evy whispered back. "He's the chief of police here in Palm Springs. You met him the other day."

John's voice came back a little louder this time. "Do you remember where you might have seen him? I'm sure his family would like to know, but so far we still can't identify him."

"Well... no, but I'm sure—"

"We're doing everything we can to identify him, but Bunny, he wasn't armed. I'm sure you and your dogs are fine. Maybe just keep them in the house a little more until this whole thing is over."

"And when will that be? Have you talked to Stewart, because I just know my ex-husband is behind all this!"

Evy looked at Chip, whose eyebrows had flown into his gracefully receding hairline.

"She thinks Stewart is involved?" Chip scoffed. "Ridiculous woman."

Evy shrugged. "Didn't his dog just win Best of Breed in the standard poodle group?"

"Well yes, but I hardly think—"

"Shhh." Evy raised her finger to her lips.

It was John again. "Bunny, I know you suspect Stewart, but we've questioned him. There's no evidence that he or any of his people had anything to do with Baron's disappearance."

"I just want him back, John."

Evy's heart broke at the pain in Bunny's voice.

"I know some people look at Baron and see an investment or a competitor, but he's my dog. I hand-fed him when he was sick. His whole life, he..." Her voice broke. "I want Baron back. I want him back so much."

"Oh Bunny." Evy's heart broke. She turned to Chip. "You know, it's so easy to think that some of these owners only care about the trophies, but—"

"Don't get too sentimental." Chip stopped her. "Bunny is as ruthless as the rest. I have no doubt she cared for Baron, but trust me, she saw that dog as an investment. An investment that will have her owing money to people if the dog isn't recovered."

"What does that mean?" Evy was still listening at the door, but the voices were receding. "Why would Bunny owe anyone money for Baron? Isn't he her dog?"

"Oh, he is. And so are is his *issue*, so to speak." Chip rose and began fixing his hair in the mirror. "I know for a fact that there are three bitches in the competition this week who have contracts with Baron for breeding during their next heat. Those spots are reserved months in advance and are very expensive."

"So if Baron isn't found, Bunny will owe those people money?"

"She always insisted on money up front before she would reserve a breeding spot." Chip looked at Evy in the mirror. "She could easily owe them thirty thousand dollars."

"Ten thousand a pop for Baron to bang their bitches?" Evy's jaw dropped. "Are you kidding me?"

"You forget that just one puppy sired by Baron and a decent bitch—and Bunny only bred Baron to the best—would easily sell for between seven to nine thousand dollars. His stud fee is unusually high because his breeding line is from royalty and Americans seem to care about such things."

"Holy shit." She looked at her mostly clean shoe. "Literally."

83

EVY HAD ALMOST ESCAPED THE EVENT THAT NIGHT when a highly avoided voice called her name.

"Evy!"

She stopped in her tracks. Dammit!

She turned to see John Marcos walking past the large-breed grooming area, dodging a massive cloud of husky fur that came billowing from an enthusiastic brusher.

He was picking the short white hairs off his jacket when he caught up with her. "Hey."

"You're going to need something stronger to keep the hairs off your clothes," she said. "I just carry a roll of duct tape with me around here."

"I'll keep that in mind."

They stood facing each other awkwardly.

"You called my name," Evy said.

"I did. Heard anything interesting around here lately?"

She thought for a moment. "Did you know the puli and the Bergamasco shepherd both have corded coats, but they've got completely different types of hair?"

He blinked. "I did not know that."

"In fact, technically pulis have cords and Bergamascos have locks. They don't even call them the same thing."

"Why are we talking about dog hairstyles?"

"You asked if I'd heard anything interesting around here, and I thought that was interesting."

He raised one eyebrow. "Oh yeah, weird dog trivia is definitely what I had in mind when I asked that question."

Evy shifted the tote and the paperwork she was carrying. "You know, I like arguing with you enough that if you weren't a cop, I might actually find you attractive, but you are, and I can't get past that."

"Just because I've arrested some of your family members—"

"Yeah, we Landas kind of take that personally."

John chuckled. "So you'd never date me—not that I want to date you; I'm not a masochist—because I'm a cop, but you're hanging out with Rafe Howell." He nodded with a little smile on his face. "Interesting."

Oh shit. "Is Rafe a cop?"

John frowned. "Well... no. I guess he's not."

"Wait, why are we talking about who I'm hanging out with? That's none of your business, and I don't want to be hearing about Rafe from you, I'd rather hear about Rafe from Rafe, thank you very much."

John shrugged. "Okay. Whatever. Have you heard anything *unspoken* about the missing dog or the collar or who Coma Guy is?"

"No. How is Coma Guy?"

"No change. Stable but not waking up."

"Has anyone reported him missing?"

"Not in the valley. We've checked all the outstanding reports. Even checked in LA. No one fits the description we have." John shook his head. "It's frustrating."

"He thought the name Sarah. I told you that, right?"

"You did. Have you heard anything *with your telepathy*, Evy?"

She knew that's what he was really asking, and she felt guilty, but it wasn't the right time for her to be experimenting. "I told you I take medication for that now. I'm going to work on... that stuff after the dog show, but right now I have too many things going on. I have to keep taking my medication."

"Seriously? Nothing slips through?" He stared at her intently.

Evy blinked. "What are you doing?"

He kept staring.

"Are you trying to send me telepathic messages?"

"Yes."

"I just took my second pill; it's not going to work."

He huffed out a breath. "Dammit, Evy, I could really use some

85

help on this, and Julia says the only ghosts hanging around here are crusty dog people." He stared at her. "What is that face?"

Evy stuck out her lower lip a little. "I'm kind of sad that she hasn't seen any dog ghosts. I feel like ghost dogs would be awesome."

"You're such a strange woman."

"I know."

"And I don't want to ask Vivian to help since she has so much on her plate—"

"You better fucking not." Evy stuck a pointed finger directly in his face. "She was neck-deep in that Booster Club conspiracy shit and her mother was threatened by a sociopath. You better not ask her for any more help."

"Bunny Barker is breathing down my neck!"

"Bunny is a barely-five-foot-tall blond society lady who's as dainty as one of her poodles, John. Get over it."

"Fine." He glared. "There are other pressures too. I'm getting a lot of shit from the mayor because Bunny is the president of the kennel club and a personal friend. He seems to think this *theft* reflects poorly on the town and the show, which is currently looking for a national broadcasting deal. He threw around phrases like the West Coast Westminster, which I know would likely be a huge moneymaker for the city. So give me a break."

"Give *me* a break. I'm not going to use my telepathy and risk my mental health in the middle of a very important job so I can help you find a missing dog and a fancy collar. If I overhear anything through normal means about people with a grudge against Bunny or..." She blinked. "Wait, I already did."

He leaned closer. "You know someone with a beef against Bunny?"

"Uh, a couple of possibilities. Chip was saying there were only so many spots to highlight individual dogs and winners for the broadcast because of time, and the station deferred to Bunny to pick the slots. The director says she's got a really good eye for which dogs will do well on camera, but inevitably some of the breed winners get pissed. So maybe ask around about that."

"Okay, I will." He took out a notebook and started scribbling. "You said a couple of possibilities?"

"I met a local groomer that Bunny nearly ran out of business because she cut one of her dogs. It sounds like there's some bad blood there. Bunny hires groomers all the way from LA because no one in town will work with her now. They all apparently have grudges against her."

He nodded. "Okay, that's good. I'll look into it. If you hear anything else—"

"I'll tell you," she said. "Promise. If I remember, because I am kind of working here and I have a lot on my plate." She lifted the gigantic three-ring binder that Keke had flung in her direction for the live broadcast starting the next day. "Speaking of that, I really need to get home."

"Right." He nodded. "Can I help you to your car?"

"No, I'll manage, but thanks. If I had Geoff with me, I'd take the help, but I just have this stuff."

"Where is the old guy? Kind of miss seeing him around, staring at me with those creepy painted eyes."

"He only seems creepy to you because Geoff is a good judge of character." She pushed the convention center door open. "See you, Marcos."

"Landa." He leaned against the door and watched her walk into the Palm Springs night, keeping an eye on her until she was safe in her car and the engine was running.

He gave her a wave, then let the door swing shut.

John Marcos might be a cop, but his mother or sisters had raised him to be a gentleman, and Evy had to respect that. That didn't mean she had to like him, but she could respect him a little.

Chapter Ten

E vy lay on the couch in the front room, her tiny aunt sitting near her feet and patting her legs.

"...think you're doing the right thing after all."

Evy blinked her eyes open. The room was dark and Geoff was sitting in the chair opposite the couch. "Marie, are you talking to Geoffrey?"

"I was, dear. How are you feeling now?"

"Better?" The headache she'd been battling had subsided, but she knew it would just come back tomorrow. "Why did I take this job?"

"Because you're a professional and you'll be brilliant at it." Marie had never been the kind to sugarcoat reality for Evy, but then her blunt honesty could also be reassuring. "They hired you because they knew you'd bring some life to this show, and they were right. Don't let little people distract you."

"Thanks, Marie."

"Did you hear me telling Geoff my plans?"

She shook her head. "What plans?"

"The traffic this week is horrendous. I'm going up to Las Vegas to gamble with Cousin Chichi."

"Marie." Evy sat up. "Are you sure that's a good idea?" Cousin Chichi was a brilliant card counter, but subtle she was not.

"There's a new casino on the south end of the strip that she's never visited." Marie patted Evy's leg. "I'm sure it'll be fine."

Evy mentally groaned, but both her aunt and Cousin Chichi were in their eighties. She wasn't going to change their mind. "When you get back, we need to talk about the roof. It needs to be dealt with before the winter because I don't think it can take another year of rain without a leak happening."

"We can figure it out when you're finished with the dog business and I'm back with some money."

It was hard to argue with her aunt that gambling every couple of months in Las Vegas wasn't a valid retirement plan when it had been working for the past fifteen years. Whenever there was a big expense coming for the house, a windfall or a chunk of money would just seem to magically appear for Aunt Marie.

It wasn't how Evy wanted to plan her retirement, but it was probably her only option unless she and Geoff wanted to start playing competitive poker.

Actually...

No. That would be unethical.

Probably?

"I met a fun guy." Evy stretched and sat up. She needed to wake up before it was time to go to bed again. "His name's Rafe. He's the son of Genevieve de Winter's friend Marina."

"I don't know her, but Genevieve has good instincts about people. Does Sergio know him?"

"I think a little?" Evy rubbed her eyes. "We're just having fun." Except she was already thinking about calling Rafe, which was weird. "When are you leaving for Vegas?"

"Tonight."

Evy looked at her watch, which had stopped again, so she looked at the wall clock. "It's nine o'clock at night."

"I took a nap, dear, and it's only four hours. I'm meeting

Chichi in Twenty-Nine Palms, and her grandson is driving from there."

Her family was something else. "Okay, I guess you have a plan. Just be careful, okay?"

"Don't be silly, Evy." Marie patted her ankle again. "There's nothing to worry about."

Inside Marie's head, Evy heard very distinctly: *We even brought a getaway driver this time.*

"Marie, I heard that!" Evy stood up. "Chichi's grandson is not a getaway driver, he's only twenty. You better not be planning—"

"Oh stop." Marie shot a dirty look at Geoff. "See if I tell you my plans next time, old man." She looked back at Evy. "I'm glad you'll be practicing with Geoffrey. You've been putting off dealing with your telepathy for too long."

"Because I never wanted it, and I don't know why you cursed—"

"Zhhhhh." Marie made a zipping sound with her mouth and snapped her fingers at Evy. "I did nothing; the universe decides what gifts fall to what woman, and this gift was yours. It's far past time that you learn to utilize it."

"Utilize it? Do you know what it's like hearing random people's thoughts all the time? It will make me crazy, Marie."

"Not with Geoff's help." She motioned to the dummy. "You act like you're in this alone, but you have Julia and Vivian. You have Maud and me and Geoff. You'll be fine." Marie stood and reached for the flowered duffel bag that was sitting on the floor. "I'm going to head to Chichi's house. Call that nice young man you're spending time with and get some bed acrobatics, Evy. You need exercise or you'll turn into an old woman."

Who needed a normal family when you had a gang of geriatric psychics, con artists, and professional gamblers at your back?

"Sure thing, Marie."

The old woman pointed at Geoff. "And don't be afraid to call in the reinforcements. Geoff is here for you when you need him."

"Right." She walked to the door and waved as Marie jumped into her ancient Honda Civic and flipped on the lights. "Be safe!" She watched her elderly aunt back out of the drive. "Make good choices..."

Maybe she was imagining things, but she heard the faint sound of laughter drifting from the house.

She thought about it for five minutes and decided to call Rafe.

"Hey, sexy." She smiled when she heard his voice on the phone. "Want to escape the doghouse?"

"Your place is amazing." Rafe looked through the 1970s relic that was Marie's midcentury bungalow. "I love it. It's like a time capsule."

"My aunt is the original owner, so it's definitely like a time capsule." Evy tried not to be self-conscious as Rafe walked through to the kitchen. "Can I get you a drink? Beer? Cold water?"

Rafe spun around, took her mouth in a sudden kiss that was bursting with happiness. Evy nearly laughed at his enthusiasm, but she was too distracted by the thrill of energy that ran down her spine.

He backed her into the fridge and slid his hands down from her waist to cup her bottom. He hitched her hips against his, and Evy felt the firm erection pressing against his jeans.

"I don't need a beer." He released her mouth and nipped at her jawline. "I've been thinking about being with you again for days now."

Evy hooked an arm around his neck and returned his kiss. "We've only known each other a couple of days."

He pulled back and frowned. "Have we? It feels longer to me. In a good way."

Evy smiled. "There is something about you..." It was an ease, an awareness. "Have we met before?"

"I don't think so, but it feels like we have, doesn't it?"

She shook her head and pushed him away a little. "It does, and I don't say that to many people."

Rafe took her cue and sat at the bar while Evy opened the fridge. "I don't either. I'm not usually a trusting sort, and I don't sense you are either."

"You're not wrong, but I try not to be *too* suspicious." She grabbed a pitcher of cold water from the fridge. "Since you didn't claim a beer, you're getting water."

"Sounds perfect." He looked around. "Your house is spotless and has no pet dander. You wouldn't believe how grateful I am for that."

"I'm glad you noticed the lack of pet dander." Evy smiled. "I consider it one of my triumphs in life."

"You mock me, but..." He shook his head gravely.

Evy smiled. "I wouldn't say my aunt and I are neat freaks, but it's a small house and we live together, so if we don't keep it pretty neat, it gets overwhelming."

"Where is your fabled aunt?"

"She took off to Vegas for a couple of days and told me to call you for acrobatic entertainment." Evy grabbed two glasses from a cupboard. "She's a character."

Rafe laughed. "It sounds like it." He leaned on the bar. "I'm glad you called, and not just for acrobatic entertainment."

Evy felt her phone buzzing in her pocket. "Sorry, let me just..." She pulled it out and saw Chip's name. "I'm sorry, I have to take this—it's work."

Rafe waved a hand. "No worries." He walked to the fridge and nudged Evy away from the glasses and the water. "I'll get the drinks; you talk."

She smiled as he made himself at home and she tapped on Chip's name to answer the phone. "Hey, partner, what's up?"

"When Bunny calls you, ignore her. She's on an absolute tear, and she does not have the power she claims. She's been absolutely raving at me. I think it might be dementia."

The sound of another call was coming through. Evy looked at the phone. "She's calling me."

Chip sighed. "If I were you, I'd ignore it. She just spent twenty minutes yelling at me because she thinks I'm working with her ex-husband to hide Baron from her and that this is all a conspiracy to discredit her breeding program."

Evy's eyes flew open. "Oh my God."

"I'm not one to throw around accusations like someone has gone absolutely mad, but I genuinely think something has gone wrong with the woman. She's not acting like herself."

Evy sighed and shook her head when Rafe turned to look at her with concern. "Well, maybe I'll be able to calm her down." The call waiting stopped beeping in Evy's ear. "She is supposed to give a little speech at the beginning of the ceremony tomorrow, right?"

"She is."

"Let me try to talk with her. Like you mentioned, you worked with her ex in the past, and I'm sure she's feeling—" The phone was beeping again. "Oh my God, she's calling me again."

"Ignore her."

"Let me try to talk to her."

"Good luck." Chip hung up, and Evy switched the phone over to the other line. "Hello?"

"Miss Landa? Miss Landa, I need to speak with you about the program tomorrow."

"Of course, Mrs. Barker. What can I help you with? Chip and I have rehearsed our introduction thoroughly with Keke, the assistant director, and we're both feeling good about it. Did you have some concerns about your speech? I saw the draft and thought it sounded great."

It had sounded boring and wooden, but Evy imagined it was exactly what most dog-show lovers had come to expect from the opening of a dog show. After all, the whole point of purebred dogs was tradition and continuity, not cutting-edge humor.

Bunny acted like Evy hadn't even spoken. "I want *you* to know that *I* know Chip and Stewart are working together. I know who's behind this, and they're not going to get away with this, and if they tell you anything about Baron's bloodline, you just ignore them if you know what's good for you. Baron is exactly the dog I say he is. After all, would Zara give him the time of day if there was anything different? No, she wouldn't, and you and I both know it."

Evy was gobsmacked. "Bunny, I don't—"

"You're not a dog person, so maybe you don't know all the things that go on, but I am telling you, Miss Lane, there are people who want to see my downfall, including that Lorain Matthews—maybe she's involved with this too—and they will stop at nothing to keep me from exposing their secrets. I know where the bodies are buried. *Literally.*"

"Literally?" She shook her head when Rafe sent her a questioning look. "Bunny, I think all of us want the same thing, right? We want a fun, successful dog show this week to celebrate—"

"Don't you tell me what I want! I've been showing dogs since before you were born! If I wanted your patronizing tone, I'd—"

The call dropped and Evy was grateful. She set her phone down on the counter and blinked. "Oh my dog, that woman is insane."

"Bunny?" Rafe cocked his head. "If you ask my mother, she's been on the edge for years."

Evy was still trying to process the call. "What was that? That was so crazy."

"What was she saying?"

"Something about Chip and her ex working together. Something about Baron and his bloodlines? Something about... knowing who's behind all this? Behind what? Baron's disappearance? If she knew that, why would she call me? Why not call the police?"

Rafe's eyes flashed. "She said she knew who took Baron?"

"If that's even what she meant. It was too much to understand, Rafe." Evy shook her head. "I mean, she's completely out there. Maybe she's just overwhelmed with the show. The woman didn't sound like herself. I think the stress is getting to her."

"Huh." Rafe was frowning. "That's... Huh."

Evy suddenly remembered that she didn't know what Rafe did for a living and John Marcos had insinuated that whatever Rafe did, it was something like being a cop.

And now he was looking keenly interested in Bunny's phone call.

She sat at the bar, and Rafe handed her a glass of water. "What do you do for a living?"

His eyes danced. "You're giving in already? No guesses? No speculation about secret agents or car salesmen or—"

"Just need to know." She sipped her water. "Sorry, someone implied today that you weren't someone I would want to spend time with and—"

"Who said that?" His frown was fast and severe. "Who implied—?"

"Can you just..." She smiled. "Can you just tell me?"

He laughed a little and leaned on the counter. "I'm an insurance agent."

Evy smiled. "An insurance agent?"

He nodded. "Yes."

"That is... so not exciting."

And a relief. Evy could handle spending time with an insurance agent. That was normal. Boring. A real adult would have that job. An adult without a criminal record.

Rafe was starting to look worried. "I did warn you that the reality likely wouldn't live up to the speculation."

She sipped her water and smiled. "I guess the fax machine makes sense now."

He smiled, and it was brilliant. "I'm never going to live that down, am I?"

Chapter Eleven

"It's the day you've all been howling for!" Evy stared at the camera, fully in the moment as the music played in her earpiece and the excitement of the crowd filtered past her shields. "Welcome to the first group judging of the Desert Fancy Dog Show in beautiful Palm Springs, California!"

"I'm Chip Dunklin."

"And I'm EV Lane. Over the next five days, we'll be your guides to the wonderful world of these hounds and herding breeds."

Chip chimed in. "The toys and the terriers."

"And all the other wonderful purebred dogs that are joining us from all over the world this week." Evy kept her gaze trained on the black eye of the camera. "We're live from the Palm Springs Convention Center and Celebration Hall. Keep with us for all the most exciting dog news and opening remarks with the president of the Desert Fancy Dog Show, Mrs. Bunny Butterfield Barker, who will be joining us to officially open the show right after this commercial break."

Chip said. "This week the desert has gone to the dogs."

Keke pointed at them. "And we're out. Commercial for ninety, and I can't find Bunny." She looked around, lifting her headphones from her ears. "Where's Bunny?"

Evy's eyes raced around the stage. "She was supposed to be here already."

"Backup plan!" Keke shouted. "Where's the vice president of the club?"

A wan man in a bow tie and a pair of wire-framed glasses stammered from the production area. "I can't find Bunny in her greenroom, but I'm the vice president. I'm Connor Wilson III, and—"

"You'll have to read it." Keke pulled the man over to the makeup gal. "Make him look alive, Shawna."

"You got it."

The woman went to rapid work on the man as the timer ticked down and Chip turned to Evy.

"What on earth?" he asked with a frown. "It's not like Bunny to miss her moment."

"Have you seen her this morning?" Evy kept one eye on the clock. "The VP is going to read the welcome statement, then we go right into announcing the hound group, right?"

"Yes." Chip straightened his tie and glanced at his notes. "Did you get all the pronunciations I sent you?"

"I did. Thanks for that; these international entries are keeping things interesting." Evy smiled as the makeup gal ran over to touch up her face. "You're a star, Shawna."

"No, I make you look like one." The woman winked. "I wonder what's up with Bunny. She's a complete no-show today. Knocked on her door an hour ago and got nothing."

Chip waved Shawna over. "She must be out on the floor this morning."

"And miss her cue to open the group judging?" Something about this wasn't adding up. Evy glanced at the clock. "We're back in ten."

Shawna disappeared and Keke grabbed their attention, snapping her fingers and pointing to the sky-blue podium where the nervous-looking vice president appeared to be looking at cue cards.

"In five, four, three…" Two fingers went up, then one.

"Good morning," the pale man said. "And welcome to the Desert Fancy Kennel Club Dog Show on our thirty-sixth annual event. As you may know, the Desert Fancy Kennel Club was formed in 1976 with the goal of enhancing the lives of all canine companions, celebrating dogs of all kinds, promoting responsible ownership, and preserving historic breeds. On this day, we welcome you…"

The man droned on as Evy's trouble radar spun in alarm. There was something wrong. Bunny Barker, the president of the club, would not just miss the opening of the live broadcast, but there was little that Evy could do to look for the woman. She wanted to call John Marcos, Vivian, or Julia, but she couldn't. She was live in ten seconds, and her cohost was looking at her like she was the awkward cousin that was going to kill his chances of impressing grandma.

Chip's face lit up as soon as the camera turned to him. "Thank you for that wonderful introduction, Mr. Wilson, and from here, let's go directly to one of the most lovable and familiar groups of dogs we'll see today, the hounds!"

Evy did her best to meet Chip's energy. "These may be nothing but hound dogs, Chip, but I see some impressive animals in the ring today."

"From beagles to bloodhounds and everything in between, Evy. This is a diverse group of champions, and we'll be highlighting all the breeds joining us today, from the more familiar dogs like the greyhound to obscure entries like the borzoi."

"And don't forget, Chip. If a problem comes along, you must whippet."

Her partner grimaced, but he didn't miss a beat. "Indeed."

EVY RIPPED THE MIC FROM HER EAR. "WHAT THE HELL IS going on? No one can find Bunny?"

Chip's face was grim. "Bunny was supposed to be in the breed highlight segment after the hound judging today. Originally she was going to show Baron, but even with Baron gone, she was still scheduled to show Zara."

"No way would she have missed that." Evy pulled out her phone. "I'm calling John Marcos." Her mind instantly went to Coma Guy. What if he really had been after Bunny and since he didn't succeed, someone else went after her? Why did she seem so unhinged the night before on the phone? What the heck was going on?

"No one has seen Bunny or Zara anywhere in the building. Do you think I should try calling Curtis, Zara's handler?" Chip was starting to look nervous. "You don't think something's happened to Bunny, do you? I feel horrible for implying she was losing it, but I was so exhausted last night, I just—"

"Wait." Evy held up a hand as John Marcos answered his phone. "John, this is Evy. Bunny is missing from the show. Can you send someone over to her house to check on her?"

"That seems out of character," John said. "This is the big day, right?"

"Yes, she missed the opening and a breed highlight thing with her dog. Something is up, and I have to be back on camera in thirty minutes."

"I'll send an officer over to her house and another one to the show." He sounded appropriately concerned. "Go do your thing, and I'll call you later when we find her. I'm sure there's nothing to worry about. She's in her eighties. She might just be feeling off. She might have fallen and hurt herself. We'll find her."

Evy was dead certain something was wrong, but she didn't have time to think about it because the herding group was in thirty minutes and she caught Rafe running at her from the corner of her eye with a giant smile on his face.

"Did you see her?"

"I did!" Evy walked over and gave him a big hug. "Afghan hound for the win. I hope you know that I was completely unbiased in my commentary."

"You were great. So funny." Rafe was glowing. "My mom is over the moon." He realized he was ignoring Chip. "Cheers. Sorry." He stuck out his hand. "How are you, Chip?"

Chip frowned. "I'm sorry, have we...?"

The corner of Rafe's mouth turned up. "I'm Rafe Howell. My mum owns Soraya."

"Ah, the hound group winner." Chip brightened. "Well done, she's a stunning bitch."

Evy didn't care how long she lived, she would never get used to the casual use of *bitch* among dog people.

"Thank you so much. I'll pass that along to my mother."

"I have to say, you *do* look very familiar." Chip narrowed his eyes. "Are you a handler?"

"Not when I can avoid it. But my mother has been breeding and showing dogs for over twenty years, and she sometimes ropes me in."

"Oh wait. Soraya. Your mother must be Marina *Wesley* then. Of course. Remarkable bitch, that Afghan hound. A strong contender for Best in Show with Baron out of the running."

Rafe smiled. "I'm sure my mum would say she was a strong contender with or without Baron."

"Of course." Chip turned to Evy. "I'm going to run back to the greenroom for a moment of peace. Can I grab anything for you?"

"Maybe a bottle of water?"

"Oh here." Rafe handed her a bottle from his pocket. "I figured you might be parched from all the talking."

Evy turned to Chip. "I'm good then. See you back at the booth in fifteen?"

"See you."

Chip slipped away, and Evy turned to Rafe. "I'm not sure I'm supposed to be fraternizing with the competitors." She winked and stood on her toes to press a fast kiss to his mouth. "But I won't tell if you don't."

"Sounds like a plan." Rafe was clearly still buzzing. "I was surprised that Bunny didn't do her usual spiel. Where is she?"

"No idea." Evy started walking through the herding group area where the handlers and dogs were bouncing with preparations for their moment in the spotlight. "I actually just called the chief of police because I'm a little worried. After her weird outburst last night, I wonder if something is wrong."

"Well, she is getting older, and the stress has to be getting to her." Rafe sidestepped a sheltie handler whose hair was standing on end. "I think the stress is getting to everyone."

"Just the herding group left today, and then Chip is filming some features with Best in Breed winners, but I can go." She bumped her hip with his. "Want to grab dinner somewhere?"

"That sounds wonderful, but I'm sure my mum will want to go out with everyone to celebrate Soraya's win." He raised two hopeful eyebrows. "Would you like to come along?"

Evy looked around the convention center and saw more than one set of eyes looking at her and Rafe. "I better not." She dropped her voice. "No one can really say anything because I'm obviously not judging the dogs, but I don't want to be seen in anyone's camp if that makes sense, and going out to celebrate one winner might be a little too obvious."

"That's very wise and professional of you." He bent to her ear. "Can I come over to your place later and be very unprofessional?"

"That sounds like an excellent plan." She spotted Keke coming toward her. "I better get back to my booth. Looks like the AD is looking for me."

Rafe touched her shoulder, then melted into the crowd.

Evy turned to see the harried woman waving her over. "What's up?"

"They messed up the recorded filler and we only have five more minutes. Can you banter with Chip for a few?"

"You got it."

After all, they were paying her well to banter, so banter she would.

THE JUDGE WAS SQUARE. TECHNICALLY, RECTANGULAR. Her shoulders were angular, her head was angular, and she walked with a loping gait that reminded Evy of a short giraffe, not a dog or a dog person.

"Interesting bit of dog trivia, Evy, but the Australian shepherd is misnamed," Chip said brightly. "Did you know that?"

"I did not. What do you mean, Chip?"

"They were originally bred here in the United States, though they are a very popular working animal Down Under. Australian shepherds are commonly used in ranching and on sheep farms; it's an excellent drover."

The fluffy dog bounced down the show ring, his attention fixed on the blue-suited handler who led him.

"And of course," Evy added, "we can't forget its most well-known role."

"As a companion dog?"

"Oh no, Chip. The Aussie's most beloved role would be starring in charming movies featuring small talking pigs who believe they're sheepdogs." She smiled at him and saw the eye roll, but she ignored it. "That'll do, Chip. That'll do."

The judge pointed at the Australian shepherd, then at the dog with long flocked hair. "The Bergamasco please." The crowd began to clap. "And the Finnish Lapphund next."

The dogs began to step out with their handlers, bouncing around with excitement. There was more and more clapping from the crowd and a few supportive shouts.

"The Belgian sheepdog and the Old English sheepdog." She pointed to the large pile of fluff that made Evy's nose twitch. "And the Pembroke Welsh corgi." She pointed at the six dogs. "I'd like all of you once more around the ring please. Keep an even pace."

Chip kept his voice low, allowing the sound of the judge's microphone to break through as she spoke. "Judge Low is a reserved judge, but these are clearly her top six dogs. I'm not surprised to see Badger in there. He's the Pembroke Welsh corgi and a crowd favorite, as you can see."

"Corgis are popular dogs, but they can be troublemakers, right?"

Chip chuckled. "They're a breed that will get into trouble if they're not kept occupied."

"Not unlike many of my male relatives, Chip." Her cohost stammered, so Evy moved on. "So the judge wants to see all the dogs walk one more time?"

"Yes, the herding group are athletic dogs, so the way that they run, the way they move, it's an important part of their breed standard and Judge Low will want to see that."

"It's a little like a fashion runway, isn't it?" Evy smiled. "Let's hope no one starts break-dance fighting."

"That sounds like an American joke, Evy."

"It definitely is, Chip." She smiled. "I sense lots of energy in this group."

Chip said, "You're not wrong. Many of these dogs aren't just family companions but are active working dogs or compete in agility competitions."

"And by agility, we mean obstacle courses for dogs, not canine yoga, correct?"

"That... is correct."

"Though obviously yoga with your dog is also a fun pastime."

The judge was looking at the lineup of dogs, walking up and down the ring with her loping gait. She stood, cocked her head, and pointed at the corgi. "The Pembroke Welsh corgi is one." She pointed at the Aussie next. "Aussie is two." The crowd began to go wild. "The Old English is third and the Bergamasco fourth. That's the order I want them."

The handlers and the dogs both began to celebrate as the dogs and competitors began to crowd around the wiggling corgi, congratulating the handler as the judge walked over and passed the winner a massive blue ribbon.

The audience in the convention center got even louder, and the music began to rise in Evy's ear.

"And there we have it, the first full day of group judging, Evy, and we have two wonderful winners, the stunning Afghan hound, Soraya from Denver, Colorado, handled by Karim Azimi, and this darling little corgi, Badger, handled by his owner, Liam Davies, coming all the way from Wales in the UK. Both dogs will be moving on to the Best in Show competition on Sunday afternoon."

"Right here at the Desert Fancy Kennel Club Dog Show." Their exit music began to play in her ear, so Evy started to wrap up. "Thank you to viewers at home for joining us this afternoon. I'm EV Lane."

"And I'm Chip Dunklin. We'll see you tomorrow for a busy day with some of our most popular groups, isn't that right, Evy?"

"We'll see group judging for the toy group, the terriers, and the non-sporting group." Evy kept her smile plastered on her face. "And I don't know about you, but I can't wait."

More music, Evy kept her face frozen.

"Aaaaand we're out." Keke clapped. "Well done, both of you. Really great today. Get rested up—you're going to have a big day tomorrow."

Evy turned to Chip. "One down, three to go."

"Dog yoga?" He closed his eyes. "Really?"

"Hey, you were brought in to be respectable and informative. I was brought in to keep the crew from falling asleep." She patted his shoulder. "We both have our roles."

She walked to the greenroom and grabbed her phone from her locker, hoping to buzz Vivian and Julia. She was desperate for a drink and a vent session.

Instead, she saw five missed calls from John Marcos on her screen.

Shit.

She dialed him back and waited as the phone rang.

"Evy?"

"I saw the missed calls; I just got done over here. What's wrong?"

"I need you over at Bunny's house," he said. "Vivian and Julia are already here."

She closed her eyes. "What happened?"

"You weren't wrong to worry," he said. "Bunny's dead."

Chapter Twelve

B unny Butterfield Barker might have been a divorced woman, but you wouldn't have known it from her house, where a grand family portrait looked down from the round entry hall. Bunny, her ex-husband, and two pure white standard poodles dominated the wall. Every other frame was filled with pictures of her, her ex-husband, and different poodles with elaborate haircuts. It looked like the Barkers had been breeding standard poodles since the 1970s.

"You're Evy Landa?" the uniformed officer asked. "Chief Marcos's consultant, right?"

Was that what she was? Evy nodded, and the officer waved her in.

"This way," he said. "They're in back."

Evy followed the officer into the house, noting dozens of formal dog portraits lining the hall and the living room at the Barker mansion. The house had been updated sometime in the 1990s, and the overall vibe was Italian country house with grapevines, wine bottles, and rustic Italian artwork everywhere.

And dogs. So many dogs.

Evy walked past the dining room, the formal living room, a

library, and a game room with a large pool table before the hallway opened up into a great room with a living and entertaining area stretching out to the right and a lavish chef's kitchen on the left.

People in white jumpsuits wandered around the place while uniformed officers stood along the walls. Evy saw John, Julia, and Vivian through the back windows, standing off to the side by a crystal-blue pool while large work lights were set up to the left, surrounded by white sheets.

Evy had a sudden, grim understanding that Bunny's body must be under the lights.

"Excuse me." A white suit nudged her to the side. "I'm sorry, but you need to move."

Evy looked down and saw yellow placards near her feet that appeared to be marking several drops of blood. "Oh God, I'm sorry."

"You're fine, just move this way." The woman in the white suit motioned her forward. "Make sure you see Tricia before you leave so we can get elimination prints and samples from you, okay?"

"Elimination...? Okay." What was this? She'd been at crime scenes before—an unfortunate number of them—but nothing like this. Of course, no one had ever called her a "consultant" before either.

"Evy Landa?" An officer waved her over. "Just walk right out to the back through those doors. The chief is expecting you."

"Right." She walked out the french doors and saw Julia turn her head.

Thank God. Evy didn't know what was going on, but with Julia and Vivian with her, at least she didn't feel lost. "Hey."

John looked up from his ever-present notebook. "Thanks for coming."

"I don't understand. Bunny?"

John nodded over toward the work lights. "She's there. The crime scene techs are still working the scene. I told them to put up the sheets. It's bad. She fought back, but whoever did this must have been really angry."

Evy turned to Julia, who was a medium and had experience with traumatized ghosts. "Is she here?"

"She is." Julia's voice was soft. "But she isn't speaking or communicating with me. It's strange. When she was alive, she always had such a huge presence."

Bunny was gone now, her vibrant presence reduced to a broken body and a silent ghost.

Evy looked at John. "Do they know what happened yet?"

"From what I've seen so far, it looks like she took a blow to the head in the kitchen with a cast-iron pan that was on the stove," John said. "She managed to make it outside, but her attacker must have followed her. None of her neighbors reported hearing anything, but this neighborhood is pretty spread out, and the trees and bushes muffle sound."

Vivian was pale, her eyes fixed on the white sheets around Bunny's body. "Richard and I were at my place last night. He came home and went to bed. He didn't hear anything."

John put a hand on her shoulder. "We'll have to wait to see what the time of death was, but the medical examiner thinks it was probably late last night sometime."

"She died out here?"

John's voice was grim. "She was on the ground, and there was a couch pillow near her. Whoever beat her up wanted to make sure she was dead."

Evy frowned. "What about her dogs?"

John looked up. "They're not attack dogs, Evy. There were bloody dog footprints around the body, but no signs that they took a bite out of anyone. Nothing like that."

Julia asked, "Were there signs of a break-in?"

John shook his head. "We're picking up a lot of hair and finger-prints, but from what Bunny said to me when we questioned her after Baron went missing, she had people in and out of here for the past two weeks because of the dog show. There's probably a ton of physical evidence, and it'll take time to sort through it."

Vivian said, "But there were no signs of a break-in and the dogs were out?"

John nodded. "Correct."

"We've met Bunny's poodles before," Evy said. "Uh... Roman and Zara."

He nodded. "They were lying by Bunny's body when the officer got here. Just lying there. Both of them covered in blood from her head wound. Animal control officers have them now."

There was something utterly heartbreaking about the image of Bunny's dogs standing guard over her body. There was something else, but Evy couldn't think. There were too many lights. Too many people. She was tired, hadn't taken her meds, and her shields were starting to slip.

...sick fucker...

...old woman like that...

...so much damn money. Jesus, I can't even pay rent and...

Evy pressed her fingers to her temple and stepped farther away from the bustling officers and techs. "I may not be much use with so many people here."

Vivian was the one who made the connection that had escaped Evy. "I know you're right about the two dogs not being attack dogs, but they were very protective of Bunny," she said. "Especially Roman. He's the black one with the short hair."

John nodded. "Yeah, he didn't want to let my guy anywhere near the body. We had to get animal control to take him. The other one was a little mellower, but not much."

Julia said, "What Vivian's getting at is that neither one of them would allow a stranger to hurt Bunny. She had them very well trained."

"Got it." John got his notebook out again. "No signs of a break-in. Dogs not reacting to a stranger. You think Bunny knew her killer."

Vivian rubbed her temples. "Is there any other evidence in the house? Anything out of place?"

John looked at his notebook. "There were two mugs out and a teapot."

"Tea?" Evy sat in a pool chair. "She didn't drink tea."

He shrugged. "Maybe she did late at night."

Julia was staring into the distance. "I've never seen a ghost like this. She's completely detached. She has no desire to connect with me at all. She's not looking at her body. She's standing under that olive tree and not even acknowledging me."

John Marcos sighed and sat next to Evy on a pool lounger. "Okay, here's the deal, ladies. Usually you end up in the middle of these things whether I like it or not. This time I'm inviting you in. We have a brutal murder here. Bunny fought back, and there was no attempt made to hide the body. This strikes me as a crime of passion. She knew her attacker, but the woman pissed a lot of people off, and the attack appears to have happened late at night, which means that most people aren't going to have verifiable alibis. There are likely going to be a lot of suspects, and I need your help."

"You have mine." Julia looked at Vivian and Evy. "Girls?"

"I'll help too," Vivian said. "I don't know how much I'll be able to help, but I can try."

Evy was silent. She'd told John that she wasn't going to risk her sanity over a missing dog and a missing Cartier necklace, but now someone was dead. Someone Evy had kind of liked and admired was dead, an old woman who loved her dogs and didn't do anything to deserve to be beaten to death.

But the medication was working...

And Geoffrey's help might work too. With him, she might just be able to control her telepathy without it becoming overwhelming. She might be able to find Bunny's killer. She might keep someone else from getting hurt.

Evy let out a long sigh. "Fine. I'll try."

John nodded. "Thank you."

"But you need to pay her," Vivian said. "If you want her to consult with the police, you need to pay her. The telepathy tires her out, and it's stressful."

Evy blinked. "Uh, Vivian—"

"That's fair," John said. "We don't have a department scale for psychics, per se, but the going rate for an additional investigator is usually about one hundred fifty an hour." He looked at Evy. "You'll have to keep track of your own hours, but I'll approve it as long as it doesn't seem crazy."

"One hundred fifty an hour?" Evy's eyes went wide. "Are you—?"

"Good," Vivian said. "That seems reasonable. I'll hook Evy up with some hours-tracking software. She'll invoice you once the case is over."

Julia was still staring into the distance, probably watching Bunny's ghost. "It's literally painful for me to look at her. I have to figure out a way to get her spirit talking."

"The dogs," Evy said. "She adored those dogs."

Vivian nodded. "Agreed. The dogs might help. We need Roman and Zara."

John frowned. "That might be difficult. Animal control already contacted her ex-husband, and he's claimed the dogs. As soon as they're processed and released by the crime scene techs, he wants to take them."

"What about Bunny's handler for the show?" Evy asked. "Curtis something?"

"No one has been able to contact him for days, and trust me, we're trying." John's mouth was set in a straight line. "He's been out of touch since Baron went missing."

"So he's a suspect?" Evy asked.

"Bunny said he went to visit family in Oregon when he found out she didn't need him for the show, but we have to question him."

"Isn't her ex a suspect too?" Vivian asked. "I mean, how could he not be a suspect?"

"You're right," Evy said. "He can't take the dogs."

"You're essentially letting two witnesses go with a person of interest in the case," Vivian said. "I'm not sure it's a good idea."

"What are we supposed to do with them?" John asked. "I don't want these animals at the shelter if someone wants to take them home. And legally, he's probably got a good claim since he was one of the original owners."

Vivian raised a hand. "I have an idea."

RICHARD WAS LOUNGING NEAR THE POOL, READING THE newspaper while Henry bounced next to him in a play saucer. He looked up over his reading glasses after Vivian made her proposal.

"Poodles?"

"Two of them," Vivian said. "Roman and Zara, Bunny's dogs. It would just be for a little while so we can investigate her ex."

"Vivi, I *know* Stewart. He would never—"

"I know you like him, Rich, but the police have to interview him. We have to eliminate him as a suspect."

Richard set down the newspaper; he looked distraught. "Poor Bunny. This is god-awful; I can't imagine who would do this. I know it's not Stewart. He and Bunny had their problems, but at the end of the day, I know he still carried a great deal of respect and admiration for her. They were married for fifty years."

"It's not just investigating Stewart." Julia sat next to Richard. "Bunny's ghost is still at the house, but she's traumatized. She won't talk to me. I think once the police leave if I could bring the dogs over there—if she could see them—she might open up. We might be able to get her to identify her killer."

Richard looked at Vivian, back at Julia. Then over to Henry. He sighed. "What do you think, Henry?"

Henry gummed a bright green butterfly that was stuck to his play saucer and gurgled something in baby.

"Right." Richard shrugged. "I guess we can keep the dogs for a little while. I'll check with Madison, but I know she grew up with animals. I doubt she'll mind. Is John okay with all this?"

"He says he can hold Stewart Barker off for a few days, give him some excuses about chain of custody or something. He's hoping that Stewart will have an alibi they can easily check."

"The man is eighty-five. Do they really think he'd...?" Richard glanced at Henry and lowered his voice. "Do they really think he'd beat his ex-wife to death?"

"Maybe not personally, but Stewart has plenty of people who work for him," Julia said. "And according to John, they'd had ongoing arguments about the dogs, about money, about all sorts of stuff."

Evy closed her eyes and massaged her temples. "Stewart Barker's dog won Best in Breed at the dog show, and he's a favorite to win the non-sporting group tomorrow. Maybe Bunny discovered that her ex was behind Baron's disappearance and they had a fight that blew up."

Richard frowned. "Did they ever discover who that man was behind her house?"

"No."

"And the dog still hasn't shown up?" Richard's frown grew more pronounced.

"Nope." Evy opened her eyes. "In fact, if all this led back to Baron, I wouldn't be surprised."

Evy's medication was starting to wear off, which meant that Julia's perky voice was starting to pop through her mental shields. Richard was a nice dull background noise, thank God, but Vivian was starting to be audible too.

Julia asked, "You really think that all this could be because of dog-show stuff?"

Evy raised her eyebrows. "Have you met these people? They're kind of..."

"Insane?" Vivian walked over and lifted Henry from his play saucer. "Obsessed? I need to get him to bed."

Richard looked up and hooked his finger in Vivian's belt loop. "It's late. Just put him to sleep in the nursery and stay here tonight."

Vivian smiled. "I'll take you up on that if there are dinner leftovers. I fed Henry, but forgot to feed myself."

"Lasagna and salad in the fridge."

Evy smiled. "You two are so cute."

Richard and Vivian both looked at her and rolled their eyes in unison.

"Forget *us*." Vivian pointed at Evy. "Why don't you tell us about *your* new friend? You're finally dating a grown-up?"

"Awww." Julia smiled. "She's moved on from sexy valets and waiters." She reached for Vivian's hand. "Our girl is growing up."

"Both of you are obnoxious." Evy shrugged. "Rafe and I aren't dating. Dating seems so... relationship-y. We're hanging out."

Julia laughed. "I thought I was the most relationship-averse person I knew, but you have me beat by a mile."

"What can I say? I like having options."

Richard looked amused. "Who are you seeing? Anyone I know?"

"Uh, maybe?" Evy was relieved to move off the topic of Bunny's murder. At least gossiping about Rafe seemed safe and nontraumatic. "He's the son of one of Genevieve de Winter's friends, Marina something. She breeds Afghan hounds, and she's here for the week."

"Marina Wesley?" Richard nodded. "I've met her; another good friend of Bunny's back in the day. Her son is Ralph something? The insurance investigator?"

Evy blinked. "Uh... what?"

"I think his name was Ralph, but I may have that—"

"Did you say he's a... an investigator?" Evy leaned forward. "Did you say he's an insurance *investigator*?"

Fuck her, this was why John was acting so smug. An insurance investigator was an awful lot like a cop. And it definitely wasn't much like an insurance *agent*, which was what Rafe had told her.

"I believe so. Bunny was speaking with me about him because he was the investigator assigned to her case. Ralph's the one who suggested a reward. I'm surprised he wasn't over there tonight. I've seen him driving around, and I know he's been in contact with the police."

Evy sat back in her chair, feeling like she'd just been gut-punched. "Right. Yeah, that makes sense."

Julia and Vivian knew something was up. "What's going on?" Julia asked. "Did he not tell you why he was in town?"

"Rafe told me he was an insurance *agent*," Evy said. "Kind of left out the part about working with the cops." And now she was wondering how much Rafe had been attracted to her and how much was a convenient "in" at the dog show. God knows she'd given him access to areas where a regular civilian couldn't go.

"I'll be right back." Vivian pointed at Evy. "Don't overreact to this, okay? I've been around him when he's with you. Just don't jump to conclusions."

Richard sat up. "I don't know that I'd say Ralph—"

"Rafe."

"Rafe then—was working with the police. I've worked with insurance investigators in the past; they're not law enforcement. If anything, they're more like bounty hunters. Their only interest is keeping the insurer from having to pay out on a claim. Whatever way it takes to restore property to the insured, they'll take it. Their interests and law enforcement often do not align."

Evy couldn't help but feel betrayed. "Would you ever describe an insurance investigator as an insurance *agent*?"

Julia shook her head. "I would not classify those things in the same way. No."

"So he lied to me." Evy stood. "Good to know."

"He lied," Richard said. "But he might have had a good reason."

"Is there ever a good reason to lie?" Evy asked.

"Yes," Julia said. "Often there are good reasons to lie. Do you tell everyone about your telepathy?"

"That's not the same thing; I don't *want* to hear people's thoughts."

"But you could if you wanted to," Richard said. "You could read Rafe's thoughts any time you wanted. Or mine. Or Julia's. Have you told him that? We all know and we're fine with it, but that's a level of scrutiny few people are prepared for."

Chapter Thirteen

Evy steeled herself the next morning, staring at Geoff in the front living room. A woman was dead. A dog was missing. A nameless man was in the hospital.

And this all seemed to circle around the dog show that she was hosting.

"Okay, Geoff, we're doing this."

Obviously he didn't talk back, but Evy felt a sense of calm assurance that steadied her. "I'm going to depend on you to keep me focused." She spoke to Geoffrey even though he couldn't speak back. "I took half my medication this morning, so I should be able to shield *some*—and it also just seemed like a bad idea to go off the meds cold turkey—but that should open me up to some of people's thoughts if you can help."

Her dummy remained silent. Which wasn't a surprise.

Evy stood and started packing Geoff into a large rucksack. "If you can hang with me and keep the voices focused, we might be able to help figure out who killed Bunny. I guess I'll have to figure out a system to show you who I want to listen to." She frowned. "And when I'm on camera, just keep all the voices away as much as possible. I do not want to make a fool of myself on live television. At least, not any more than I usually do."

Evy might have been imagining it, but she felt a sense of amusement, and she didn't think it was coming from her own head.

"This is weird." She looked at her dummy. "Okay, let's go catch bad guys."

Evy packed up her car and drove to the venue with two extra hours under her belt. She wouldn't be on camera until ten o'clock, but she wanted time to get acclimated to the venue without all her medication. She needed to spend some time with Keke and Chip. She needed to wander around the grooming area and see if she could figure out if any of the groomers who had beef with Bunny had taken that anger to the next level.

"I guess it's going to look like I'm talking to myself a lot." She suddenly realized she didn't need to look like an idiot. "Oh right!" She reached for the earbuds in her purse. "I can't have this in when I'm on camera, but I'll keep one in, and it'll look like I'm just one of those obnoxious people taking phone calls everywhere." She glanced at Geoff's rucksack in the rearview mirror. "This can work." She looked forward again. "I'm already talking to myself."

She arrived at the convention center and took a few deep breaths before she exited the Caddy. She noticed a greater police presence at the venue; no doubt the news about Bunny was already making the rounds.

In fact, she had Geoff slung over her shoulder when Keke found her.

"Oh my God, Evy, did you hear about Bunny?" The younger woman looked upset. "Can you believe this? I don't know what to think! You don't think it has anything to do with...?" Keke looked around.

Evy felt a quiet channel open, and her ears popped.

...fucking crazy dog-show people and now one of them went and killed that bitchy lady—damn Keke, that's just wrong you don't

119

speak ill of the dead that way. If Nana heard you she'd be the one on a killing—

"It's horrible," Evy blurted. "I heard about it last night, 'cause I know John Marcos a little bit and my friend Vivian lives in Bunny's neighborhood."

"Do they have any idea who did it?" *...better fucking catch whoever did this shit I do not want to be working with a murderer they do not pay me enough how much is Connor getting paid is what I want to know...*

Geoff was keeping his attention steady on Keke, but Evy still had whiplash listening to both the spoken and unspoken thoughts. Thank God Keke didn't seem to have anything to do with the murder, not that Evy had suspected her.

"I don't know," she told Keke. "I'm sure they're looking at everyone who had arguments with Bunny, but that was a lot of people."

"All I know is that vice president guy? The thin one with the bow tie? He hasn't been able to stop crying all morning. People may have bitched about Bunny, but I think most of them depended on her."

"I get the same feeling."

Geoffrey seemed to have drifted away from Keke, probably sensing that she wasn't a suspect. It allowed Evy to have a more normal conversation with the woman. There was a white noise kind of sound in the background, but nothing Evy couldn't think past.

Keke took a deep breath. "You gonna be ready for the broadcast? The show must go on, according to the network. I think Chip is already putting some kind of statement together."

"Chip's here already?"

"Oh yeah, he got here like half an hour ago. He already knew about Bunny—word travels fast around here."

"Chip used to work with her. Bunny and her ex-husband. He worked as a handler for them."

"Are they looking at Bunny's ex?" Keke frowned. "Damn, that man is probably as old as Bunny was. Who's ninety and looking to murder their wife? That's just wrong."

Evy laughed. "I don't think he's quite that old, but yeah. I have a feeling he's not the prime suspect or anything."

Keke sighed. "Just... Poor Bunny. First her dog and now her life. What the hell is this world coming to, right?"

It's going to shit, Keke, and I have to listen to it all. Evy nodded toward the back wall. "I'm going to go put my stuff in the greenroom. Is Chip in there?"

"I'm not sure, but I'll see you later." She tapped Evy on the shoulder with her ever-present clipboard. "Don't forget to get that perfect face made up. You're looking a little rough this morning."

"Your flattery means everything to me."

Keke cracked a laugh. "I only speak the truth. Later."

Evy walked to the back wall, then decided to take a detour through the grooming area. She immediately spotted the clutch of groomers who seemed to have been Bunny's mortal enemies. They were bunched under the Desert Fancy Groomers' Association banner, and Lorain Matthews, the dog-show organizer, was standing among them.

"Okay, Geoffrey," Evy muttered. "Go do your thing."

She felt a mild sense of confusion pushed toward her.

"I don't know who to focus on first." Evy surveyed the group. "Uh, try Lorain, the clipboard lady. Focus on her for now."

Evy wandered over and immediately sensed Lorain's inner voice.

...just a disaster...

...how to be gracious?

There was a jumbled sense of images and memories, but Lorain's thoughts popped up like balloons.

...regret being a bitch and everyone is going to judge...

...so typical Bunny ruining everything...

"Evy!" Lorain waved at her. "How are you? You've heard the news about Bunny?"

"I have." Evy walked over, unsure of what Lorain's inner thoughts indicated. "I know you and she weren't the best of friends, but this is so tragic."

"It is. We didn't get along, but I had so much admiration for the success Bunny brought to the club."

One of the groomers snorted. It was a woman with dark curly hair and a horsey face.

Evy turned to her. "Sorry, is there something funny about a woman being dead?"

The woman shook her head. "Bunny was a bitch. Lorain, I know you're trying to be nice, but seriously?"

"Daphne, you and Bunny had your differences, but—"

"She accused me of sleeping with her *husband*, Lorain! That woman probably had a heart attack brought on by choking on her own hate or something. And she was like ninety years old."

Zero in, Geoffrey. Evy turned to Daphne. "She was in her eighties, and she was murdered."

Everyone fell silent, even the horse-faced woman named Daphne, who had the grace to look slightly sorry. "Okay, that's horrible. I hadn't heard that—I thought it was a stroke or something."

"She was beaten to death in her home, managed to crawl to her backyard to try to get help, but her killer smothered her. And her dogs were lying next to her body when the police found her."

Lorain gasped, and all the groomers began to whisper.

"What?"

"I hadn't heard that."

"Did they find Baron? Is it the same person who took her dog?"

"Have they arrested anyone?"

Lorain's thoughts tuned in loud and clear. ...*most horrible way I can imagine was she in pain? She was probably in so much pain*

*and her poor dogs I am never living alone I know Rodger is probably
sleeping with his secretary again but if I leave him now I'll die alone
just like Bunny and...*

Evy blinked at the rush of Lorain's thoughts and tried to
mentally prod Geoffrey. *Come on, man. Focus on Daphne!*

Daphne grimaced. "Okay, obviously no one is happy Bunny is
dead, but that woman walked through life making enemies and
lists of people who pissed her off." She folded her arms over her
chest. "Bunny Barker thought she was better than anyone in this
town with all her international friends and her house in London
and her dogs with royal DNA. I mean, she invited all these foreign
entries to the show this year, which meant people who are actually
part of the club didn't get a spot." Daphne shrugged. "She had a
lot of enemies; that's all I'm saying."

*...fucking hag got what was coming to her if I hadn't wanted to
just glad they can't pin this on me first time in ages my mother-in-
law finally came in handy will they ask? They won't ask I'm a
nobody one of those fancy people probably had to do with that ridiculous collar...*

The woman's thoughts were a jumble, but it sounded like at
least this groomer had an alibi. Evy stared at her. "So who do you
think did it?"

"Probably whoever took that ridiculous dog and his collar,"
Daphne said.

"Bunny was smart." Lorain jumped in to say something positive. "Maybe she figured out who took Baron, and they killed her
before she could tell the cops."

That wasn't an entirely idiotic theory, but Evy wasn't going to
tell the woman that. "What about you?" She pointed her chin at
Daphne. "Maybe you killed Bunny."

The woman laughed. "I was at my mother-in-law's for dinner
last night. I may have hated that bitch, but I have an alibi."

"Bunny wasn't killed last night," Evy said. "They found her
last night; she was killed the night before."

The woman's expression fell. "What the hell?"

Not so confident now.

Still, Evy ruled her out as a suspect based her thoughts. There had been no hint of deception. In fact, Daphne the groomer was hiding far less than most others at the show.

And the woman was far from the only groomer with a grudge. Evy looked around the group, most of whom looked confused. There were two though. Two whose expressions were carefully blank, and she wasn't reading anything from their minds.

The Hudson woman Evy had met the other day and a man who resembled her were standing silently along the edge of the group. The Hudsons, who had lost their store because they'd dared cross Bunny Barker. They were still working, but they didn't have a physical location anymore, and Bunny had been the reason. Maybe their mobile grooming van had pulled up to Bunny's house a couple of nights before.

Evy glanced at Tamara Hudson, then at Daphne. "I don't know about you guys, but I'd think about coming up with an alibi if I were you."

"And with that outstretched hand, Tito the Havanese takes the toy group title!" Chip exclaimed over the roaring crowd. "What a contest today. I don't know about you, Evy, but I did not see that coming."

Evy didn't know how you saw any of this coming since all the judging seemed completely random to her, but she didn't think that would play well on air. "With that many fancy haircuts, Chip, I don't know how Judge Offenburger could pick a winner."

"Small dogs, big attitudes." Chip chuckled. "But that just goes to show that there is always a twist at the dog show."

"There sure is, Chip." *Kill me. Kill me now. That would be a twist.*

"The papillon, Veruca's Salon, was highly favored to win today, but Tito the Havanese came out of nowhere—all the way from Dubai—impressing Judge Clarence Offenburger and taking command of the winner's circle."

"What do you think Tito's chances are to win the whole show, Chip? I mean, I know I'll be raising a shot of Tito's later to celebrate, but will the judges for Best in Show be doing the same?"

Chip kept his smile frozen. "I'm sure the judges are all celebrating this wonderful little dog in their own way, just as they celebrate all the group winners at this contest. An interesting bit of trivia, this is the first group win for a Havanese in the history of the Desert Fancy Kennel Club, though it's one of the more popular breeds in the organization."

"It's no surprise to me that Tito is popular at the club, Chip." Evy could literally feel her cohost squirming and she loved it. She saw Keke giving her the hand motion to wrap up the banter. "We're taking a quick break, everyone, and then we'll be back with the terriers. We'll raise the woof for one of the most active groups out there, so hang in there and be ready with the a-paws." Evy elbowed Chip. "A-paws. Get it?"

Chip was dying. "I sure did, Evy. We'll be right back with the terriers."

A fist pump from Keke. "And we're out. We've got thirty minutes of prerecorded footage while they set up the next ring. Take a break."

Evy stretched her neck and reached for a bottle of water.

"I knew you'd have vodka jokes," Chip said. "But even I underestimated how many."

"The dog's name is Tito, Chip. *Tito*." Evy shrugged. "I'm supposed to pass that up?"

"I suppose not." He grimaced. "This all feels horrible and macabre."

Evy knew Chip was talking about Bunny. They hadn't had time to talk before the broadcast, but Evy could see the lines around Chip's eyes and mouth. He was clearly upset. "Have you talked to Bunny's ex?"

"Stewart?" Chip shook his head. "What do you say to the man? He and the woman fought like... well, cats and dogs, I suppose, but they were together for fifty years. I know he must be devastated by the news."

"So you don't think he had anything to do with it?" Evy wished she could peek into Chip's thoughts, but she'd tucked Geoff away and had as many shields in place as possible.

"God no." Chip winced. "The man's idea of confrontation was a lawsuit, not a fistfight. He was a litigator for forty years; his violence in his world was a legal brief."

Chip was naturally hard to read, which wasn't unusual for a lot of people, so Evy knew she'd need Geoffrey's help if she wanted any insight into his thoughts.

"So who do you think did it?"

"What do you mean?" Chip blinked. "Did the police say Bunny was targeted? I assumed that it was a burglar who broke into her house. You're saying that..." He frowned. "No, that's not possible. Who would hurt Bunny?"

He seemed to realize how many people might hate the woman as soon as the words left his mouth. Chip's face fell. "I mean... Well, it's just that I can't imagine anyone doing that. Surely it was a burglar or something of that sort."

Evy shrugged and kept her voice low. "According to my friend who works with the police, there were no signs of a break-in and the biggest clue is the dogs."

"The dogs?" Chip's face was pale. "What about the dogs? What happened to them?"

"They're fine, but you know Bunny's dogs." Evy looked around. "They were protective. Whoever hurt Bunny was someone the dogs trusted."

"Right." Chip frowned. "I hadn't even thought of that. So... it had to be a friend or a family... I mean Stewart would have known Roman and Zara, but I can't imagine—"

"I'm just saying that he had motive, didn't he?" Evy shrugged. "I mean, this all goes back to Baron. If Bunny found out that Stewart had taken Baron—"

"Why would he?" Chip snorted. "Baron wasn't a threat to him. Trust me."

"I mean, you know the dog-show world better than I do. Who's favored to win the non-sporting group with Baron out of the race?" Evy raised her eyebrows. "From what you've said, Stewart's dog is a shoo-in."

Chip frowned. "Evy, I hate to say this because it's literally my livelihood, but this is a *dog show*. No one is killing the competition to win a dog show."

Evy noticed someone pushing through the production crew and turned her head to see Rafe heading toward her.

A spike of anger in her gut.

Shit. Not now.

Evy didn't have the mental energy to deal with him right now, and she didn't know what she'd say. She had two more groups to announce with Chip, and she didn't want to deal with Rafe the Liar Howell.

"Hey Chip, I'm heading back to the greenroom for a few minutes. Just tell anyone who comes around that I disappeared for a bit." She stood and walked off the stage.

"Of course." The corner of Chip's mouth turned up. "Feeling a little *ruff*?"

She pointed at him. "See? I'm rubbing off on you. Hold that energy for the terriers, Dunklin."

"Go away." Chip waved her off with a rueful smile. "I'll misdirect any admirers who come looking."

"And I'll collie you later."

Chapter Fourteen

The camera swung closer as the crowd continued a continuous round of applause.

"And with that win, we have five of our seven finalists," Chip proclaimed. "Through a storm of controversy and mystery, the incredible Hercules, the champion standard poodle handled by Kurt Peterson for Barker Breeding Group, has won the non-sporting group. A well-deserved win for a young champion who has made quite a name for himself in winners' circles around the country."

"That controversy," Evy added, "is of course the disappearance of crowd favorite, Baron the standard poodle, who just happens to be Hercules's father, isn't that right, Chip?"

"That's correct. Those champion lines run strong, and our new winner comes from a very old family of poodles dating back to sixteenth century German royalty."

"Fascinating." Evy tried to keep her expression neutral as the crowd continued to celebrate and Hercules's handler made the handshaking rounds. "Would you say that Hercules is a favorite going into the Best in Show competition on Sunday?"

"It's hard to imagine trying to pick any one of these dogs as somehow better than another." Chip glanced at Evy, then back at the camera. "They're all so different and all represent their breed and group so wonderfully, but I would say that Hercules is definitely a contender."

"You heard it here." Evy looked at the camera. "More drama, more competition, and more dogs are coming at you tomorrow afternoon when we present the last two group competitions, the sporting and the working groups!"

She was too tired for quips, jokes, or puns. It had been a day of incredible pressure, high emotion, and more than one breakdown.

Chip had exploded at the makeup girl just for asking him to roll up his shirtsleeve. Keke had to deal with Lorain hovering over every single change she made to the program. And Evy was silently juggling half a dozen people's thoughts as she simultaneously tried to laugh, smile, and pretend she cared about the upset in the terrier group judging where the tiny miniature schnauzer, Jade Beauty, took home the blue ribbon instead of the crowd favorite bull terrier, Jester.

Evy waited for the camera light to go out, then ripped her earpiece from her head and bolted from the table. "I'll see everyone tomorrow."

There was no wrap-up Evy wanted to go over. She wanted no notes. Thursday had been their busiest day on the program, and after getting the news about Bunny, it only made everything more complicated.

Her head was pounding. Her body was aching. She was hungry, exhausted, and wanted to curl into a ball somewhere dark where no one could find her.

She left Geoff and her backpack in her locker, walked straight to her car, and got in, nearly leaving her body when someone tapped on the window. *Jesus Christ on a cracker!*

John Marcos peered through the car window, his eyebrow raised. "Sorry."

"I don't want to talk to you." Evy put her head on her steering wheel. "I am exhausted; I have a horrible headache. Plus I don't know anything yet. Trust me, I was scanning people all day, but I don't have anything worth knowing."

"I highly doubt that."

Ugh. Why did he have to be right? Evy rolled down the window and leaned on the car door. "Okay, I probably didn't identify anyone as a strong suspect, but I maybe eliminated some people. Does that help?"

"Immensely."

Evy closed her eyes and thought back on the day. "Lorain Matthews is probably not involved. She and Bunny had a couple of very public fights, but today she was more annoyed than satisfied about Bunny's death. She's the show organizer, and she didn't read guilty to me. She was mostly thinking about how inconvenient it was that Bunny died this week." Evy frowned. "Put it this way—I wouldn't put it past her to murder Bunny, but I don't think she'd have done it the week of the show."

"That actually makes sense to me. Anyone else you get a read on?"

"Keke, our assistant director, was definitely not involved."

"What about Chip Dunklin? He worked with Stewart Barker a few years ago."

"I didn't get a read on Chip because I was focused on the show, but he was shocked by her death and he thought it was because of a burglary or something."

John nodded. "And the dog-show lady that Bunny was complaining about?"

"That's the Lorain I mentioned."

"Right." He made a note in his notebook. "Anyone else ruled out?"

"I didn't have much time to go around the vendor area, but there are two groomers you should check out. Tamara and Kevin Hudson. Bunny basically made them lose their business, and they weren't on good terms. They'd probably be worth questioning."

He wrote down the names. "Got it. I'll pass those along to my detective."

Evy looked at him, noticing the lines around his eyes. "I suspect my day was about as peachy as yours. Any more news about Bunny's death I should know?"

"The coroner put the time between ten and midnight on Tuesday night." He leaned on the roof of her car. "Bunny didn't have any home-security surveillance, and neither did her neighbor across the street."

"Most of the people on that block are ancient."

"Yeah, we're not lucking out with doorbell cameras in the neighborhood either because most of the houses have gates, walls, or hedges that block the view of the cameras to the street."

"Damn."

"You'd think rich people would be more paranoid, but it looks like Bunny mostly depended on her dogs for security."

"Any staff at the house?"

"None live-in. The housekeeper only came one day a week; she did mention she used to come every day."

"And the gardener?"

"Also one day a week." John tapped on her car door. "Still no sign of the handler guy, Curtis, but the dogs are over at Richard's place now. Animal control released them to Vivian. I think Julia was going to try to take them over to Bunny's tomorrow. The crime scene people should be done by then."

There was something about the housekeeper and gardener that was bothering Evy. "Have you looked at Bunny's financials?"

"Why?"

"Staff cutbacks and now this insurance claim. Maybe Bunny was having money problems and putting on a good front."

"And sometimes when money is tight, people put themselves at risk without even realizing it." John nodded. "I'll see if her estate lawyer can release the records to us. I'm going to question her ex-husband tomorrow. His and Bunny's business interests were still pretty entangled; he might know more."

"Make sure to congratulate him on his win," Evy said. "Baron's son took the group championship that Baron probably would have won if he was around."

"And I'm assuming that this dog is owned by Stewart Barker?"

"And the Barker Breeding Group." Evy nodded. "Baron's son is now the official top poodle in the valley and, according to Chip, maybe the country."

"Hmm." John stared into the distance. "I can't believe there's still no sign of that damn dog." He curled his fingers on the door. "Why do I feel like that poodle is still at the middle of this crime?"

"Because he might be," Evy said. "I don't care how much Chip says that this is 'just a dog show,' people go a little crazy when they want to win. That poodle disappearing meant that a whole new winner was announced, Bunny's estate has a massive insurance claim in the waiting, and Baron the poodle is no longer the top breeding male in Palm Springs."

John tapped on her door. "Speaking of insurance claims—"

"Nope." She started to roll up her window. "Not talking with you about this."

"I'm just saying that you seemed surprised about him being a recovery agent," John said. "He didn't tell you?"

"Bye, cop."

He stepped back. "Fine. Don't talk to me, but you know he's a sneaky bastard, Evy. There's something about that guy that's not on the up and up."

"Good." Evy put her car in reverse and started to back out. "He'll fit right in with the Landa clan."

EVY WAS LOUNGING ON THE COUCH IN THE DARK WITH A sheet mask on her face when she heard someone knocking on the door. She tried to reach out mentally to see who it was—there *was* a murderer on the loose—but she hit a dark wall and remembered that she'd taken a full dose of her antianxiety medication as soon as she got home.

And she'd left Geoff at the convention center. Dammit.

Her brain was a soft, empty room with padded walls and a white noise machine in the background. Bliss.

Whoever it was knocked again.

"Who is it?" she muttered.

"Evy, it's Rafe."

Shit. Ugh, she didn't want to have to think about Rafe Howell, his cute ass, his clever tongue, or any of the reasons that might tempt her to forgive him for lying to her.

"Evy, is something wrong?"

Yes, but I don't want to explain it.

"I'm... fine."

"You don't sound fine." He moved to the window near the sofa where she was lying. "I feel like an idiot shouting in your front yard. May I come in?"

She should just open the door, cuss him out for lying, and slam it. He'd leave, right? She looked like hell, so that was probably good. He wouldn't try to come on to her when she was looking like hell.

Evy hoisted herself off the couch, stomped to the front door, unlocked it, and yanked it open. "You lied to me."

Rafe fought his way from the bushes in front of her window back to the front door. "I what? No, I didn't."

"You told me you were an insurance agent."

"I am." His eyebrows went up. "I work for Southwestern Premier Insurance. It's a boutique provider to high-end customers that insures everything from homes to—"

"Purebred dogs?" She crossed her arms over her chest. "Cartier collars? Dog semen?"

Rafe sighed. "Bunny didn't have Baron's testicles insured

directly, but she did insure the dog."

"You're not an insurance agent, you're an insurance *cop*."

"Ha!" He grinned. "Did John Marcos tell you that? He loves me, by the way. Says that I'm two steps from a criminal, which..." Rafe shrugged. "I mean, he probably has a point. I don't give a rat's arsehole about arresting anyone—I just want to get that damn dog back."

Rafe wasn't acting contrite, embarrassed, or sorry at all, which made Evy perversely angry.

"Do you really think what you did is fine? I asked you what you did for a living and you—"

"Actually." He leaned on her doorjamb. "At first you didn't ask me. You deliberately didn't. When you finally did, I gave you the simplest answer because explaining to most people what an insurance recovery agent does is somewhat complicated." He glanced at her face. "Nice sheet mask."

"I like sloths."

"We insured one of those for a time." He smiled. "That's another story. Are you angry with me?"

"Yes."

"Why?"

"Because you lied."

"I believe I have established that I did not. I *am* an insurance agent, just one who works in the field."

Damn it, he was right. Evy narrowed her eyes. "Did you flirt with me because you wanted to or because I was hosting the dog show and it might give you inside information?"

"What inside information did I mine from you that I couldn't have acquired with my mother's assistance as a top participant in the show?" His eyebrow went up. "I didn't flirt with you because you're working the show, darling. If anything, it was an inconvenience."

Evy uncrossed her arms and stuck her hands in the light grey robe she'd thrown on when she got home. "So you weren't flirting with me for nefarious or illegal purposes?"

He took a deep breath. "Would it be sexier if I had been?"

The corner of her lip twitched. "Maybe."

Rafe was trying to suppress a smile. He looked over his shoulder, then back at her. "Evy?"

"Yes?"

He stepped into the house, slamming the door shut behind him, and shoved Evy up against the wall, caging her against his body as his lips hovered an inch away from hers.

"I lied." His voice was raspy. "I lied because I had to. But nothing about my feelings was a lie. I just didn't know..."

She could barely breathe. "Didn't know what?"

"If I could trust you with the truth." He ripped the sheet mask off her face. "I'm sorry, but I cannot keep this up while talking to a sloth."

A laugh bubbled out of Evy's lips, but Rafe took her mouth in a passionate kiss that had Evy hooking her leg around his and pulling him closer. Desire and delight bubbled in her veins. She kissed Rafe back, sliding her fingers into the silky hair at the nape of his neck.

He finally pulled away with a gasp. "God, you're sexy."

"And you're really good at the secret agent, my-feelings-weren't-a-lie schtick."

"Thanks." He smiled and slid his hands down to cup her backside. "How was your day? Are you exhausted?"

"Feeling much more awake now, thanks." She walked him backward down the hall. "Did I show you my bedroom?"

"You didn't, and that's one tour I definitely wanted." He pulled the tie on her robe open and gaped when he saw the bra, panties, and garter set she hadn't taken off yet. "Are you joking? You were wearing this with a slouchy grey robe and a sloth mask?"

"I was wearing this all day." She let the robe fall from her shoulders. "I just hadn't gotten all the way undressed yet."

"My God, I'm never going to be able to picture dog-show presenters the same." He stumbled over the heels she'd kicked off when she got home. "Pretty please, Miss Landa, may I make torrid love to you in your garters and brassiere?"

"It's the accent." She fell back on the bed, placing one stocking-clad foot on Rafe's shoulder. "It's really an unfair advantage."

"You're the one with the accent, not me." His fingers trailed along her ankle, up her leg, and teased behind her knee. "If I stole those lace panties, that would be stalker-like behavior, wouldn't it?"

"Kind of?"

He knelt at the foot of the bed, placed both hands on her hips, and pulled her down until her thighs were hanging over his shoulders. "Well then." He slid his fingers on either side of the black lace that framed her sex. "I'm just going to get rid of these, and please don't look for them very closely."

She laughed, but her eyes started to cross when his tongue licked up the inside of her thigh. The stubble on his cheeks rubbed against the tender skin.

"God, you smell so good."

She shoved her hands in his dark hair as he pulled her panties away and lowered his mouth to the juncture of her thighs. He feasted there, cupping her bottom and lifting her to his mouth like a starving man.

A stream of nonsense left Evy's mouth, and she closed her eyes, focusing on the intense physical sensation and grateful that she heard nothing, felt nothing but the rising tension of her own climax growing until it crested in a wave that overwhelmed every sense and left her shuddering on the edge of her bed.

She gasped as Rafe raised his head and licked his lips. "Fuck, your climax is delicious."

"Condom." She flung her arm toward the bedside table. "In me. Got. Condom."

Rafe chuckled. "I get the idea, but I have it covered." He stood up, reached for his wallet, and took out a strip of condoms, and then he shoved down his pants, sheathed his deliciously long erection, and pulled Evy's hips back toward the edge of the bed, lifting her bottom again, sliding into her, and letting out a long, delicious groan of satisfaction.

"Evy?" He started to move in long, lazy thrusts.

"Yeah?" Please let him not be a talker. Evy couldn't concentrate on anything but the sex that night.

"Can we classify this as our first fight?" He pulled out and back with a little thrust up at the end.

Evy gasped. "Uh... sure. If you want. Sure."

"Oh good." He bit his lip and slid out, then in again. "Then about three rounds of makeup sex should do it."

Wait, wasn't he in his forties? *"Three?"*

He caressed her bare bottom, then gave it a little slap. "We'll pace ourselves, darling. After all, we've got all night."

Chapter Fifteen

She was dreaming of coffee.

"...the case file has to be updated because we're dealing with a different insured at this point, aren't we?"

Evy was sure she smelled coffee, but who had turned the news on? Did they get the BBC on cable now? Aunt Marie was so weird. Why was she watching BBC?

"If it's a living trust, that's one thing, but her heirs— No, she didn't have any children."

She blinked her eyes open and saw the remnants of the night with Rafe.

"Oh." She sat up. "Ohhhh." Evy rubbed her eyes and surveyed her bedroom. Well, it was a good thing she wasn't a neat freak because she didn't have time to deal with cleaning all this up when she had to be at work at... She glanced at the clock.

"Shit!"

She scrambled out of bed, half falling while her legs were entangled in the sheets. It was already nine o'clock, and she had to be at the convention center in an hour. "Rafe!"

"Let me call you back." He popped his head in the bedroom.

"I asked what time you needed an alarm for last night, but you were already asleep."

"That is your fault." She pointed at him. "Exhausting man."

He grinned. "You weren't complaining last night."

"No, of course I wasn't." She hissed and pulled on a pair of panties from her dresser, then stood in front of her closet and stared. "I don't know what I'm supposed to wear."

Rafe walked to her closet and stared at her hanging clothes. "They don't have wardrobe for you at the venue?"

"This isn't a national network—it's Palm Springs local." She blinked. "The brief was black, grey, or white with accents of forest green if I wanted any color. We're sitting in front of that giant kennel club logo most of the time, so it's the most neutral."

"I bet you're gorgeous in green." He flipped through her closet. "Go get coffee; I'll pick out your clothes."

She raised an eyebrow. "Oh really?"

"Hey, I'm a fashionable man." He motioned to his boxers. "Obviously."

Evy snorted and walked out to the kitchen. If she didn't like what he picked, she'd just go with the black suit she wore on Wednesday. No one was really paying attention to what she wore anyway. "Thanks for making coffee."

"Thanks for the rather fabulous night," Rafe said. "I have to admit, I was not expecting that when I came over."

"Oh really?"

"Yes, really." He had a smile in his voice. "I know the second day of judging is always the most hectic with three groups, and then add to that the news about Bunny."

She paused while grabbing a mug. "Was that what you were talking about on the phone?"

"Yes. It's an absolutely heinous crime. I'm fairly sure Bunny was trying to commit fraud, but there's no way that should have cost her life." He walked out with a kelly-green satin blouse. "Too bright?"

139

Evy looked up from stirring two spoons of sugar into her coffee. "Sadly yes. Fraud?"

"Yes." He walked back into her room. "Are you and your psychic friends helping the police?"

She nearly spit out her coffee. "What?"

Rafe walked out of her room with a grin and a cool grey-and-white ensemble that had Evy taking a second look. "You don't exactly make it a secret, Evelyn Landa. Genevieve has regaled my mother with tales of your exploits." He held up the trim grey pants, the oversized white button-down, and the grey menswear vest she'd picked up at a thrift store in Vegas. "How's this?"

She cocked her head. "Actually, with the right jewelry, I love it."

"It's a little more casual, but I think the vest will make it work with the wanker's suit."

Evy smiled. "Not a fan of Chip?"

"He was always a pretentious, smug sort of person," Rafe said. "That whole nonsense when I met him the other day and he pretended not to remember me? I've met him dozens of times at shows. He's an arse. It's not that he's working class, though that's what he'll claim. He's just an arse."

She sipped her coffee, feeling slightly calmer since she had an outfit she knew would look good. "I'm not on camera until noon, but I want to be there by ten if I can." She glanced at the clock. "I should take a shower."

He opened his mouth, then shut it. "And I will join you another day when you are not in a hurry."

"Thank you." She couldn't stop looking at him. "So you know about the psychic thing?"

"I mean, I don't know about it from you. I only know rumors." He leaned his elbows on the counter. "Telepathy? How does it work?"

"It doesn't freak you out that I can read your mind?"

He frowned. "If it were me, I think I'd try to avoid other

people's thoughts as much as possible. I never imagined you were spying." He wiggled his eyebrows. "Were you? Did you hear where I hid those lace panties from last night?"

She tossed a balled-up kitchen towel at him. "Pervert."

"Only for lace and garters—they're my weakness." He lifted the towel, folded it, then walked over and hung it on the wall oven. "Really though, are you helping the police with Bunny's murder case? That's a bit frightening to be honest. What if the murderer knows you're looking for him?"

"You say him, but it could easily be a her."

"Statistically around ninety percent of homicides are committed by men. The chances are good that a man did this." He lifted his coffee. "Though Bunny did piss off both men and women equally, so you may be on to something."

"You said she was committing fraud. Why?"

"I don't know for certain, but I'm fairly sure Bunny is the one who orchestrated Baron's disappearance along with her handler, Curtis Weathers. She wanted the insurance money for the Cartier collar."

"How much was it?"

"She and Stewart had it insured for half a million and she got it in the divorce, though there were stipulations that certain assets and dogs would revert to the ex-spouse if one died before the other."

"So Stewart had motive to kill her."

"In short? Absolutely. The Cartier collars were some of the assets that would revert."

Evy chewed over that thought. "Was Bunny having financial problems?"

"She was paying off a substantial loan on her house, which would have been solved by an insurance settlement."

"She was worried about her mortgage?" Evy's eyebrows went up. "Bunny Barker?"

"That house is worth a fortune, and Bunny had to buy Stewart's share after the divorce if she wanted to stay. They split everything fifty-fifty, so she had continuing income from Stewart's retirement and money from the firm they founded, but she had to pay him half the going market value as of five years ago when they split, which was about six hundred thousand."

"Why wouldn't she just sell the necklace?" Evy asked. "Why not sell both of them?"

"Two reasons spring to mind. Pride for one. Do you think she wanted anyone in her social circle to know that money had become an issue?"

"Oh no. Those people are all about appearances."

"That's one. And the other one was a little quirk that her ex-husband's lawyers overlooked. If she *sold* the Cartier necklaces that Stewart had commissioned for Baron and Zara, Bunny would have had to split the proceeds from them. But the policy attached to the two pieces was never changed to reflect joint ownership when they divorced. The insurance policy followed the asset and listed Bunny as the only one insured."

Evy's mouth dropped open. "So if she sold the collars, she'd have to split the money. But if one was stolen..."

Rafe nodded. "The insurance payment would be all hers."

"That's motive for fraud."

He sipped his coffee. "And that fraud might have led to murder."

Evy felt the phone in her pocket buzzing, so she took it out and saw a text from John Marcos to her, Vivian, and Julia.

Not good news.

She quickly opened her phone just as another text came through.

Coma Guy passed in his sleep last night. There was a pause as another text came through. *There were no signs of foul play. The nurses say it's possible he just succumbed to his injuries. Still no ID.*

"Bad news." She read the text to Rafe. "There goes one more lead."

"And one more life." Rafe's face was grim. "Do we really think it was natural causes?"

"Bunny was finished with a pillow over her face, so it's possible the killer used the same tactic with Coma Guy. But whether he was murdered last night or he died from his injuries, someone is still responsible for his death," Evy said. "And whoever it is, it's probably the same person who killed Bunny."

AN HOUR LATER, EVY MADE HER WAY DOWN TO THE vendor marketplace with her backpack in tow and Geoffrey beside her. She'd rescued Geoff from the greenroom and already apologized for leaving him at the convention center all night. He didn't seem too pissed off, but that could have easily been her imagination.

She didn't know how or why it had happened, but as soon as she'd opened herself to the idea of working with Geoffrey instead of seeing him as a haunt, she'd been able to feel his presence. It wasn't a distinct feeling but more an overall sense of confidence and well-being.

"Looking good, Evy!" Lorain waved at her from a corner of Vendor Row. "Love that vest." *...can't ever pull off menswear like that. Is it my boobs? It's probably my boobs. I never should have let Greg convince me to get that enhancement...*

"Thanks, Lorain." As Evy walked, she realized that the feeling she got from Geoffrey was the same feeling she remembered from the very first time she picked up Geoff and started to practice her ventriloquism. "Geoffrey, we can ignore Lorain from now on. I'm pretty sure she doesn't have anything to do with Bunny's death."

There had always been something freeing about it. Sure, everyone knew where a dummy's voice came from, but it still allowed Evy to let loose, be outrageous, and blame things on the prop.

"Excuse me."

Evy felt someone tug on her shirt and turned with a jerk.

"I'm sorry." A mousy woman with a ruffled plaid shirt was holding up her hands. "I'm so sorry, I'm just new at these things and I think..." She looked a little frantic. "My dog won the Best in Breed competition for all the Pomeranians. Like, all of them. And the show producer told me that because Poms are so popular, the television crew would be coming by to do a feature with me and Pumpkin." She smiled, and Evy saw clear braces on the woman's teeth. "That's my dog, Atherton's Pumpkin Spice Latte, which I know sounds silly, but you have to give show dogs these crazy names so they're not the same as any other dog in the entire world and Pumpkin is just—"

"I'm sorry, but I don't understand." Evy was completely lost. "Are you supposed to be somewhere this morning and you need directions?"

"No, see... I don't know what happened, but yesterday someone from the television crew came by and said that my recording had been cut because of program changes and another lady would be doing the segment on Pomeranians, and I just don't understand why that is because Pumpkin is the one who won the Best in Breed competition."

Evy didn't know for sure, but she had a feeling that Bunny had been the one to put a kibosh on the Pomeranian owner with the frumpy clothes, the mousy hair, and the clear braces. "I'm sorry, but I'm just the host. I don't do any of the scheduling. For that, you'd better talk to Lorain Matthews—she's the dog-show chairwoman, and she's kind of the organizer of all this. If you go over to the information table for the kennel club and tell them the situation, I'm sure they can help you find her."

"Oh, thank you so much!" Pumpkin's mom looked relieved. "I just didn't want to do the wrong thing." She looked around. "This is pretty fancy. Much fancier than I'm used to in New Mexico. But

I qualified, and then Pumpkin won the whole darn thing. Isn't that something?"

Evy couldn't help but smile. The Pomeranian owner was a bright spot in an otherwise very complicated morning. "Your dog must be really wonderful to impress the judges so much."

"And she's just the sweetest thing." The woman looked around. "Thanks for being friendly. Not everyone is at this show."

"I'm sorry you haven't been made more welcome." Evy glanced at the clutch of dog groomers in the corner and directed her mental attention toward them. "Are they part of the problem?"

"Oh, I wouldn't want to say."

...worst kind of people who just show up and think they know something about show dogs and they don't they just don't and it's so obvious who shouldn't be here if the organizers just had some discrimination about who they let in...

Geoffrey was picking up the mental voice of one of the dog groomers in Daphne's clique. He wasn't narrowing in on the two she'd suspected the day before though, and that's when Evy realized that the Hudson Grooming Company table was empty, the banner was gone, and nothing was left except a black-and-white placard with the booth number and a name.

"Excuse me." Evy put her hand on the woman's shoulder. "I need to get going, but you should talk to Lorain, okay?"

"Oh, of course! Thank you so much."

Evy walked toward the empty table, only to be intercepted by Daphne and her assistant. "Why are you back here?"

Evy raised an eyebrow. "'Cause I want to be. You have a problem with that?"

"I just think it's weird that you and Chip are snooping around so much. What do you have to do with the back of the curtain? You're not owners. You're not vendors. Chip isn't even a handler anymore, and there's no way he would be again after what happened in London, is there?"

145

Evy bit her lip to keep from laughing. "Sorry, I don't really keep up with the riveting gossip in the dog-show world."

Daphne's horsey face was smug. "Right. Like you're not in on the Make Chip Popular Again campaign. Whatever. At least it's going to be harder with Bunny gone. Maybe her death had a silver lining after all."

"I don't know what you're talking about." And Evy didn't want to, but then again, maybe she needed to. "And just a word of advice, try not to look so smug about a lady getting murdered when it's pretty clear you hated her."

Daphne's smirk didn't leave. "I don't have anything to hide."

But did Chip? Was he pretending to be someone he wasn't? Had Bunny found out? Chip had worked for the Stewarts and knew their dogs. Could he have been the one to break into Bunny's house and beat her to death?

"Look him up online," Daphne said. "We all know why that man isn't handling animals anymore." *...asshole leaving a mark on a poodle like that and Bunny got livid at me for one bad trim but she was helping that hot-tempered asshole regain some former glory with the higher-ups and what use would it be to...*

"I need to go." Evy glanced at the clock and realized that she had less than an hour to get made up, make her way to the broad-casting set, and go over the schedule with Chip.

She had so many questions. Was there a reason Chip was no longer a handler? She'd assumed that he'd simply retired, but maybe something else was going on.

And if he had a controversial past, why would Bunny—who was entirely focused on appearances—have hired Chip at all?

Chapter Sixteen

"**A**nd that's an end to the sporting group judging, Chip." Evy turned to her cohost with a huge smile. "A thunderous round of applause here in the convention center for the golden retriever Cleopatra and her—let's just call him vivacious—handler Sergio Oliveira."

"A bit of local gossip—Mr. Oliveira is the son of legendary screen actress Sonia Ambrosio, who was also a dog breeder many years ago."

"That's correct. Sergio grew up with golden retrievers and tried his hand at breeding rottweilers but returned to breeding goldens about sixteen years ago," Evy said. "Which may seem like an unusual switch, but I hear that switching breeds is pretty common, right, Chip?"

"Not unusual at all for breeders to expand their breeding programs over the years," Chip said. "And here we can see that Mr. Oliveira has clearly made that switch successfully. Cleopatra is an incredible dog. You can see her spirit and joy in the ring. She loves this crowd."

Keke was giving Evy the signal, so she wrapped up. "Just one more group winner to go, folks. Stick with us and we'll be back in just over half an hour to share the final group judging in... the working group!"

A few moments later Keke shouted, "And out! Take ten, everyone."

Evy pushed back from the announcers' desk with a sigh and a big stretch over her head. "That was a long one."

"And Working will be just as long or longer. Judge Hinkley is known for taking her time." Chip was looking a little ragged that afternoon. "I'm genuinely astonished that Sergio and that German pointer handler didn't come to blows."

"Right? You could feel the tension all the way up here." She eyed Chip, then nudged her backpack under the table. "So with all this drama, do you miss being in the ring with the dogs? It's a little like going from athlete to announcer, right?"

Chip blinked. "I've never been an athlete, so I can't say, but I love being in the announcer's chair. Fewer personalities to juggle."

"Is that why you left handling?"

The corner of his lip twitched. "I feel like you've been listening to gossip, Evy."

"Me?" She shrugged. "I don't know any dog-show people other than Sergio, and trust me, the gossip he shares is usually not about dogs." She leaned closer and wondered why Geoffrey seemed to be striking out. Chip was a completely blank wall. "Was there a delicious kind of *scandal* or something?"

He opened his mouth, then closed it. "I... I don't really know how to answer that."

"I was joking!" She raised her hands. "Sorry, man. Didn't mean to ask any awkward questions. God knows I've got my share of local scandal dogging me." She realized what she'd just said. "No pun actually intended that time."

"Heh." Chip's smile was weak. "Well, people get very protective of their dogs. They're like their children, I suppose. Stewart and Bunny were no different."

"Right." Evy took a deep breath. "I wonder if Bunny left her estate to her dogs. Do people really do that?"

"Oh yes." His face was tight. "In fact, more than one estate has been left to a furry friend. Families usually challenge that in court though."

"Bunny didn't have any kids though, right?"

"She didn't." Chip rose. "Forgive me, I need to take a quick break away from the lights." He smiled politely. "I'll see you shortly."

If that wasn't an escape, she didn't know what was. Evy stood and removed her earpiece, then hiked her backpack over her shoulder. "So is Chip super locked down or something?" She felt something like assurance when she felt Geoffrey hanging around. "Let's go check in with Lorain. And no, not because I think she's a murderer, Geoffrey."

She didn't suspect the show organizer of violence, but if there was gossip, Lorain was sure to be in the center of it, and she wanted to know what had happened to the Hudson siblings.

Evy wandered over to the kennel club booth, which was the largest table and banner set up behind the curtain. There were three ladies in neat grey suits handing out information and directing people to various parts of the vendor marketplace.

Since most of the group judging was done, the back of the curtain area was shifting from a tense atmosphere to something a little more friendly and festive. It was still a bench show, so dogs and handlers were everywhere, but so were carefully concealed glasses of wine, more than a few beers, and hearty conversation.

On Saturday, the show dogs would have a rest and the agility exposition would take center stage. It made for a nice change of pace while all the dogs but the finalists packed up and left the convention center.

"Evy?" Lorain waved at her. "Evy!"

Evy walked over and smiled at the harried woman. "You look like you need a drink."

"Ha! Do I ever, but no, thank you, that's really not appropriate for the timing." She held her clipboard up like a shield. "I tried to touch base with Chip this morning, but if you could mention again at the beginning of the next group judging that the vendor area is still fully running throughout the show. Crowds tend to peter off as we get closer to the finals, and I don't want the vendors to start packing up."

"I saw a few of the groomers had already left." Evy pointed toward the area where fluff and fur were still flying. "The Hudsons, right? The brother and sister with the mobile grooming bus?"

"They *did* leave." Lorain frowned. "Strange kind of thing. They said something about a show in Salt Lake City, but I don't know what they're talking about. The Utah Club already had their big show for the year, but maybe there's a smaller show I don't know about." She shrugged. "We can't actually keep them in the marketplace if they want to leave, even though we hate having those gaps, you know?" *...stupid rednecks and their idiotic truck as if I didn't know they were leaving because no one was giving them the kind of business they used to have not my fault they were the ones who killed that little pug and if they think they're coming back from something like that...*

"So have the police said anything else about Bunny?" She wondered if John Marcos had already talked to the Hudsons. "Or about Baron?"

Lorain quickly looked down at her clipboard. "You know, they haven't, but they probably know how hectic things are back here. Such a tragedy, of course, but Bunny would have wanted us to carry on."

"I'm sure she would." Evy hooked her backpack higher on her shoulder and kept walking. "I'll talk to you later."

"You're doing great, Evy!" Lorain forced a big smile. "The ratings this year have been better than ever!"

"I FOUND YOU."

Evy turned to see Sergio hovering by her ear. "Oh my dog." She turned and threw her arms around her friend's neck. "You are a sight for the sorest eyes."

"You're finished! Mostly!" He rubbed her back and squeezed her again. "How are you, doll?"

She nodded at her backpack where Geoff was peeking out. "I've been listening all day, even when I was live."

"Oh dear." Sergio frowned. "Is that why you let that catty comment about the Dogo Argentino slip out?"

"I thought a colonization joke would fly a bit better, but I forgot my cohost was English. I did not mean to be culturally offensive."

"That's okay." Sergio shrugged. "I'm Brazilian. You can insult Argentinians all you want."

"I thought that was just for soccer."

"Oh no, it's for everything." He pressed her head to his chest and covered her ear with his hand. "Is that better?"

Unfortunately, being this close to Sergio just meant that his mental monologue was that much louder.

...poor thing doesn't know how vicious oh she can probably hear me hi Evy! Oh my God is the sex with Rafe good? I always thought it probably would be strong vibes with that one but I don't think he's ever played on our team even a little he's a big fan of pussy isn't he? I can see that about him...

"For the love of Dolly, Sergio." She pushed away. "Could your internal monologue be any more intrusive?"

"Obviously yes, it *could* be." He cocked his head. "Do you want it to be?"

"No." She laughed. "And I'm not answering any of those questions."

"Whatever. Just tell me where you need to be and I'll walk you there and beat back anyone who tries to talk to you." He propped her up and put an arm around her waist. "Are you done for the night?"

"Officially yes, but I am consulting with..." She dropped her voice. "...the police about the thing."

"Oh my God, are you helping the police solve Bunny's murder?"

Evy looked at him. "Do you have any concept of secrecy or privacy at all? I mean... at all?"

He pursed his lips. "Not really, no."

"Yes, I'm helping them. I'm a consultant or something; they're actually going to pay me this time."

"Oh, that's nice. Good, because what is this vest? It looks old, Evy. Why are you wearing old clothes to professional things?"

"It's not old, it's vintage."

"Same thing." He put his hand at the small of her back and moved her through the crowd that was quickly shuffling out of the convention center now that the day's judging was done. There was a sizable number going to the vendor marketplace, but Sergio steered around them, causing Evy to nearly trip over a pair of legs from a man bent over and securing a large crate.

"Oh, I'm so sorry." She braced herself on the stranger's shoulder and held on to Sergio's arm. "It's so crowded in here."

The man looked up and frowned. "I beg your pardon, are you—?"

"Kurt!" Sergio immediately exclaimed. "How are you? Have you met EV Lane yet? She's one of the cohosts."

The man stood and straightened himself, adjusting the slim black tie that matched the pure black standard poodle he'd shown in the ring. "Of course. Miss Lane, very nice to meet you. The commentary this year has been far more lively than usual."

"I don't know if that's a compliment or veiled passive aggression, but I'll just say thanks anyway." She held out her hand. "You handle Hercules, the standard poodle, right?"

The man glanced at the crate. "I do. We were just wrapping up here. I'm meeting Mr.—"

"Kurt!" A voice bellowed from across the room. "What in God's name is taking so long? I've filed federal cases that have moved faster than..." A barrel-chested man stepped into Evy's personal space. "Who are you?"

"Evy, meet Stewart Barker." Sergio practically shoved Evy's hand out. "Stew, this is EV Lane, one of the announcers for the show this year and a friend of mine."

The man gripped her hand like it was a contest, and then he let it go with a hard shake.

"You're the woman." Stewart Barker didn't seem to have any volume but ten. "Thank God you're there to liven Chip up. I swear to God, that man gets more boring every year."

Evy could see Chip in the distance, well in earshot of Stewart Barker, trying to speak to Lorain and Keke at the club table. His shoulders went still when he heard his name bellowing from Stewart's mouth.

"Well, I'm certainly glad Chip is working with me," Evy said. "I don't know a fraction of what he does about dogs."

"Bah, just give this one all the awards." Stewart motioned to the crate. "Do that and everyone will be happy."

"Not so fast, old man." Sergio elbowed him. "My Cleo is in the ring with your fancy boy tomorrow, and she takes no prisoners."

"He's a shoo-in!" Stewart had a gleam in his eye. "I knew Bunny couldn't tie up that trophy forever. It's about time it's Hercules's shot."

"I'm so sorry about your ex-wife," Evy said. "I didn't know Bunny well, but she seemed like a force of nature."

A complicated mix of emotions ran over Stewart Barker's face. Anger. Sadness. Confusion. More anger.

"I tell you this." Stewart shoved a finger in Evy's face. "Whatever bastard did that to my Bunny, he better pray the police lock him up before I find him. I may be an old man now, but I know people, you hear me?"

Her shields were down, but the fact was that Stewart Barker's internal monologue was about as straightforward as his external rant definitely helped Evy keep her mind focused. *...fucking dregs of human waste who would hurt Bunny such a God I miss ya Bun whatever you were up to you made me laugh the fucking balls on whoever did this shit...*

"So you don't have any idea who would have hurt Bunny?" Evy asked. "The police seem to think—"

"Those fucking cops don't know their ass from their elbow." Stewart turned to Sergio. "Do you know those fuckers came to my own house and questioned me? Me? About Bunny! Those assholes."

"I'm sure they have to ask, Stew." Sergio rubbed Evy's back. "Not everyone understood that you and Bunny were still close."

"That woman made me crazy! But she was still my wife."

Evy frowned. "Hadn't you been divorced for like five years?"

"And?" Stewart was scowling. "Just 'cause I got a girlfriend doesn't mean Bunny wasn't my wife. That's a different thing, you understand?"

"Not really," Evy murmured.

"Stew, we need to get Hercules back to the house." The handler put a hand on Stewart's shoulder. "He's getting overstimulated, and he only has tomorrow to rest."

"Fucking smartest dogs in the fucking world." Stewart looked at Evy and stabbed a finger at the poodle's crate. "I thought Bunny was nuts when she started this whole business, but these dogs are smarter than most people I know."

"Do the police have any idea where Baron is?"

Stewart pounded a fist on his chest. "That dog. I don't even know what to say. It breaks my heart. Roman and Zara too. I just want them all back with me. The poor things." He turned to the handler. "Kurt, I'll get Mario to start the van." He gripped Evy's hand. "Miss Lane, it was a pleasure. I look forward to your commentary on Sunday for the Best in Show. Sergio, my dog is gonna beat your ass, and you're gonna thank him." He gave Sergio a small salute, then stomped away.

Sergio laughed a little. "You're wrong, but see you in the ring."

Kurt turned to Evy and Sergio. "The police told us they were holding on to Bunny's two other dogs until the investigation was over. I don't suppose you guys have heard where they're keeping them, have you? They're not at the shelter or something like that, are they?"

Evy answered, "They found a home to foster them in the neighborhood. They'll be very safe."

"Dogs understand death," Kurt said. "They grieve for people. I hope whoever is keeping them knows that. Stewart may come across as brash, but he adores his poodles. They need to be with him."

"I understand." Evy was inclined to think that Stewart was innocent of any wrongdoing, but if he had "people," not all of them might have been as understanding and appreciative of Bunny as Stewart appeared to be. "Kurt, do you have any idea who Bunny's heir was?"

"I think her niece and nephew?" The man shook his head. "She and her sister were close, I do know that. And the sister had two kids, a boy and a girl. I'd kind of expect her to leave the estate to them, but I don't know that for sure. Stewart would know all the legal details. Despite the yelling, they knew everything about each other."

155

Chapter Seventeen

H*eading over to try to talk with Bunny.*

It was a text that could only come from Julia.

Evy wanted to hide at home, but a woman was dead and over three days had passed with no real leads. She didn't feel responsible, but she did feel like she needed to be doing *something*. There was a murderer roaming around Palm Springs, and they'd already killed two people.

She headed to Bunny's house despite her desire to stick her head in the sand.

After pulling into Richard's driveway, she crossed the lawn and entered the front gate, where someone had left a note on the door with the code.

"Hey, guys?" Evy wandered back, still carrying Geoff in the backpack. "Geoffrey, maybe you can fill me in on anything I missed today. Julia will be here."

A positive energy floated through the night air.

The cool May night was clear, and the sky above Vista de Lirio was filled by a dense canopy of stars. Evy walked across the grass, listening for the sound of her friends.

Roman bounded up to her, letting out a small *wuf* that didn't quite make it to a full-throated bark.

"Hey, buddy."

Roman stood at attention.

Evy heard Vivian calling from a distance. "Roman?"

"He's out in front with me."

Vivian walked around the side of the house and patted her leg. "Hey, Roman. Come on back, boy. Come back to me."

The dog gave Evy another suspicious glance, then trotted off toward Vivian. Henry was sitting on her hip, babbling happily at the dogs. "I don't know how I'm going to give these two up," she said. "I love them already."

"Well, if you want to keep them, you're going to end up fighting Stewart Barker."

"I had a feeling you might bring him up." Vivian rubbed the top of Roman's curly head and bounced Henry. "Sergio texted me and Julia. Said you'd met him after the show tonight. Didn't he, Henry? He sounded like a big grumpy old man, huh? We should keep the happy curly dogs at our house, shouldn't we?"

Henry seemed to agree, and Roman licked Henry's slobbery, outstretched hand.

Evy wrinkled her nose. "He's gonna put that right in his mouth, isn't he?"

"It's almost impossible to keep them from sharing slobber." Vivian tried to clean Henry's dog-slobber hand with a wipe before he stuck it back in his mouth. "He's completely in love though. I get why people go a little nuts over these dogs."

"Well, Stewart Barker is a character, but Geoffrey and I aren't getting anything murderous from him. He seems genuinely upset and downright pissed about someone killing Bunny. Still calls her his wife and everything."

"I wonder why they got divorced." Vivian wore a small frown between her eyebrows. "I suppose it doesn't really matter; I doubt it had anything to do with her murder. Julia's out back already."

Evy lowered her voice as they rounded the house and saw Julia sitting silently in a corner near the olive tree. Zara was lying at her feet. "Any luck yet?"

"No, though apparently Bunny's ghost seems more peaceful tonight. She's happy the dogs are here."

Julia glanced at Evy and offered her a nod, but she didn't move her attention from the olive tree.

"Thanks, Mae," Julia said quietly. "Bunny, Mae is going to stay with us a while if that's okay. She says that your spirit is very torn right now, but it will get better with a little time. Can you nod?" Julia smiled. "That's great! I saw that. I did."

Mae was only one of the many ghosts that lived in Vista de Lirio, most often at Dean and Sergio's house. She was one of the friendlier spirits in the neighborhood and often followed Julia around when she was showing houses. Julia described Mae as one of the liveliest spirits she'd ever met.

Zara perked up and stood, walking to the olive tree, sniffing around, then going back to sit next to Julia. She put a single paw up and set it in Julia's lap.

"You're so sweet, Zara. You know Bunny is here, don't you?" Julia held the dog's hand and patted her fluffy head. "That's right, she'll be more with us tomorrow night, I bet." She kept talking to the dog as Vivian and Evy moved closer. "Mae was telling me that sometimes when someone has been really hurt—not just physically but emotionally—then their ghost is a little fragmented at first." She glanced at Evy. "That usually happens when there's been a personal betrayal. Sometimes it takes a spirit a little while to feel whole enough to talk."

Evy sat next to Zara and rolled up her pant legs to dangle her feet in the pool. "Then we can wait, can't we? The dog show is still going really well, Bunny."

Julia nodded. "She's interested."

"Let's see, the group winners are all chosen now. The only contest left is Best in Show. They're doing all the agility trials tomorrow since it's Saturday. Then we have the champions' brunch on Sunday morning before the Best in Show judging. In fact, Baron's son Hercules took the top prize in the non-sporting group. He'd be a proud papa, don't you think?"

"She's not sure about that. Something about that is upsetting," Julia said softly. "Maybe talk about the other dogs."

"I'm sure you remember that wonderful little mini schnauzer from London, right? Jade Beauty? Well, she and her handler got the top prize in the terrier group, so she'll be in the final too. I think you and that dog's owner were friends, right?"

"This is good. She likes the news," Julia said. "Keep it coming."

"And let's see, Sergio and his golden retriever took the prize in the sporting group. There was this absolutely gorgeous Doberman pinscher named Lulu in the working group. She was the winner there. Uh... the toy group was kind of a surprise! Apparently there was a papillon that everyone thought was sure to win, but the Havanese won in an upset. His name was Tito, and I drank a shot of vodka to celebrate."

"She just smiled. She liked the vodka-shot story."

Evy turned her face to the olive tree. "Everyone misses you at the show, Bunny. Chip and I are trying to keep it together, but Lorain is kind of lost without you. Don't tell her I said that. It's just not the same. And she's really upset that some of the vendors left early. Oof." Evy remembered the grooming area. "I don't know how you dealt with those grooming people. I was telling Chip earlier that groomers are the worst gossips, and that's saying something when you're talking about—"

"Evy, wait."

"Oh." She pursed her lips together. "Too much?"

"She's upset again. Mae can you— Okay, no worries." Julia turned to Evy. "Bunny kind of drifted away. It's okay, she stayed longer than she did this afternoon. Mae's going to hang around and see if she can coax her out again."

Evy still felt guilty. "Was it talking about missing her? I don't know how to talk to ghosts."

"That's okay." Julia sat back. "Geoffrey's here. Good to see you, sir. How was the dog show?" Julia laughed. "I'll tell her. Geoffrey says it's the most excitement he's had in ages. He's loving it in that very reserved, stuffy, Geoffrey way." She rolled her eyes. "Geoffrey, I can call you stuffy if I want. You know you are. He says you've been doing very well, and he wants to know how his help has been with the telepathy."

Evy nodded. "Pretty good. I feel more focused. I'm still taking half my meds, so I'm not crystal clear, but I think that's good. I can definitely sense when he focuses on certain people. They come in loud and clear."

"Do you have any suspects? He wants to know."

"Stewart was definitely one, but I think he's in the clear from what I was reading this afternoon. I didn't get much of a read from his handler, Kurt something, and he could be a suspect." She tried to think. "Just anyone I haven't been able to read yet. I can't get into Chip's head right now because we're on air together most of the day. I did have a thought about maybe trying to go to the hospital to visit Coma Guy and see if I could read anything, but clearly that isn't—"

"Hold that thought!" Vivian spoke up. "Richard just texted me. Can we head over to his house if Bunny is gone? John is over there, and Rafe just showed up, looking for Evy."

Evy rolled her head back and stretched her neck. "Oh right, I told him I was coming over here. Sorry."

"No worries. He's more than welcome, but apparently Rafe and John are not each other's biggest fans." Vivian bounced Henry on her lap. "We better head over so Richard doesn't get caught in the cross fire."

"Sounds good." Julia nodded. "I think Mae is going to hang out here a little bit, and if Bunny wants to talk, she'll let me know."

"Do we have to leave?" Evy wrinkled her nose. "I don't feel like hanging out with grumpy men tonight."

"I know, but all those men are looking into Bunny's murder

from one angle or another," Vivian said. "From a purely organizational perspective, it's probably a good thing if we all coordinate."

Evy let her head fall back, then looked at Vivian. "Why are you the worst?"

"You always say that when I'm right about something."

"Because it's the truth."

Evy hung back as Vivian took the lead with the two grumbling men on Richard's patio. Vivian carried an air of maternal authority that silenced both John and Rafe as soon as she walked into the backyard.

"Okay, listen. All of us want the same thing right now." Vivian glanced at her watch while simultaneously bouncing Henry on her hip. "In one minute, I'm going to go down the hall and feed Henry before I put him down to bed. The rest of you are going to meet in the kitchen—I'm sure Julia can make drinks for everyone—and you can drink, snack a little." She looked at Richard. "Are there snacks?"

"I think so?" He shrugged. "If there aren't, I'll order out."

"Great!" Vivian smiled. "Let's everyone get their notes together and we can collaborate." She looked at John pointedly. Then Rafe. "We all want the same thing here. A woman has been murdered. Another man died from his injuries. A beloved dog is missing. And someone has stolen from Bunny's estate. These things are all important and likely tied together. If we pool our knowledge, we have a better chance of making sense of this, right?"

Evy wanted to say "Yes, mom" even though Vivian was younger than she was.

John sighed. "You're right."

"Absolutely," Rafe said. "I'm on board for collaborating. I'll share whatever I can."

"Great!" Vivian smiled. "Henry, say good night to all these big grown-ups who are going to collaborate like professionals."

Henry said, "Bah bada, gahgo" and blew a raspberry.

Evy gave him a thumbs-up. If that wasn't the best way to exit a room, she didn't know what was.

Vivian disappeared into the house with Richard while Julia, Evy, John, and Rafe went through the french doors to the kitchen.

Julia made herself at home at the fridge, pulling out a bottle of white wine, a bottle of vodka, and a whiskey before she turned to John and Rafe. "Okay, what can I get you both to drink?"

"Beer," John said.

"Just water for me."

She pursed her lips. "You're boring." She turned back to the fridge and got a bottle of beer for John. "Rafe, glasses are over there; help yourself—I'm not serving you water."

Evy sat at the table while Julia made her a vodka tonic with a slice of orange. Then she poured two fingers of whiskey over crushed ice with another slice of orange before finally pouring herself a glass of white wine. She left the whiskey on the counter, then walked to the kitchen table and sat next to Evy, handing her the vodka cocktail.

"You're my favorite person in the world." Evy laid her head on Julia's shoulder. "You're a beautiful ghost therapist and my personal bartender."

"You don't deserve my awesomeness."

"I don't, but I do."

"I know."

John and Rafe were looking at both of them like they had two heads, but Evy didn't care. She adored her two best friends and didn't quite know how she'd survived forty years without them.

Richard walked into the kitchen. "She's going to be about twenty more minutes—she said we should get started." He pulled a white marker out of his pocket. "And she gave me this."

Julia jumped up. "Cool! We can use the french doors for a murder board. Good thinking."

Richard blinked. "A what?"

Julia pointed to the counter. "Your whiskey is over there. I promise the marker will wash off."

She walked over, uncapped the marker, then wrote BUNNY on top of one door, BARON/NECKLACE at the top of the other. Then she turned to all of them.

"Okay, let's start with the necklace and Baron since that happened first."

Rafe raised his hand. "I liked Bunny, but I suspected her of fraud. She took twenty thousand dollars out in cash a week before Baron went missing, and she didn't have an explanation for it other than she was helping out a friend. She never explained to me where the money went, but I think it was to hire someone to take the dog and the necklace."

Julia wrote MISSING 20K on the glass door. "Okay, John?"

"We didn't have any information about that until Bunny died because we had no reason to suspect she'd kidnap her own dog, so we had no reason to look into her finances."

Evy frowned. "Kidnap or dognap?"

"Either way," Rafe said. "The insurance company thinks it's highly probable that Baron is living the good life somewhere of Bunny's choosing with a friend or associate until the insurance pays out. Curtis, her handler, is a strong contender since no one seems to be able to find him and he had a good relationship with the dog."

Richard sipped his whiskey and frowned at the doors. "If Bunny needed the money, why couldn't she just sell the Cartier necklaces? Wouldn't that have been easier?"

Evy said, "She couldn't sell them without splitting the money with Stewart."

Richard nodded. "Makes sense; she would hate that."

Rafe said, "My working theory was that Bunny was planning

to claim the insurance money, then in a few years make the collar reappear and say she ordered another one to match Zara's." Rafe glanced at the pure black poodle. "Speaking of that, do we know where Zara's collar is?"

"It was in the safe," John said. "And the contents of Bunny's safe were taken to the police station until the case is closed. I figured that was more secure than leaving everything in an empty house."

Rafe was appeased. "Good call."

Julia got them back on track. "So Bunny probably staged Baron's dognapping to claim the insurance money, but then how does she end up dead? The dognapper is out of luck. She can't claim the insurance money if she's dead, and he's stuck with a dog that's supposed to be missing."

Rafe let out a frustrated breath. "This is where I lose the plot. Nothing about the insurance-fraud plot works if Bunny dies."

"Unless the dognapper has the necklace too," Richard said.

"Do you really think Bunny would hand over the Cartier collar *and* the priceless dog?" Julia asked.

"No," Richard said. "She wasn't a naturally trusting person. She had very few friends."

Evy asked, "Could whoever has the necklace now just sell it? Fence it?"

"It would depend on who they are," Rafe said. "And what kind of connections they have. It's a custom-made Cartier collar. It's one of a kind, so it would make waves on the open market."

"They'd need a black market sale," John said.

"Almost certainly," Rafe said. "And it's not like your average Palm Springs society maven is likely to have connections like that, nor is a professional dog handler like Curtis Weathers."

"So probably Bunny wasn't planning to sell the necklace," Richard said. "Probably she was just going to claim the insurance."

"I..." An idea was tickling the back of Evy's head, but she wasn't sure if it was feasible. "Never mind."

"Nope," John said. "If you have an idea, shout it out. We still have no idea how we got from insurance fraud to murder."

"Who benefits from Bunny dying?"

"Stewart Barker," John said. "Her niece and nephew, but we have no evidence they were involved. They live in New York."

Evy blurted out, "I think Bunny was going to sell the necklace."

John frowned. "But the insurance payout—"

"Would have covered the house loan." Evy nodded. "But what about her lifestyle? The housekeeper. The gardener. Do you really think Bunny Barker wanted to keep picking up her own dog's poop in the yard?"

Julia shook her head. "No way."

"But think about this show." Evy leaned forward. "What's different this year from any other year they've held it?"

Julia sat up straight. "The international competitors."

Rafe raised one eyebrow. "It *would* be easier to fence the collar if you got it out of the country."

Richard nodded. "There are private collectors in Europe who would be interested in something like that. And if not there, then you have the Middle East and Asia."

John asked, "Did Bunny have those kinds of connections?"

"Maybe not," Evy said. "But Bunny's dog club is hosting one of the biggest dog shows in the country while making a point to invite participants from all over the globe." She looked at John and Rafe. "Why settle for a half a million when you could have a full million?"

Julia smiled. "You think Bunny was going to claim the insurance *and* sell the necklace."

"A million dollars is a hell of a supplement to her retirement savings. What if the whole international theme of the dog show this year was set up so she could steal her own necklace, sell it with a partner overseas, and get the money from the sale *and* the money from the insurance payout?"

John and Rafe exchanged glances.

"It's possible," John said. "There are people from at least two dozen countries in town right now."

Evy looked at Rafe. "And Bunny was friends with all of them, right?"

"I'd say she knew some of them for forty or fifty years." Rafe rubbed his jaw. "All that equipment, all the luggage... one sparkly collar. It would be easy to sneak something out in the chaos."

"But the partner got greedy," Julia said. "Whatever Bunny was paying wasn't going to cut it. He or she wanted more than their share, and when Bunny didn't agree..."

"He killed her," Evy said. "Or she killed her. If we're right, it has to be someone involved with the show."

"Which means"—Richard finally spoke up—"that you folks have about two more days to figure this out." He raised his eyebrows. "After that, your suspects are going to start flying away."

Chapter Eighteen

On Sunday morning, Evy was a guest of honor at the Desert Fancy Kennel Club Champions' Brunch, a yearly event to celebrate the seven group winners for the Best in Show competition, their owners, the handlers and even the dogs themselves. It was held in a patio garden of the Monte Verde Country Club. Normally Bunny would have been the hostess as the president of the club, but this year Lorain Matthews had taken over the event.

Lorain waved Evy over as soon as she arrived with Rafe as her plus one.

"Evy, thank God you're here." Lorain already looked frazzled, and it was only nine thirty. "Okay, we're going to have to play diplomat a little bit this morning. Remember, we have lots of competitive people. The handlers and dogs aren't usually a problem, but the owners can be a little..."

"Bitchy?" Evy supplied.

"Sensitive is what I was going to say." Lorain looked like she was nursing a headache. "But that other word might work too."

"I'll do my best. You know Rafe Bamford-Howell, right? His mother Marina is one of the owners."

Lorain's face drained of color. "I'm sure your mother is lovely."

Rafe only looked amused. "She is, but you're right. All the rest of them?" He leaned closer. "Complete drama queens." He winked at Lorain, and her cheeks flushed a little. "Evy and I will be more than happy to circulate and keep things casual and friendly."

Lorain fluttered away, and Evy angled her eyes at Rafe. "You're good at that."

"What? Reassuring stressed people?"

"Charming women." She shoved her hands in the pockets of her crisp grey suit. "Are you charming me?"

"I certainly hope so." He moved his hand to her lower back as they walked into the room, sliding a finger under the back of her jacket and teasing his thumb along her spine. "I've been putting in my best effort."

"There's you being unfair with that accent again."

"I keep telling you, you're the one with the accent." He moved his hand and waved at someone across the room. "Speaking of accents, let's introduce you to Liam."

Evy turned and spotted the most pleasantly plump man she'd ever seen. If "jolly professor" had a dictionary entry, his picture would be next to it. "Oh my God, that's Badger the corgi's handler!"

"And owner." Rafe walked them across the room. "Liam Davies is one of the most genuine individuals you'll ever meet at one of these things. No pretense at all; he just loves dogs."

They reached the table, and the professor stood, reaching out his hand.

"Rafe." He shook Rafe's hand, then turned to Evy. "And the marvelous EV Lane! So nice to finally meet you. Liam Davies. You've been giving Chip a good run, haven't you?"

"I don't know what that means, but I love your dog." She looked at Badger, who was busy sniffing under the table, his fluffy backside wiggling as he snuffled. "I'm so happy he won."

"You're very kind. You're a good little man, aren't you,

Badger?" Liam shook the short lead that was holding the dog, who looked over his shoulder at his owner, huffed, then went back to investigating the carpet for snacks.

Rafe and Evy sat at two of the empty chairs at the table. "Liam, I was telling Evy that you're one of the nicest people in the circuit and I'm glad your fame hasn't changed you." He turned to Evy. "Badger just won a very prestigious prize in the UK a few months ago."

"Still just a small-town dog from Cardiff though." Liam smiled. "I have to say, it's been quite something to travel all the way out to California. My first time here, and I'm feeling a bit like the country bumpkin in the big city."

"Oh, Palm Springs is not that big," Evy said. "Have you been to Los Angeles?"

"We flew in there." Liam nodded. "Badger and me. Then Ms. Barker came and whisked us away with her driver. It's quite the unusual landscape in the desert, isn't it?"

"Bunny brought you in herself?" A hint of a smile curved up the corner of Rafe's mouth. "That was very kind."

"Wasn't it?" Liam looked around. "I believe she sponsored several of the top competitors this year, all to foster the international spirit of the show. That's the way she phrased it."

Evy nodded. "I know that was a bit of a push this year, making the show more international. Kind of as a way to raise the club's profile, I think."

"Yes, it's a good strategy." Liam pointed across the room at a tall couple standing next to the Doberman pinscher. "Geerta and Marc Weber are from Munich—Lulu's owners—Bunny sponsored their entry fee for the show." He looked around more and gestured to an elegantly dressed woman in a long cream dress. "And that's Rania al Ahmadi from Dubai. She's Tito's owner, and she has a very extensive Havanese breeding program. Determined to elevate the breed's global profile, and I'm sure she'll do it. Isn't she glamorous?" Liam blushed a little. "She was very complimentary of Badger."

Evy raised an eyebrow. "It doesn't look like she needs a sponsor for anything."

Rania al Ahmadi wore diamonds like she'd been born with them. Her wardrobe might seem casual that morning, but it was simple in a way that screamed exorbitant amounts of money.

"Oh no," Liam continued. "I believe her development company was a show sponsor this year. But Bunny reached out personally to Rania. They're friends." Liam grimaced. "*Were* friends. I just can't believe any of this happened." He looked sorrowful. "It doesn't seem real, does it?"

"I know what you mean." Rafe shook his head. "Such a senseless act."

"And to such a kind woman." Liam pursed his lips and shook Badger's lead. "Wasn't she, Badger? Just a sweet woman who loved dogs. Was it a burglar or something like that?"

"They think it might have had something to do with Baron's disappearance," Rafe said. "And his collar. You know anything about that, Liam?"

"Oh, if you're asking for gossip, I don't know anything." He chortled. "I'm not one for intrigue! Probably because I'm horrible at keeping secrets." His smile fell. "Everyone knows that. I told Bunny when she told me she wanted to sponsor me. I told her: Don't expect me to not share it, Bunny!"

Evy asked, "Did she ask you to keep it a secret?"

"Not... precisely. But I got the feeling she didn't want everyone to know that she was being so generous. I can't help it though, can I? When someone is kind, I just want to give them the credit."

Evy smiled. Liam Davies was so sweet she wanted to hug him and take him home to serve him tea. And Evy didn't even like tea.

Rafe knew how to mine a source though; she had to give him credit. He leaned one elbow on the table and scanned the room.

"So who else did Bunny reach out to personally? You and the Webers obviously. Rania and her entourage..."

"Well..." Liam cocked his head. "It's funny you ask. Other than the three American competitors here, I think every single one of the Best in Show finalists are people Bunny knew personally." Liam turned to Rafe. "She really did know how to pick winners, didn't she?"

Rafe glanced at Evy. "She really, really did."

THE BOW-TIED VICE PRESIDENT WAS GIVING A SPEECH to the winners, and it seemed to go on and on.

And on.

Evy's eyes were beginning to droop, so she reached for the porcelain coffeepot, only to have it scooped up by an attentive server who refilled her cup before she could blink.

"Thank you," she whispered.

The server smiled and stepped back to her position along the edge of the patio.

"And without Bunny's generosity of spirit, tenacity, and vision to make the Desert Fancy Kennel Club Open a world-renowned competition of reputation, high standards, and international dog appreciation, we would not be here today." The bow-tied man put his reading glasses together and lifted a mimosa. "To Bunny Butterfield Barker."

"To Bunny," the party responded, then there was polite applause as the vice president stepped down from the podium and Lorain stepped up.

Rafe leaned toward Evy's ear. He directed his eyes at the table across from them where one of the other owners was sitting. "The Lomaxes."

"Who— Oh!" Evy nodded. "Right."

It was another British couple Liam had mentioned. The man

was pale, narrow-faced, and in his midsixties. The woman was the same one Evy and Chip had met at the television station, an aristocratic beauty with dark brown skin and a heart-shaped face; she wore a head wrap that looked West African.

"Juliet and Edgar Lomax, mini schnauzer breeders," Rafe said. "Very high dollar. The breed is getting very popular in London the past few years. He was big in an energy company, and I believe she was a lawyer before they had children. Now their kids are grown and she's all about the dogs. Incredibly competitive and highly focused. Juliet and Bunny started showing dogs around the same time."

"The handler?" Evy eyed a woman in an immaculately cut forest-green suit.

"American, if you can believe it. She went to school in the UK. Her name's Kenzie Hawthorn. She's their handler, and I believe she runs their kennel as well. Their dog Jade Beauty came in second to Liam and Badger in that big show he just won, and they'd love to beat him this time."

"Okay, so Bunny recruited Liam. Should we assume she recruited the Lomaxes as well?"

"I think that's a safe bet with Bunny and Juliet being so close."

The table next to the Lomaxes was occupied by the party representing Hercules, the standard poodle. Stewart Barker was there along with a heavily made-up blond woman in her early thirties, his handler Kurt Peterson, a woman who seemed to be with Kurt, and two other men in matching polo shirts paying strict attention to Lorain's speech.

"Stewart's here," Evy said. "Along with a crowd."

"You met Kurt already. I believe that's Kurt's wife. Girlfriend? Not sure, but they've been together a while. They're normal folks."

"Did he bring muscle with him?" Evy glanced at the broadly built men in polo shirts.

Rafe chuckled. "Pretty sure those are just employees of the kennel."

"They're big guys."

"Well, maybe they're muscle too."

Evy turned her attention to the German couple who were sitting in front of them, just next to Lorain's podium. "The Webers. Liam said Bunny sponsored them too?"

"They're not from money. Owner-handlers like Liam. Geerta is usually the one who shows Lulu, but sometimes Marc will step in. They both have fairly normal jobs. Engineers or architects, something like that."

"So not likely to have illicit black market connections to fence a stolen Cartier?"

Lorain's voice broke through their whispers. "And we cherish that time and dedication. She brought so much joy to so many that it would be wrong to focus on the ending of her life instead of on the great organization she built and the show that drew so many of us together." Lorain paused, and the party offered polite applause.

"Of the four foreign finalists for Best in Show" —Rafe leaned closer as Lorain continued to speak— "I'd say that Rania and the Lomaxes are the most likely to have any connections to the black market. Rania also has a private plane, which would make smuggling *anything* easier. I believe the Lomaxes fly commercial."

Evy saw Chip from the corner of her eye. He was staring at her and Rafe with a scowl.

"Shhh." Evy hushed her date. "Chip is gonna get me in trouble."

"Oh, poor Chip." Rafe chuckled a little. "Ever the prefect."

"What's that?"

He whispered, "I'll tell you later."

"...so we feel her presence in every happy bark and bounce. We celebrate the joy she took in these wonderful animals that offer their companionship, and we celebrate the seven competitors here who represent the finest of purebred-dog breeding from around the world."

More applause as Lorain looked up. "Could we have all the owners step forward please? If you could bring your dogs with you, that would be perfect."

One by one, seven parties stepped forward. First was Sergio with his gloriously happy golden retriever Cleopatra, who was far too friendly to be queen of anything but Sergio's kitchen.

Then came Liam and Badger, shuffling to the front and shaking hands with everyone. Liam even bent down and offered his hand to Cleo, who happily shook with a lolling tongue and a doggy grin.

Rania al Ahmadi walked up next, tall and elegant with an immaculately brushed Havanese in her arms, the little spry dog Tito with his gorgeous cream-and-grey coat brushed out to look like falling silk. Rania might have been an elegant lady, but her face glowed with pride as people applauded for her and her dog.

Next came the low-key Weber couple, their Doberman Lulu alert and relaxed with the straightest posture Evy had ever seen on a dog. Geerta and Marc shook hands with everyone in the line of champions, exchanging small pleasantries before they stood next to Rania.

Rafe's mother Marina was next with the stunning Soraya, the Afghan hound's luxurious coat flowing like a satin gown as she walked to the front.

Marina was followed by Mrs. Lomax holding the pert, chocolate-brown Jade, whose curving whiskers seemed to quiver with excitement as everyone clapped.

And finally Stewart Barker stepped forward with Hercules, both the dog and the man holding their heads high. There was extra applause for them, no doubt on account of Bunny's loss. Stewart looked a little red in the face, but he nodded brusquely at the crowd and shook hands with the rest of the owners as Hercules followed along like a faithful lieutenant.

Rafe stretched out his legs and reached for Evy's hand. "A fine-looking group of suspects, don't you think?"

"You're including your mother and Sergio in the suspect pool?"

"Anything's possible with purebred-dog breeders, Landa. Anything."

Chapter Nineteen

"And we're back today for our final competition in the Desert Fancy Kennel Club Open." Chip sparkled into the camera. "I'm Chip Dunklin."

"And I'm EV Lane." She shined her brightest smile toward the giant black eye of the live camera. "Welcome back for the final round, where seven champions compete under the gaze of a live audience to find out who will take home the trophy this year for Best in Show."

"We have seven marvelous dogs competing this year, and they'll be ranked by one of the best judges in the business, Evy. Just a really remarkable professional, Judge Angus Mason from Chicago."

Evy watched as cameras moved around the floor of the convention center. The stands were packed with attendees. Since there was only one round today, it was by far the best attended.

The hubbub behind the scenes was equally chaotic. Vendors were in full swing and much of the past two hours had been a rush of first-time attendees swarming the vendor tent in the few hours before the Best in Show judging.

As Chip wrapped up the introduction of Judge Mason, Evy

tried to keep her wits about her. She could feel Geoffrey nearby, but he hadn't connected with any of the dozens of people surrounding Evy. She'd had little luck at the breakfast that morning; the competitors had all been too focused on the afternoon's competition.

Now all she could do was hang on for dear life as four prime suspects in Bunny's death—she couldn't imagine Sergio, Rafe's mother, or Liam being involved—clapped politely from the front rows as their handlers trotted each dog around the show ring.

"Cut to background on the miniature schnauzer," Keke called. "Three minutes."

Evy took a deep breath, stepped away from the desk, and stood quickly, swinging her arms and stretching her neck. "You good?"

"I'm ready to fly back to London if that's what you're asking," Chip said. "Five days is too long; they should have done the Best in Show judging yesterday."

"I have no idea how that goes, but I have a feeling they wanted to sell as many tickets for today as possible."

"I suppose that's true."

"Chip and Evy, you're back in one."

Evy sat at the table again, pleased to see she was still put together and had managed to avoid getting dog hair on her neat black suit.

"Did they already do background on the owners?" Chip asked.

"Worked into the prerecord." Keke held up her hand to count down the camera.

"Such an impressive and bright little dog," Chip said. "A good shot at the Best in Show title, I think."

Evy decided to ad-lib a bit. "Chip, someone told me this morning that mini schnauzers are one of the most popular dogs in London. As a native, can you confirm?"

He glanced at her but went with it. "I can. It's a popular dog to see on walks and in the local dog parks. An active little breed, but its small size means that it's an apartment-friendly dog as well."

"Good to know."

They turned back to the ring and cut to the judge, who was finishing the examination of Jade, the adorable brown mini schnauzer.

"Just a very impressive competitor," Chip said. "She has a bright future in front of her, though she may be just a tad young for the Best in Show title this year."

"But still a champion, right?"

"A champion, no doubt. In fact, these dogs are the champions of champions of champions. It's a highly selective process."

"I'm ready for the hound," the judge said.

The camera cut off and the prerecorded video for the Afghan hound played.

"When are you flying out?" Evy asked.

"I have a flight out of LAX tomorrow afternoon," Chip answered. "The red-eye to Heathrow."

"Nice, so you're not too far from being back at home."

Chip shook his head. "More than ready."

"And you're back in..." Keke counted down.

The camera turned on. "Afghan Hounds are one of those breeds you get if you really loved braiding your dolls' hair as a kid," Evy said. "Those coats look like a lot of work."

Chip chuckled. "In fact, they are. But what a glorious animal."

The hound began a trot around the ring.

"Look at the way the hair flows around this dog. Afghan hounds were historically used to hunt down rabbits and gazelles in the mountainous regions of Central Asia. They are a sight hound, though they've been popular in purebred-dog circles since almost the beginning of kennel club competition."

"Has an Afghan hound ever won the Desert Fancy title, Chip?"

"No, though this particular dog, Soraya, has taken this group competition for three years in a row, which is almost unheard of."

"The judge looks impressed."

They cut to the judge's microphone as he examined the animal. "Once more around the ring please."

The crowd applauded as the stunning animal loped gracefully around the ring, her silky hair flowing around her.

The light on their camera cut out as the director shifted the show to the Havanese prerecorded segment.

"Did you check with the police about leaving?" Evy asked. "Remember, Chief Marcos was saying he didn't want us to leave town."

"Honestly" —Chip kept his voice low— "they have to know I didn't have anything to do with Bunny's death. Stewart's thugs already came to my place a few days ago and grilled me."

"Stewart has thugs?"

Chip frowned. "Of course he does."

Keke shouted. "And we're back!"

Evy was juggling too many thoughts in her head. Stewart had thugs. Bunny's ex had suspected that Chip might have hurt Bunny. Chip was getting ready to flee the country—or just go home, but flee the country seemed more dramatic.

Her brain was everywhere.

Live streaming the dogs.

Bantering with Chip.

Watching the judge.

Watching the owners.

More dogs.

More crowds.

Finally the judge was having all the dogs run around the ring one more time. He stared at them. Looked at a small notebook. Then looked at the dogs again. He walked across the ring and bent over a large book sitting on the trophy table.

"And we have a winner." Chip was buzzing in excitement.

"Any guesses, Chip?"

"It's anyone's prize, Evy. Every single one of these dogs is a champion, and I do not envy Judge Mason; I have no idea who he's picked this afternoon."

There was a pause and dead silence as the judge walked back to his position; then his hand went up, his finger fell...

"The Pembroke Welsh corgi."

The crowd erupted in applause as Liam and Badger danced across the ring. Evy jumped out of her seat and clapped, grateful that all the cameras were focused on the show ring.

"It's Liam! Liam and Badger won the show!"

"If there was going to be an upset this year, this was it!" Chip spoke up over the roaring crowd and the cheers from the production area. "What a charming and wonderful story, and what a delightful dog."

"So where do we go from here?" Evy asked.

She was leaning against Rafe's arm and lounging on the patio at Sergio and Dean's house, celebrating with her friends as Soraya bounced around the extensive grounds with Sergio's retrievers, Genevieve's poodle, and Paco, who was very curious about the Afghan hound.

It was a dog party loosely chaperoned by Genevieve and Marina while the rest of them drank and watched the sunset from the patio.

Vivian sipped a Paloma. "We still have no idea who killed Bunny. All we have are guesses about the motive and what it could all have to do with Baron's disappearance. Stewart is picking up the dogs tomorrow. John said he couldn't hold him off any longer."

Julia said, "I still haven't made any progress with Bunny's ghost."

"And Baron is still missing."

"Along with the necklace," Julia said.

"And don't forget Coma Guy," Rafe added. "Poor Coma Guy."

"I went by the hospital earlier today with John," Julia said. "No ghost around, but he never woke up, so he never really connected with that location. It's not surprising his ghost isn't there."

"Wait, what kind of ghost activity is at the hospital?" Evy asked.

Julia shook her head. "Don't ask."

Sergio turned to Dean. "What did John say about the investigation?"

Dean said, "He asked everyone to stay in town, but unless he has evidence to charge someone, he can't really keep them from leaving."

Rafe sat up, easing Evy off his arm. "Okay, we know that Bunny paid someone twenty thousand the week before the show."

"Probably Curtis Weathers, her handler," Julia said.

Sergio nodded. "That fits. Curtis would do anything Bunny asked; that's why she worked with him. Hell, she probably wouldn't have even had to pay him. If she said jump, Curtis would ask how high."

Rafe said, "But we have to assume that whoever Bunny gave the necklace to is likely the person who killed her, and they're still going to have to move that necklace out of the country."

"So there were three people in the conspiracy," Evy said. "Bunny and Curtis to hide Baron, and Bunny and someone else to steal the necklace and commit the fraud. Do you think Curtis knows who Bunny's other partner was?"

"I doubt it," Sergio said. "He'd hide a dog, but I feel like insurance fraud is probably out of his league."

Rafe continued, "But we do know Bunny orchestrated numerous international competitors to come to the dog show, probably to help her sell the Cartier collar. It's probable that one of them has it."

Evy said, "I saw some collars that looked like Harry Winston at that show. If you tossed Baron's collar in there with a bunch like that, it would blend right in."

"So smuggling it out with another dog owner would be smart," Julia said. "But it would have to be someone you trusted one hundred percent."

Evy grimaced. "Someone she *shouldn't* have trusted."

"Yeah," Julia said. "She obviously trusted the wrong person, but she *thought* they were safe."

"So who was closest to Bunny?" Rafe asked. "Sergio?"

He pursed his lips. "Liam adored her, but he didn't know her that well. The Webers are pretty new to the scene. I'd guess Rania or Juliet."

"Who are probably both leaving tomorrow." Evy rubbed her temples. "So is Chip; he's on the red-eye tomorrow to Heathrow. I should have read all of them earlier. Then I'd know."

"You were working," Vivian said. "John can't expect you to throw away your career to help him."

"Not even to catch a murderer?" Evy shook her head. "I've been a chicken, dipping my toes into the telepathy without really committing. I should go to their rental houses tonight and question them. I can make up some excuse. I'll call John and tell him to go with me maybe?"

Rafe sat up straight. "You don't have to go to their houses; I know where both of them will be. Where all of them will be." He looked at Evy. "There's a reception tonight at Monte Verde. Mum was invited, but she begged off. Liam texted me about it, asked me if we were going. All the group winners, some of the bigwigs from the club. Sponsors. They're all there."

Sergio frowned. "I forgot about that."

Dean was amused. "You forgot about a fancy cocktail party?"

Sergio shrugged. "I've seen all those people too much this week. Why on earth would I want to spend *more* time with them?"

"I wasn't invited." Evy made a face. "I bet Chip was, but I wasn't."

"Who cares?" Rafe leaned toward Evy. "Throw on your best dress, darling. Let's go crash a party we weren't invited to."

"If I want to use my telepathy, I have to bring Geoff. He's not the most subtle accessory when we're talking about evening wear."

Rafe grinned. "Even better." He pulled her to her feet. "I've got the perfect plan."

Chapter Twenty

"Are you sure I look okay?"

Rafe looked her up and down, from the tips of her patent leather heels to the crystal waterfall earrings she'd worn with her black suit. "You look stunning, and so does Geoff."

Evy had changed Geoff's suit to his tuxedo for the occasion, and she was shaking off the jitters. "I haven't done this in over two years." She started doing mouth stretches and adjusted Geoff's seat on her arm. "I'm going to be rusty."

Rafe frowned. "Do you want to try the backpack idea?"

Geoff turned to Rafe. "Not on your life, pal."

The words jumped out of Evy's mouth and into Geoff's automatically. She hadn't even thought about it, it just happened.

"Like riding a bike," she whispered.

The corner of Rafe's mouth turned up. "That was both spooky and cool."

"What's wrong with this one?" Geoff asked. "Never seen a dummy before?"

"I don't know," Evy said.

"Well," Geoff said, "he must not have any mirrors in his house!" Geoff turned to Rafe and cackled.

Rafe's eyes lit up. "Brilliant."

"Sorry," Evy said. "It's... Geoff."

"There's no way they don't let us in. You're amazing."

"I know you're talking about me," Geoff said. "Let's do this thing."

Evy shrugged. "He's always been more confident than me."

The three of them walked up the front steps of the Monte Verde Country Club, Rafe flashing the inscribed invitation the club had sent his mother. Security took one look at them, their gazes lingering on Geoff for a second, and then one of the guards pointed at Evy.

"Damn, yo! You're EV Lane! I saw you announcing the pet show." He smacked his buddy on the arm. "Dude, I told you she was the lady who did the comedy thing at my granddad's home a couple of years ago."

"Oh right." The security guard nodded. "Nice. That's awesome about the TV gig."

"Thanks, guys!" She nudged Rafe. "I know I'm technically only supposed to have a plus one, but it's more like plus one and a half." She looked at Geoff. "We cool?"

The first security guard busted up laughing. "Dude, the little man's even dressed for the occasion. I can't hate." He gestured them past the green velvet ropes. "Have a great night, ma'am."

Rafe put his hand on her back and hurried them both inside before anyone looked too closely at their invitation.

"Wait, did he just *ma'am* me?" Evy looked over her shoulder. "He can't be more than ten years younger than me!"

"You performed for his grandfather, darling. I'm afraid you've stepped over a threshold."

"Hey, Rafe," Geoff said.

"Yes, Geoff?"

"Did I ever tell you I like older women?"

185

Rafe's eyebrows went up. "No, I don't think you've mentioned that."

"It's true." Geoff looked up at Evy, then back at Rafe. "They're used to disappointment in life, so they're ready for me."

Rafe snorted. "Both depressing and likely accurate."

Evy said, "You're telling me." She spotted the signs for the Desert Fancy Kennel Club party. "You know, despite my devil-may-care attitude, I don't make it a habit to crash fancy parties. Have you done this thing before?"

"I'm the poor relative of a minor British aristocratic family," Rafe said. "Of course I have."

He strode into the party, nodding at Lorain, whose eyes went wide when she saw Evy and Geoff. "Don't wait for them," he muttered. "I'll distract them, you take the stage."

"Oh God, oh God, oh God." Evy was trying not to hyperventilate.

"What are you panicking about?" Geoff sounded disgusted. "You think this is a tough crowd, you should see the Senior Tanning Club at Desert Vistas." Geoff let out his familiar cackling laugh.

He'd always been braver than Evy. She listened to Geoff's urging and walked to the front of the room, waving at Chip and Liam when she passed them, and took to the stage, aiming straight for the microphone without looking left or right.

Evy walked right up to the podium, tapped the mic, and adjusted it. "This thing working?"

A light flipped on, and she brought out her thousand-watt smile. "I can't believe you all invited me here with Geoff tonight." A few people in the crowd clapped, clearly not knowing this wasn't on the program. "You all know he's a cat person, so—"

"Cats rule and dogs drool!" Geoff blared from her arm. "I'm looking at you, English mastiffs."

Evy cleared her throat as the laughter started. "Now Geoff, you know these are dog people." She gestured at the crowd. "Our audience tonight owns some of the most award-winning dogs on the planet."

"Let me ask you something." Geoff looked at the crowd, then at Evy. "Any of these genius award winners know how to use the bathroom yet?"

"The dogs?"

"The owners!"

The crowd laughed, and Geoff let out a wheezing chuckle, turning his head to look at the crowd. "These dogs got you played, humans! You think they're your dogs; you're their servants!"

The crowd laughed again as Evy tried to placate Geoff. "Geoff, you know that dogs can provide priceless companionship for humans." She glanced at the crowd and appealed to them. "I mean, wouldn't you say that's right?" The crowd clapped. "Dogs are man's best friend."

"Not Stewart Barker," Geoff said. "Why call a dog your best friend when you've got that gorgeous blonde on your arm?" Geoff turned to Stewart as the crowd laughed. "Hubba-hubba. Now that's what *I* call a best friend."

Evy pretended to wince and turned to Stewart and his girl-friend. "I am so sorry; he doesn't mean to be disrespectful."

"Of course I do!" Geoff threw back. "They both know I'm not actually the one talking!"

More laughter while Evy closed her eyes and pretended to be exasperated.

"You know, I thought you were retired." Evy looked at the dummy. "Didn't you tell me you wanted to retire? What happened?"

Geoff turned his head toward Chip. "I saw the dummy you got for your new partner and figured I needed to rescue you."

The crowd roared with laughter, and Chip gave Evy a good-natured smile.

"Geoff!" She shook her head at Chip. "He's just jealous, Chip."

Chip laughed and raised both his hands. "What can I say?" he told the crowd. "I can't compete with anyone who wears a tuxedo that well."

EVY DIDN'T PUSH HER LUCK. SHE DID A SNAPPY FIFTEEN-minute set that left the crowd wanting, then stepped off the stage with her blood buzzing.

God, she'd missed this! As she walked through the crowd of well-wishers, she twisted to avoid Lorain, who was watching her with narrowed eyes, and turned to Rania al Ahmadi, who was sipping a martini and flirting with Rafe.

"Here we go, Geoffrey," she whispered. "I need into her brain." She waved at Rafe. "Honey!"

Rafe's eyebrows went up. "Darling. You were incredible."

Rania was smiling. She'd been dressed in luxurious neutrals for the brunch that morning, but tonight she was wearing a brilliant emerald green.

"I loved your show," she gushed. "What fun. I had no idea that you did the…" She motioned to her mouth. "What do you call it?"

"Ventriloquism," Evy said. "It's something I've practiced since I was a kid. I used to use my little brother for a dummy; now I use Geoff." She winked at Rafe. "Or Rafe if he sits on my arm like this."

Rania laughed again. *…delightful woman and such a nice catch for Rafe though I'm sure his grandmother would prefer someone with money the estate in Scotland needs a sizable investment not a recognizable personality but Fared might enjoy an option for parties rather than the same celebrities…*

"So Rania." Evy broke through the mental stream of consciousness. "I understand you and Bunny were friends." She let her face relax into an expression of concern. "How are you doing?"

…intrusive questions Bunny and Stewart such a tragedy… Rania

blinked. "It's... I mean, it's horrible of course. I don't really think I've processed it to be honest." *...have to make friends with Lorain? Not sure what kind of organization without Bunny...* "Bunny and I were friends, but I always sponsored the club's events as well. My husband and I have a winter home here."

"Oh, I didn't know that! So you're *really* part of the club."

"I always come for the show, and we usually spend a month or so here around the holidays. I do love American Christmas." She turned to Rafe. "How's your mother, Rafe? I was sorry she decided not to attend tonight."

"She wanted something a little more low-key with Genevieve tonight, so she sent me as the designated family representative." He winked at Rania. "I've been instructed to fill her in on all the gossip later."

...tell Marina how charming he is serious about this woman? That would be a surprise and is he still investigating for that insurance company tell Juliet to avoid him and not really interested in him poking around... "And how's your sister?"

"Doing well in Denver. She loves the mountain life."

"It's a great city." Rania turned to Evy. "Miss Lane, do you have a card with you by any chance? I think my husband might be quite interested in hiring you for a corporate event or two. Do you travel?"

"Whenever I can." Evy felt like she'd gotten quite a bit from Rania, but none of it pointed directly at her being Bunny's coconspirator. There were some suspicious thoughts though. And what had she been thinking about Juliet? "I think I have a card here." She pulled an old business card from a small pocket sewn into the back of Geoff's jacket, quickly checking the number to see if it was correct. "Yeah, this is mine."

Rania smiled and took the card. "I'm going to say hello to a few more people; then I'll be taking my leave, but it was so nice to talk to you both." She looked at Geoff. "And nice to meet you, Geoffrey."

"I hate to see you leave, but I think I'm gonna love watching you walk away if you know what I mean."

"Geoff!" Evy covered his eyes. "There's no excuse for him; I'm sorry."

Rania laughed and waved as she walked away. Evy turned to Rafe. "It is a good view; she's gorgeous."

"And rich. And very status conscious. And did you get anything interesting?"

"Some, but let's not stop now. She said something about Juliet."

"Lomax." Rafe nodded. "I see her."

They drifted through the crowd, making their way toward Edgar and Juliet Lomax, who were both dressed in elegant black. Juliet's hair was wrapped in a gold-threaded turban, and a diamond-studded choker set off her long neck.

Everything about the Lomaxes screamed old money, from the custom suit Edgar was wearing to the satin opera gloves that set off Juliet's formfitting gown.

"Mrs. Lomax," Rafe said, intruding on a conversation. "I've been instructed by my mother to offer my congratulations on Jade's showing tonight. She commented on her stack specifically. Said she'd never seen a young dog show their lines so well."

Juliet smiled. "That's so kind, Rafe. Tell Marina I send her my regards." Her attention shifted to Evy. "And Miss Lane, I've attended countless dog shows over the years; you managed to make this one less dreary. I know Bunny had her doubts about you, but had she been able to see your performance, I have no doubt she would have approved."

Evy felt her heart warm a little. "Thank you. I understand you and Bunny were good friends."

Edgar laughed a little. "Thick as thieves," he said. "My Juliet and Bunny were very close." He put his arm around his wife. "This show has been difficult."

Juliet's face was a carefully controlled mask. "Which is why

190

owners are always best served by hiring professionals like our wonderful handler Kenzie." *...dear God get me out of this room all these self-congratulatory plebeians if Bunny could see—God Bunny! —this hideous town why did you ever stay here should have left the minute Stewart let you go...*

Edgar said, "She's right of course. We can always depend on Kenzie to get the best out of Jade."

Something on the other side of the room caught Juliet's attention, and Evy zeroed in, trying to read her thoughts, but she ran into a hard, dark wall.

"Forgive me, Rafe." Juliet put a hand on Rafe's arm. "Edgar, the sponsorship rep from IAMS is speaking with Liam. We need to get over there before he signs a contract." She looked at Evy. "He's lovely but a complete amateur and one of our tier signing a bad contract affects negotiations for us all."

"Oh right." Evy nodded.

"Edgar," she hissed and pulled her husband away.

"Well," Rafe remarked. "It's pretty clear where her priorities lie. Business over sentiment."

"She kept a good face up, but her thoughts were pretty broken up over Bunny."

"Evy?"

She turned and saw Chip heading toward her. "Hey partner!"

"Not partner anymore." Chip gestured to Geoff. "Clearly you've replaced me."

Evy smiled. "You're flying back to London tomorrow; I had to."

Chip hung his hands in his pockets, looking amused. "Does he like dog puns more than I do?"

"Hell yeah, pretty boy." Geoff turned to Chip. "What're you looking at? Just 'cause I got all the looks in the gang—"

"Thanks, Geoff." Evy slapped a hand over his mouth. "Obviously you can see why we needed a break."

His face was all amusement. "I don't know whether to be

concerned or impressed that you so clearly have a split personality."

Evy was trying to probe Chip's mind, but there was nothing. It was like poking at a thick velvet curtain. She sensed that movement, thoughts, and emotions were flowing behind that barrier, but she couldn't quite hear them.

"Chip, you remember Rafe?"

"Of course." He raised his glass. "And how did you like the show? Your mother's dog showed extremely well." Chip looked over his shoulder at Liam. "Sometimes I think even the judges get caught up in the story about a dog. Everyone does love an underdog."

It was maddening but not unheard of. Richard and Dean had similar brains, so she tried not to be suspicious, but it was hard not to let her mind run wild in the absence of anything solid she could read.

"My mother knows Liam and his family, so she was thoroughly delighted that he took home the trophy," Rafe said. "What about you? Did you have a secret favorite?"

"Well, after working so closely with the Barkers, I had to admit I was rooting for Hercules, but he's young still. He'll have many more shows to shine."

"I have a new respect for poodles," Evy said. "They really are fantastic dogs."

"You have a friend in the police department, correct?" Chip sipped his cocktail. "Have they made any progress finding Baron?"

"None, but they're looking into Curtis Weathers, Bunny's handler. They think he may have taken the dog."

"Such a tragedy," Chip said. "To be honest, I don't know if I'll return after this year."

Rafe cocked his head. "Oh?"

"So many memories." Chip swirled the ice around his glass. "So much tragedy." He raises his glass toward Evy. "But it was a pleasure working with you, Evy. A unique experience." He patted her shoulder and drifted away.

Evy wrinkled her nose. "Why—I mean how—does he manage to make something sound like a compliment but it feels like an insult?"

"Easy." Rafe was watching Chip's retreating figure with narrowed eyes. "He's British."

"I mean, I know this was my first TV hosting gig, but I think I did all right. Everyone I've talked to tells me that I'm the one—"

"Evy, stop being insecure about your performance." Rafe nudged her shoulder, so she turned to watch the crowd. "How did you miss him?"

Her eyes went wide. "Chip?"

"Oh, he's definitely involved."

"What... I mean, why would— How do you know that?"

"My gut." He tapped her temple. "Anything up here? I'm kind of doubting it because I bet that man has mental shields on mental shields."

"How did you know that?"

"Because he's a liar." The corner of Rafe's mouth turned up. "Old Chip is definitely hiding something."

Chapter Twenty-One

On Monday morning, Evy met John in front of the La Serenissima Guest Quarters in La Quinta, a midrange country club where Chip Dunklin had been renting a cottage. The cottages were connected to La Serenissima Golf Club and scattered over the south course, each one a self-contained apartment with luxurious amenities and lush landscaping.

"Okay." The police chief got out of his car with a resigned expression. "What's our angle here? I remind you, I don't have a warrant."

"Can you just ask him if you can search his house?" Evy asked. "Can you ask management?"

"Not while he's renting the place," John said. "We can ask, but he's not obliged to let us in. A judge will say he has a presumption of privacy in any place he rents. We can't search it until after he checks out."

"Which would be after he destroys any evidence of Bunny's murder," Evy said. "Rafe and I are pretty sure he's involved." Well, Rafe was more convinced than Evy was, but something about Chip gave her pause too. His mental walls were airtight, and it made her suspicious. "And it's not just Chip. I think

Rania and Juliet are both hiding things too. Rania more than Juliet."

"Make up your mind," John said. "Is it Chip, Rania, or Juliet? What did you hear?"

She took a deep breath. "Not much to be honest. At least from Chip. He's pretty shut down, which is not necessarily incriminating—some people are just naturally that way, you kind of are—but there's just a... vibe." She bit her lip. That sounded stupid even to her own ears. "It's hard to explain."

John stared at her. "A vibe? A telepathic vibe?"

"Yes?"

He closed his eyes and shook his head. "This is what I get for hiring a psychic." He slammed his door. "Okay, let's go ask Chip Dunklin pretty please if he'll let us search his room. For funsies."

"Your sarcasm is not appreciated." Evy put on her sunglasses and closed her own car door. "It's a good thing you can't hear what *I'm* thinking right now."

"This was that insurance investigator's idea, wasn't it?"

"This was my idea. Even if he says no, maybe something he's thinking will slip out and give us a reasonable..."

"Reasonable what?"

"Clue?" *Ugh!* Why did he make her feel so incompetent? "John, just trust me on this, okay? Chip's involved in this somehow."

"Okay, I believe you, but we have to prove it. He's in number three." John pointed to a white bungalow with a red Spanish-tile roof and colorful pots with cacti and succulents around the entry patio. A fountain trickled in the small courtyard between cottages three and five.

John knocked on the heavy mission-style door, but there was no sound from inside. He glanced at Evy. "I can't break in, so don't ask."

"Such a rule follower," she muttered. Evy tried to peek in the windows, but the drapes were tightly drawn. She saw some kind of artificial light along the edges of the drapes. Chip had to be there. "Try again? He's flying out tonight, so I'm sure he's awake. He's probably packing."

John knocked again, and this time he announced himself. "Mr. Dunklin, it's Palm Springs PD. I have a few questions for you about Bunny Barker."

Evy whispered, "Should you tell him it's about Bunny?"

"What else would we want to question him about?" John leaned against the corner of the wall. "A parking ticket?"

"I'm going to look around back."

"Evy, you cannot—"

"I'm just going to peek in the windows!" She rolled her eyes. "I haven't broken into a house in twenty years," she muttered. "So suspicious."

"Lots of people have *never* broken into a house," he said. "Just throwing that out there."

Evy walked along the landscaping, following the edge of the cottage around to the back where the yard opened out onto the golf course and a distant spraying fountain in the middle of the rolling hills and greens.

There was a window on the side with drapes shut just as tightly as those around the front door. Evy kept following the garden beds around to the back patio, which was more reddish tile glazed with age and decorated with even more plants.

She walked over to the french doors that opened onto the course. A shade cover was already protecting the glass from the desert glare, but she pressed her hands to the seam of the curtains and peered through.

A frozen hand on the ground.

A broken glass that had shattered on Saltillo tile.

The cuff of a formal white tuxedo shirt.

"Chip!" She pounded her bare hands on the glass door. "Chip! Wake up! John, get back here!"

Footsteps raced around the back of the house. "Evy?"

"He's on the ground! I see him on the ground!" She looked for anything to break the glass, lifting up a pot. "John, help me!"

He walked over and yanked on the french doors; they opened easily. "Not locked. Call 911. Tell them we need an ambulance. Mr. Dunklin?"

John rushed into the room, batting away the curtains that covered the french doors, and Evy followed him, her phone already at her ear. Chip was on the ground, and she knew in her gut he was already dead.

"911, what's your emergency?"

"We need an ambulance." Her voice felt like a whisper. "I'm with Chief John Marcos in La Quinta. Uh... there's a man collapsed on the ground. I think he might be dead."

"Can you check his pulse?"

"John, his pulse?"

He was on his knees, his fingers at Chip's neck. She stared as he turned to her and shook his head.

"Ma'am, can you check his breathing or—?"

"He's dead." The hand holding the phone felt limp; the phone was suddenly the heaviest thing in the world. "He's..."

John held out his hand, and Evy handed him the phone.

"This is John Marcos of Palm Springs PD. We need an ambulance to La Serenissima Golf Resort over in La Quinta. Over by the guest cottages. Number three. The victim is cold, probably been dead for hours."

He answered a few more questions as Evy stared at the lifeless body.

Chip was still in his suit from the night before; his eyes were open, his lips were pulled back in a macabre grin, and there was white residue around his mouth. He'd fallen on the floor, and the glass he'd been holding had broken into several pieces. There was a pool of liquid under the glass shards and a few drops of blood.

"Probable poison—please contact the crime lab too, and poison control. Don't touch anything!"

She turned and saw John was speaking to her.

"Evy, don't touch a thing."

She shook her head, still shocked by the vision of Chip's body lifeless on the ground. "I saw him last night. He's still wearing the same suit."

John kept his eyes on her, but he was still speaking on the phone. "Do you need— Yeah." He paused. Nodded. "Yeah, Mancini if he's available. Thanks. I'll be here."

He hung up the phone and held it out to Evy. "Keep it in your pocket, okay? They might call back."

"He was wearing these clothes last night."

"That's probably when he was poisoned."

Evy stared at Chip's body. "He wasn't the murderer," she said. "Poor Chip."

JOHN SHOOK HIS HEAD AS HE SPOKE QUIETLY TO EVY ON the back patio. "This scene is impeccable. At Bunny's house there were hairs, fingerprints. This place is immaculate."

"Someone cleaned up."

John nodded. "Meticulously."

"And he was poisoned?" Evy wanted Julia and Vivian, but they hadn't come to pick her up yet. Julia had texted her she was on the way only a few minutes ago.

"They'll have to test his blood to be sure, but it looks like poisoning. Did you see how his teeth were gritted?"

"Yeah." She'd be having nightmares about it. "So Bunny's killer struck again. I really think you need to autopsy Coma Guy."

"Already being done," he said. "The lab's a little impacted. We don't usually have three dead bodies coming at us in one week."

"Not since the Booster Club."

John pulled a chair over and sat across from her as the crime scene people bustled in and out of the cottage. "How are you?"

"Not good." She wanted to be home, and she couldn't get the image of Chip's agonized face out of her brain. "I just saw him last night. This doesn't seem real."

"You mentioned seeing him at a party, right? Where was it?"

"He was at Monte Verde. There was a reception for the bigwigs at the kennel club. Sponsorship people there. Club donors. Stuff like that. Rafe and I crashed it and I did a bit with Geoff—"

"Oh yeah?" He smiled. "How'd it go?"

"Killed it." She winced. "Bad choice of words. I wanted to read Chip, Juliet Lomax, and Rania al Ahmadi because we figured they were the most likely people to have been Bunny's partner in the insurance fraud."

"I know Bunny was friends with the Lomax woman and the gal from Dubai, but why did you suspect Chip?"

"Partly because I hadn't been able to read him last week since we were on air every time we were together. But he'd also worked with Bunny and her ex in the past. She knew him, he knew the dogs, so they wouldn't have barked. He was from London. There were rumors that Bunny was trying to kind of rehabilitate Chip's career because I kind of think she'd been the one to kill it."

"She killed his career?"

"There was some rumor about him hurting a dog."

John frowned. "That sounds like Chip would hate Bunny for killing his career, not want to conspire with her."

"Yeah." Evy shrugged. "But maybe he needed the money and Bunny knew it."

"I'll look into his financials, but it might be complicated since he lived in the UK." He stretched his neck from one side to the other, then narrowed his eyes as he looked out over the golf course. "You know, I've talked to Stew Barker before, but I think we need to go talk to him again. At least Chip's murder did us one solid."

Evy frowned. "What's that?"

"He was still in his clothes from that party last night?"

"Yeah."

"So it's likely that whoever poisoned him—and whoever killed Bunny—was there. That means that everyone at that party is a suspect, and I can justify making them all stay in town until we figure this out."

The light turned on. "You can keep everyone at the dog show from leaving the country."

"Yep. Hope you don't mind listening in on questioning, Landa, because you're going to be earning your keep as a consultant starting right now."

She pulled out her phone and called her cousin. "I guess Danny's going to be covering my pools the rest of the week."

"Don't worry, you can bill me." The corner of his mouth turned up. "But I'm gonna make you earn your psychic keep, so make sure you bring the dummy, and I'm not talking about Rafe."

Chapter Twenty-Two

Evy was sleeping in on Tuesday morning, trying to wind down from the rush of activity the week before, the party and performance on Sunday night, then the trauma of finding Chip dead on his living room floor.

She was trying to figure out how she felt about Chip dying. She wouldn't have called him a friend, but they'd definitely been friendly. She'd considered him a colleague and a good one. He'd been really kind, showing her the ropes of the dog-show world, and they'd had a good time writing bits together.

All in all, she hadn't liked suspecting him, but it seemed willfully ignorant to assume the man wasn't involved in any of this when he knew all the players so well. The dogs, the people, and the sticky dynamics of the industry.

She heard her phone buzzing on her bedside table and grabbed it.

Marcos.

Evy sighed and answered the phone. "What is it?"

"Are you alone?"

"Aunt Marie is supposed to be getting back today, but yeah."

"The medical examiner finally ID'd Coma Guy. Want to go talk to his wife with me?"

She winced. "Not really, but okay."

"You're a consultant, Evy. Don't forget to bring Geoff. I'll swing by your house in half an hour. Is that enough time?"

She glanced at the mirror on her dressing table and ran a hand through her hair. "Yeah, that works."

He said goodbye; then Evy sat up, swung her legs over the side of the bed, and told her phone to call Julia and Vivian.

Julia answered first. "Hey. How you doing?"

The faint ringing in back stopped and Vivian picked up. "Hello?"

"Group call," Evy said. "I don't want to have to explain twice."

"What's going on?" Julia asked. "Is it something about Chip?"

"Oddly enough, it's about Coma Guy."

"Oh!" Vivian's voice got brighter. "Did they find out who he was?"

"Yes, but John didn't tell me on the phone. He's picking me up in a half an hour and we're going to talk to the guy's wife."

"When you get his home address, pass it along," Julia said. "I can try to swing by later and see if his ghost is hanging around the house."

"Good idea," Vivian said. "Have you had any progress with Bunny's ghost?"

"She's talking a little bit, but not about anything to do with her attack. She mostly talks about her dogs. Talks about Baron in the past tense, which is a little concerning."

"That *is* concerning." Evy frowned. "Have either of you found anything about the handler, Curt Weathers?"

Julia said, "You might ask Rafe about him. I think I overheard him say something to Sergio about tracking him down. He finally got some kind of lead on the guy."

"I'll ask." She wanted to see Rafe anyway. He'd asked to come over the night before, but she'd begged off. If Rafe came over, she'd want to have sex with him, and she found that slightly perverse since she'd just found the dead body of her coworker.

Vivian said, "I don't really have much going on today. My parents have Henry for a sleepover, so Richard and I are just hanging out here."

"Call John," Evy blurted out. "We're going to talk to a dead guy's wife. It might be good to have an empath there."

JOHN THOUGHT THE IDEA OF BRINGING VIVIAN ALONG was a good one, so he and Evy swung by Casa de Lirio on the way to La Quinta to visit the estranged wife of Shawn Dumas, the man who'd died in the hospital after a beating behind Bunny's house.

Sarah Dumas sat on a tan leather couch, holding a mug of coffee between her two hands. Vivian sat next to her, and Evy and John sat in chairs on either side.

She was a petite woman in her midthirties with short blond hair and bright blue eyes. Tan in a way that told Evy she liked the outdoors. Much of her house seemed to be dedicated to bikes, mountain biking, and other sports.

"It doesn't feel real," she said.

John started. "Mrs. Dumas—"

"Please just call me Sarah." She shook her head. "Shawn and I were separated, and it was going to end in divorce so..." She frowned. "Does that make me a suspect? God, it probably looks awful that I didn't report him missing, but he doesn't live here anymore. He'd gotten his own place over in Palm Desert, nearer to his job."

John gave her his notebook. "Would you mind writing down the address for me? We'll have officers go over and search it. See if we can find any more information about who might have hurt him."

"Sure." She reached for the notebook and scribbled on it while

Evy tried to read her. Unfortunately, all she was thinking about was trying to figure out her new phone so she could find her ex's address.

Eventually she handed it back to John. "This is where I was forwarding his mail."

John stood. "If you give me a minute, I'm going to just call the station real quick."

"Sure, yeah."

John stepped out of the room while Evy and Vivian stayed with Sarah.

She looked at them. "Are you two cops? No offense, but you don't look like cops."

"We're consultants," Vivian said. "I work with grieving families, so sometimes Chief Marcos will have me accompany him to meetings like this."

"Right." Sarah looked between Evy and Vivian. "That's actually really nice. You don't see stuff like that on TV, but I guess all that's made up, right?"

"Most of it." Evy nodded. "Yeah."

"You know, I kind of thought it was weird that Shawn wasn't texting me every day, but I was hoping like hell that he'd finally decided to move on." She snorted. "Can you believe I was hoping my husband got a girlfriend?" Her smile was bitter. "Probably tells you a lot about our marriage, huh?"

Evy delved into Sarah's brain, and her mind was flooded with memories and thoughts of her husband. *...have to call his mom and dad God there has to be a funeral I don't think he told them anything was even wrong should I just move his stuff back here and pretend nothing happened? His parents are Catholic they'd probably appreciate that this is so crazy fucking Shawn manages to mess up my whole life just by dying what the hell?*

Vivian broke into Sarah's internal monologue. "Is there anyone we can call for you? I sense that you're a little overwhelmed. Is there a friend or a family member who might be able to help?"

"Where do you work?" Evy asked. "John can probably call them if you needed him to. He can explain."

"I'll be fine," Sarah said. "Thank you for offering though. I work as a supervising RN at a long-term care facility in Rancho Mirage, and I don't go on shift until this afternoon. I'll be okay."

John Marcos walked back into the room. "And where did Shawn work, Miss—Sarah?"

"Um..." She frowned. "A couple of places. He never really seemed to stick with one thing. He went to school to be an EMT, but that didn't seem to make him happy. I used to tell him he should try to get hired by the police because he liked ordering people around." She shrugged. "No offense."

John smiled. "None taken."

"He did night security at this storage place, but he had another job at a dog-boarding kennel that he liked better. He loved animals." Her eyes went wide. "Oh my God, his dog."

John's eyebrows went up. "He has a dog in his apartment?"

"Yes," Sarah said. "And it's a pit bull mix, but I promise she's the sweetest thing. Oh my God, I hope she's okay. I wonder if one of the neighbors grabbed her. Or maybe he took her to work; he did that sometimes when he worked at the kennel because she loved being around the other dogs."

"I'll call the officers heading over there." John stood again. "Let them know she's friendly."

"Her name's Frida," Sarah said. "I'm going to call the kennel place too. Hopefully they have her. When was Shawn attacked? It's been over a week now? Oh my God, I hope that poor dog is okay."

Evy's instincts were pinging all over the place. "What kennel did you say Shawn worked at?"

"Uh..." Sarah was scrolling through her phone. "I don't think I did. It was connected to this big purebred-breeding business, but they do short- and long-term boarding too. It's Barker something. Barker Kennels? In Rancho Mirage. Something like that. I always thought that was kind of a dumb name, but whatever." She touched her phone and put it on speaker. "Hello? Hi, this is Shawn Dumas's ex-wife. Do you have Frida there at the kennel, his pit bull mix? She's grey and has a white chest. Her ears are unclipped. Do you have her there?"

Evy was holding her breath when a voice on the other line answered.

"Yeah." The man sounded annoyed. "We've been trying to call him for a week now. He dropped her off for one night and then never picked her up the next day. Plus he hasn't been into work for like a week. We were about to call animal control."

Sarah's shoulders sagged in relief. "It's fine. I'll be over there to pick her up. Shawn—"

John touched her shoulder and shook his head.

"Uh... I'll come by in a little bit and take care of the bill and get Frida," Sarah said. "If that's okay."

"Lady, at this point your ex has been fired and we're about to hand this dog over to the city, so if you want to pick her up, that's fine by me."

He hung up, and Sarah let her phone drop to her lap. "You didn't want me to let them know he's dead?"

"Stewart Barker is the owner of that kennel," Evy told her. "And we're going to head over to question him. I think Chief Marcos would prefer that he be the one to tell them that Shawn has died."

Her eyebrows went up. "You think someone at the kennel might be involved with Shawn's death?"

"We don't know anything for sure right now," John said. "Let's just say that dogs are a recurring theme in this investigation."

STEWART BARKER SAT AT HIS KITCHEN TABLE, HIS backbone ramrod straight and a black poodle with equally formal posture sitting next to him. "Shawn Dumas?"

"He worked for your kennel, Mr. Barker." John sat across from him, and Evy sat at his side. "He was the man found beaten behind your ex-wife's house a little over a week ago."

Evy tried to read Stewart Barker, but unlike the other day, the man was locked down tight. He was definitely hiding something, and she didn't even need telepathy to figure that out.

Stewart might not have been talking, but John had more to say.

"He died from complications relating to that beating in the hospital on Friday night; we just found out who he was this morning. Are you trying to tell me that one of your employees being beaten to a pulp behind your ex-wife's house was purely a coincidence? I'm not buying it, Mr. Barker, so don't try to sell it."

Stewart's shoulders loosened a little. "I sent Dumas over to see if Bunny was hiding Baron at the house. I didn't know what to think, but the dog was missing and something about it seemed off to me. He called me and said he didn't see the dog on the property and the only ones around were Zara and Roman. The only people were Bunny, a friend, and her gardener. I was irritated and told him to go home. I had no idea..." He shook his head. "I had no idea something had happened to him. He hadn't worked for me long, and sometimes people just take off."

"We published details about the man in the newspaper," John said. "His dog was at the kennel, and he wasn't answering his phone. Why didn't you come forward to identify him?"

"I didn't see it," Stewart said. "I don't read the paper much, and no one told me his dog hadn't been picked up. The agreement was between Dumas and me." He waved a hand. "Check my phone records if you want. You'll see he called me that night."

"What happened to Baron?" John said.

"Obviously I don't know."

"Did you take him? Or did Shawn Dumas take him and then you decided to get rid of a loose end?"

"That's ridiculous!" Stewart pounded his fist on the table. "I'm as worried about that dog as you are. And that Chip fellow..." He shook his finger. "I heard about that one too. He was dirty, I'm telling you. He called me, said he knew something about Baron, but he wanted money."

"He called you about Baron?" Evy asked. "What did you do?"

"I told him to fuck off." Stewart's eyes were cold. "You got information for me or you don't. This is one of my dogs, Miss Lane. That's like holding a kid for ransom and asking the parents to pay for information. I told him where he could put his information. Probably all bullshit anyway."

"When was this?" John asked. "When did Chip call you?"

"I think it was Saturday." Stewart stared at the table, then nodded. "Yeah, it was right after the police came here the first time asking about Baron, acting like I'd stolen him or something." Stewart shook his head. "As if I'd take that dog away from Zara. That's the night I sent Dumas over to check out the house and he called me. So I knew Chip was full of shit."

"The timeline fits." Evy turned to John. "Baron disappeared on Friday, we went over to Bunny's on Saturday to check on her, and that's when we found Shawn Dumas in the backyard."

Stewart pointed at her. "You found him?"

"Yeah." Evy nodded. "He wasn't dead. In fact, it seemed like he was getting better. What exactly did you tell Shawn Dumas to do, Mr. Barker?"

The old man shrugged. "Poke around the house and the grounds, see if the dog was still there. That's all."

"He said Bunny had a friend with her," Evy said. "Did he say who it was?"

"No." Stewart frowned. "And I didn't ask. Bunny has a lot of friends." His face fell. "*Had* a lot of friends."

Nothing she could gather from Stewart Barker told Evy he was telling them anything but the truth. He was pissed about Shawn and still angry and worried about Baron. He was also heartbroken about Bunny.

But Shawn Dumas had been watching the house on Saturday, and he might have seen Bunny's coconspirator, which meant it was likely *that* person was the one who had beaten up Shawn Dumas or ordered someone to do it.

Was Juliet Lomax or Rania al Ahmadi capable of beating a muscular man like Shawn Dumas badly? That seemed far-fetched.

But at least one of them traveled with some pretty intimidating security.

Evy waited until she and John were back at the car to tell him.

"Rania al Ahmadi," Evy said. "I think she was Bunny's partner."

"I was thinking the same thing," John said. "Shawn Dumas wasn't a commando, but he wasn't a small guy either. Rania travels with some pretty hefty security."

"She also travels by private jet," Evy said. "We need to find out where she is."

Chapter Twenty-Three

E vy was sitting in her living room, a cold towel over her eyes, when the front door opened.

"I'm home, sweetie."

She peeked out from behind the towel to see Aunt Marie walk into the house and set down a large duffel bag and a brown grocery bag on the counter.

"What is that?"

"Just some money for the house."

She sat up and let the towel fall from her eyes. "Marie."

"Chichi had a good weekend! How was yours? How's Geoff?"

"Is that a grocery bag full of cash?" Evy hissed. "Don't tell me that you won legitimately and the casino gave Chichi a bagful of cash."

"Of course they didn't," Marie said. "The bank did. That's why it took an extra day."

She covered her eyes again. "I don't want to know."

"Always a good policy in this family. Julia called me about Bunny, but then I heard there was another murder?"

"Three if you count Bunny, Coma Guy—who we now know was named Shawn Dumas—and now Chip."

"Do you know who did it?"

"We think Bunny got double-crossed by her partner, who may be one of the owners from the dog show. I'm waiting for John to call me. This woman travels by private plane, so keeping her in the country could be a challenge."

"So you found the dog?"

"No, we still haven't found the dog." Evy was exhausted and she was anxious, waiting for John to call her. He'd told all the suspects that they were required to stay in town, but if Rania al Ahmadi wanted to get on her private jet and fly out of the country, there was very little stopping her. John didn't have the power to seize her passport, and the woman had connections.

"I'm proud of you, Evy." The couch dipped.

Evy took the towel off her eyes. "For what?"

"For using your gifts. For working with the police to solve these murders. I know it's difficult."

Evy let out a long breath. "Thanks. About the money, is it going to be enough for the roof? Because I have some savings, and I'll be getting a big check from the dog show, so—"

"Please." Marie patted her leg. "It's not your job to replace the roof until you inherit this place. Until then, I have it covered."

Evy blinked. "What?"

"There's more than enough to replace the roof, and I want to pay you back for what you contributed to the air-conditioning repair last summer. I know you said it wasn't much, but—"

"Did you say I'm inheriting the house?" Evy sat up. "You never told me that."

Marie looked at her like she had two heads. "Evy, I don't have any kids. You're the one who lives here. You're the one who drives me to doctor's appointments and makes sure I remember to eat and—"

"I didn't want to assume! I'm not your only niece."

"Sweetheart." Marie chuckled. "Who else would I leave the

house to? You're the executor of all my estate. I probably should have talked to you about it before, but I know you're busy."

"You think I'm responsible enough to be the executor of your estate?"

"Well, it's nothing like Genevieve's or Sergio's mother's, mind you. It's a pretty modest prospect, but I have put away a bit over the years, and I trust you to handle everything." Marie smiled. "Evy, you're one of the most responsible people I know. Definitely one of the most responsible in the family."

"Just because I've avoided arrest—"

"Not just because of that." She leaned toward Evy. "You took Marty's little pool-cleaning business and made it one of the best-reviewed pool services in the valley. I've read your Yelp reviews. You're in high demand."

"I don't have time for any new customers; it's just me."

"You could expand if you hired Danny full time." She raised her hands. "But that's all I'll say; you know your business. Added to all that, you're a celebrity now! You're hosting television shows; you're back doing comedy again. Evelyn, the sky is the limit for you."

She let out a breathy laugh. "I never feel like I have anything together. Ever. I always feel like other people are more... I don't know—it just seems like all the rest of my friends are better at life than me."

"Why? Because they have traditional jobs? Traditional paths?" Marie touched her cheek. "That's not you, Evy. It was never going to be you. Don't be like the other ones; you're far more than that." Marie stood. "Enough wallowing. I think you need to call that policeman. Find out what is going on and stick your nose in it."

"That does seem to be one of my strengths in life."

Rania al Ahmadi sat in the police interrogation room in Palm Springs, sipping a can of ginger ale and looking as out of place as a queen at a backyard barbecue.

Evy watched her from behind the two-way mirror.

"She parked her private jet in Chino instead of Palm Springs. Took me a second to find it," John said, "but once I did, they confirmed that her pilot had filed a flight plan to take off this afternoon."

"Dubai?"

"A stop in Istanbul to refuel, then Dubai. She'd have been out of our reach in two hours if I hadn't been able to find her. The dogs were already loaded on the plane." He took out a silver attaché case. "And so was this."

"What is it?"

"I don't know; it's locked and it'll take some time to open it without damaging it. Since I don't know what's inside, I don't exactly want to take a hacksaw to it, you know? I'm hoping Mrs. al Ahmadi might volunteer to open it herself."

"Good luck with that." She looked at the woman on the other side of the mirror. "Do you really want me, like, *in* there with you?"

"Are her shields as solid as Chip's were?"

"Not even close, but her thoughts are only about half understandable to me."

"Why?" He shook his head. "Of course. She's not a native English speaker."

"It's about half and half from what I've picked up so far."

"Half is better than nothing." He picked up the case. "Let's go see what Mrs. al Ahmadi was so eager to get out of the country."

They walked around the corner to enter the interrogation room. Rania al Ahmadi barely looked at them.

"Mrs. al Ahmadi, thank you for—"

"Mrs. Ahmadi is sufficient. It's what I go by in the US. Or you may call me Madam Rania." She folded her hands and looked at John patiently. "Not Mrs. al Ahmadi. It sounds ignorant."

John sat down and smiled. "Thank you for correcting me. I'll remember that."

She inclined her head slightly. "The comic woman from the dog show is here. Why?"

"She's a police consultant."

"Interesting." Rania turned to Evy. "Were you spying on the show?"

"No." Evy leaned her elbows on the table. "I guess you could say that I'm... unusually observant. Chief Marcos asked me to help out."

"Hmm." Rania said nothing else.

John spoke again. "Mrs. Ahmadi, you understand that you're not being arrested or detained at the moment?"

She looked around the taupe walls of the interrogation room. "I *am* being detained."

"Because you were trying to leave the country. If you want to leave the station right now and go back to your house here in Palm Springs, I have no problem with that."

Rania considered that idea for a few moments. "My husband is quite furious right now and is telling me that I shouldn't say anything to you. He's already called our attorney."

John folded his hands over the manila folder on the table. "Would you like to wait for him or her? We can do that."

"I don't want to be here at all. I am unhappy, exhausted, and grieving a dear friend. I want to go home to my husband, my children, and my dogs. I am hoping that by talking to you, this process might all go faster and you will let me leave."

...have the case I checked with the company's legal counsel and she gave it to me so there's really nothing they can do not even sure why I am here have to do with Bunny? Oh my friend... Rania's internal monologue drifted into Arabic.

"We appreciate that." John spoke, interrupting Rania's reverie.

"Mrs. Ahmadi, I asked you to stay in town after Chip Dunklin was killed. My officer spoke directly to you. Was there something about that message that wasn't clear?"

"I would assume that you wanted my party to stay in Palm Springs because you need to question us about Chip's murder, but since I know none of us had anything to do with that, and I have items with me of a delicate nature, I ignored you and decided to go home." She spread her hands. "Clearly that did not work."

"Why did you keep your plane in Chino instead of Palm Springs?"

"That was my husband's request," she said. "The mechanic we have used for years recently moved to that airport, and Haider wanted this man to service the plane. It was due for a checkup. No nefarious purpose intended."

"I'm sure we can find someone to verify that." John was flipping through a file. "You and Bunny Barker were close friends, were you not?"

Rania's gaze kept darting to the silver attaché case. "We were, yes. For nearly twenty years. Bunny was the first person to invite me to show my dogs at one of her competitions. Since I was not connected to a European club, many other shows were not so welcoming. Since then we've done business together. I have sponsored the show here, and she has consulted on my breeding program and in training my handlers."

"That's a strong connection," Evy said.

Rania raised an eyebrow. "I valued our friendship very much. While I may not be a demonstrative person, I was devastated when I heard about her death. Haider and I were both very upset. Quite angry, in fact. You still haven't arrested anyone."

John continued. "You were aware that Baron, her standard poodle, went missing. Along with his platinum, diamond, and onyx collar."

"It was a custom-designed piece and stunningly beautiful." A small frowned marred her forehead. "I am aware. Have you made any progress finding Baron?" There was a flicker of anger in Rania's eyes. "Bunny would have wanted Stewart to take care of him."

"Does the name Curtis Weathers sound familiar?"

"Of course." *...asking about Curtis has something happened to Curtis too dear God in heaven this town is a death trap want to go home...* "Curtis is Bunny's handler. Has something happened to him too?"

John frowned but didn't answer. "How about the name Shawn Dumas?"

...murderer? Is this man the one who hurt Bunny and Chip?

"No," Rania said. "I have not heard of him."

Evy nudged John's foot with her own. She glanced at him and shook her head slightly.

He murmured, "You sure?"

Evy nodded. Nothing about Rania's internal monologue connected her with Shawn's murder, Bunny's death, or Chip's. While she wasn't exactly forthcoming with emotion or information, she wasn't hiding murderous intent.

John brought the attaché case up on the table and sighed. "Mrs. Ahmadi, my consultant here doesn't seem to think you have anything to do with the crimes that have happened this week."

Rania turned to Evy. "She is a perceptive person. Obviously, I do not. I simply want to get home."

"What's in this case, Mrs. Ahmadi?"

She cocked her head. "As I mentioned, it is delicate and nothing that relates to you."

He closed his eyes. "If you could just open it—"

"I don't have to. I'm no longer the subject of your investigation." Rania looked at Evy. "Correct?"

"You're not," Evy said. "But I *can* say that if you just tell him, this will all go a lot faster and you'll be able to head home without any other hiccups." She looked at John. "Right?"

"We need to question her security team."

Evy shook her head. "No, we don't. They wouldn't do anything without her knowing about it."

John looked at Rania, who nodded.

"The comic woman is correct. My security is extensive, but I don't send them out to murder people, especially those I consider friends." A shadow in Rania's eyes. "Though now I wish I had sent one or two to Bunny's house. She was a fiercely independent woman. She thought nothing could touch her. Obviously she was wrong."

John put his hand on the attaché case. He looked tired and frustrated. "Mrs. Ahmadi, if you could just tell me what's in the case—"

"Dog sperm."

Evy snorted and John took his hand off the case.

"I beg your pardon?"

"Did you not hear me?" Rania was clearly amused. "Dog. Sperm. Biological samples from three breeding Havanese males to be precise. For artificial insemination of my bitches. Two of the samples are from Florida and one is from New York. Would you like to see the pertinent receipts?"

John opened his mouth, then closed it.

"Is that why you don't want to open it?" Evy asked. "I assume they're frozen or something?"

"They are, Miss Lane. The trip back to Dubai is long, and I will have to open the case there when I go through customs. I would prefer to not disturb the cooling mechanism any more often than necessary."

While her features were carefully composed, internally Rania al Ahmadi was laughing at John Marcos. She loved his expression, and she was resisting the urge to laugh in his face.

"Right." John carefully slid the attaché case across the table toward Rania. "I would like to get copies of the receipts and proper permits for the biological samples." He cleared his throat. "For my report."

"Of course, Chief Marcos." She glanced at the door. "May I go now?"

"Yeah, that's fine."

John shuffled his papers as Rania rose, took the silver case, and turned to Evy. "I still have your card, Miss Lane. I trust that your consulting work here does not preclude you from taking comedy and hosting jobs?"

"Oh yeah," Evy said. "This is kind of a side hustle."

"Good." Her eyes turned intense. "You *are* very perceptive. I feel slightly better knowing that you are trying to solve Bunny's murder. She was a friend."

"I have friends, Mrs. Ahmadi." Evy's voice was soft. "I understand."

"I think you do." She nodded at John, then at Evy. "Good afternoon to both of you."

Chapter Twenty-Four

Almost as soon as Evy left the station, Vivian called her.

"You need to get over to Casa de Lirio."

"What's wrong?" Evy unlocked her car and slid inside the beast. "I just left the police station, and it's not Rania. Remind me to tell you about the dog sperm. The look on John's face—"

"Curtis Weathers showed up at Bunny's house, got all confused, and wandered over to Richard's. He has the dog with him."

"Holy shit! Do you want me to get John?"

"Uh..." There was talking in the background. "Not just yet. It's complicated."

Evy understood complicated. "Okay, I'll be right there. I'll call Rafe and—"

"Maybe... Uh, maybe not Rafe either. Not just yet anyway."

Evy was even more confused. "Well, did you call Julia?"

"Oh yeah. I pulled her away from an open house this afternoon and she's pissed, but we need her."

"Vivian, what the hell is going on?"

"You'll find out when you get here, but put it this way: Bunny's got some explaining to do."

CURTIS WEATHERS WAS A THIN YOUNG MAN WITH A pale, angular face, gorgeous cheekbones, and black hair that was nearly as elaborately coiffed as a standard poodle. He sat on the couch in Richard's living room with Baron's head laid plaintively in his lap. He looked like he was about twenty years old, and he was terrified.

"I didn't start to get worried until Saturday," he said quietly. "I took him up to my brother's place in Oregon because I'd been wanting to visit anyway and Butch loves riding in the car, so it seemed perfect."

Evy frowned. "Butch?"

Curtis lifted his eyes to hers, then looked to Vivian and Richard. "I... I don't want to get in trouble. Bunny said I wouldn't get in trouble."

Richard frowned. "Why would you get in trouble? She told you to take the dog, didn't she?"

"Yes, but..." He sighed. "I knew about Baron."

Evy felt her heart sink. "What about Baron?"

"Bunny's dead." The young man choked. "There's no point in lying about it anymore. This isn't Baron. Baron died in his sleep about three months ago."

Evy's jaw dropped. "What?"

Vivian murmured, "Oh my God."

Julia blinked rapidly. "Well, that's a twist."

"She found..." The young man struggled for a moment. "A friend put her in contact with a discreet breeder who had a dog a little younger than Baron, but he looked really similar. At least, it was enough to fool people, you know? But it wouldn't have been enough to fool the judges at the show. That's why he had to disappear."

Evy touched Geoff in the backpack. "Read him," she said under her breath before leaning forward. "Curtis, why would she do this? Why would she try to pass off this other dog as Baron? And what happened to him?"

...gonna get into so much trouble I should have gone to college my mom was so right this is so messed up Bunny said I could trust her she said she had a plan and I just went God I'm so stupid and I'm going to jail what will happen to Butch if I...

Curtis shook his head vehemently. "We don't know what happened to Baron. According to his last checkup, he was perfectly healthy. There was *no* reason for him to die, but he did."

Evy sat back in her seat. "Holy shit."

"I think part of the reason Bunny did what she did was just... she couldn't face it. She loved him so much. I don't think she wanted to admit that Baron was actually dead." His shoulders sank. "But part of it was the money."

Evy remembered what Chip had said about Bunny always asking for money up front for breeding contracts. "How much had she taken?"

"About forty-five thousand, and she didn't have it. The house cost a fortune to maintain, and she just didn't have it."

"For what?" Vivian asked.

"For breeding Baron," Evy said. "Baron had some very expensive balls."

"And Baron wasn't providing any more puppies," Julia said. "But Bunny had people who'd already paid for Baron's sperm."

"She couldn't cover the bill," Richard said, "but if Baron was dognapped..."

Curtis said, "Baron was insured against anything other than natural causes. An insurance payout wouldn't have been a lot, but it would have at least covered the breeding contracts." He blinked back tears. "But my idea was to just get him away from the dog show so no one would know Baron wasn't Baron. Then he could show up again and it would be fine. Everything could go back to what it was."

Julia cocked her head. "But Curtis, you'd still be cheating people."

He looked up with tears in his eyes. "I didn't want Bunny to file an insurance claim! I knew that was illegal. The breeding stuff?" He shrugged. "Breeders do shady shit all the time, but Bunny never did." He petted the head of the poodle on his lap. "Look at this dog. He's beautiful! He's as show-worthy as Baron was; he just doesn't have that stupid German pedigree going back two hundred years. Who cares?" Curtis shook his head. "Fooling breeders didn't bother me as much, but I worried that Bunny would get into trouble if she filed a claim for Baron with the insurance company."

Richard asked, "What about the collar? The Cartier?"

Curtis frowned. "What about it?"

"Bunny filed a claim on that too."

His eyes went wide. "I didn't know about that. I just assumed she put the collar in her safe. I was always worried when I took him out that he'd be a target because of it, you know? I told her all the time that she should only keep the collars on Baron and Zara when they were at events." He rubbed his face. "Oh my God, do the police think I stole the collar?" He stood up in a panic. "I promise I didn't steal it! I didn't steal Butch either. She told me to take him."

"Right now it's your word against a dead woman's," Julia said. "That could be a problem."

"No! Chip Dunklin knew too! He found out—I don't know how—and he was holding it over Bunny's head."

"Wait." Evy slid forward in her seat. "Are you telling me that Chip was blackmailing Bunny?"

"Yeah. He knew that Butch wasn't Baron. He and Bunny met a couple of times right before I left. Right after the appearance at the TV station, he came over."

"No," Vivian said. "That doesn't make sense."

"I don't know if it makes sense or not," Curtis said. "I just know that Chip showed up one night and said he'd figured it out and unless Bunny cut him in on the insurance, he was going to the cops." Curtis snapped his fingers. "Maybe Chip murdered Bunny!"

"Only Chip is dead too," Evy said. "He was murdered Sunday night."

"No." Curtis sank into the sofa again. "That's horrible. I mean, he was an asshole, but no one deserves to die just because they're an asshole."

Julia was staring into space. "If Chip was blackmailing Bunny, he had no motive to kill her. The whole point of blackmail is getting stuff from the target. If the target's dead, you get nothing."

Evy asked, "Who was the friend, Curtis? The one who hooked her up with the breeder who replaced Baron?" Evy was thinking that since Curtis didn't have the Cartier, whoever had conspired with Bunny was still holding the collar.

"I don't know," Chip said. "I never knew. Bunny never told me, but..." He frowned. "She did give me a phone number for just in case. She said to only call it if something went wrong and I couldn't get ahold of her." He pulled out his phone. "I called it a couple of days ago, but no one answered or called back."

"What was the number?" Evy was already getting out her phone. "Maybe we can call it."

"No," Vivian said. "It would be better if we handed all this information over to John." She looked at Curtis. "You didn't do anything wrong. If what you told us is all correct, all you did was follow your employer's orders, and you brought Baron—uh, Butch—back. So you should be in the clear."

"I agree," Richard said. "I don't think John Marcos is going to arrest you for doing what Bunny asked you to do."

"You don't know that," Curtis said. "And honestly? Bunny

dead, Chip dead, and some guy behind her pool got beaten up too?"

"But he's dead now." Evy grimaced. "Sorry. We forgot that one."

"I'm fucked," Curtis said. "I'm completely fucked."

"Not yet," Richard said. "But Curtis, I'm going to advise you to stay here for a night or two. Or at least until we know what Chief Marcos wants to do."

VIVIAN, JULIA, AND EVY MARCHED OVER TO BUNNY'S house while Richard got Curtis settled in one of the guest rooms.

"Okay, Bunny." Julia was muttering under her breath. "You've got some explaining to do."

"Why would she do this?" Vivian said. "It's... crazy. It's crazy, elaborate, unnecessary—I mean, her dog died! It's tragic, but she set this bizarre Fake Baron plot up, and now look what's happened!"

"I'm telling you," Evy said, "there are people who own dogs, and then there are Dog People. And the dog people are more than a little unbalanced."

They reached the backyard of Bunny's house and walked directly to the corner where Julia was heading.

"Bunny," Julia called out. "We need to talk. Curtis came back to Palm Springs, and he has a story to tell."

There was silence to Evy's ears, of course, but she could hear a faint white noise in the background since she'd left Geoff back at Richard's house.

"I don't care that you don't want to talk about upsetting things." Julia was arguing with the ghost. "I will buy that you might not remember what happened when you died, but don't tell me you can't explain about replacing Baron with Butch."

Vivian and Evy sat down on pool loungers while Julia continued to badger Bunny's ghost.

"It's always weird watching her do this," Vivian said. "I mean, I know she's not hallucinating, but still."

"It doesn't look great." Evy leaned back. "Should we call Rafe?"

"I think you need to. I don't think the insurance company can go after Curtis, can they? Or at least Rafe won't. The dog is back, and I'm sure there's some way they can test if it's Baron or not. Doggie DNA?"

"They'll probably contact Stewart," Evy said. "He has Baron and Zara's offspring."

"This is so messed up."

"We need evidence," Julia said. "Come on, Bunny. Please don't make the police dig up Baron's body. No one wants that."

She paced back and forth under the olive tree, pointing at the ground for emphasis.

"You know, now that we know Baron is buried there," Evy said. "It so totally looks like a dog graveyard."

"There's even a statue."

While there wasn't a grave marker, there was a cast stone garden statue of a black poodle just under three feet tall. Beside it, a stone bench sat in the shade of the olive tree, overlooking the rolling lawn at the back of Bunny's estate.

"Do you think that she was planning to bury Zara there too?" Evy asked.

"Maybe." Vivian looked at Julia. "I think she's making progress."

"—tell us what you know or Curtis is going to end up getting into trouble. No, don't worry about us verifying it. We'll figure out how to do that, but right now we need to know where the necklace is and what Chip knew about the theft."

Julia turned and waved Evy and Vivian over after Bunny's ghost responded. "Okay, I think she's ready to talk."

They walked over to the olive tree, and Vivian sat on the bench. "Bunny, you picked a beautiful place for Baron. I know you must have loved him so much."

Evy folded her arms over her chest and waited.

Julia said, "Everything that Curtis shared was correct. Baron died in his sleep, and neither of them knew what had happened. Curtis had been staying in the guest room at the house for weeks, but he hadn't noticed Baron acting unwell any more than Bunny had."

"It could have been anything," Evy said. "A random stroke. A heart attack. An infection that no one caught. Sometimes there aren't any answers."

"And Bunny says if she hadn't been so distraught, she might have tried to have the vet perform a necropsy, but she panicked about the breeding contracts. Plus she was worried that Baron might have had a genetic defect they hadn't spotted before, and if that happened—"

"Then any dog that Baron had sired would have a tainted bloodline," Evy said. "She couldn't take the chance."

Vivian asked, "Whose idea was the impostor?"

Julia waited a beat, listening. "She says it was a friend, but she won't say who. She said they were only trying to help."

"And Chip?"

There was another long pause. "She's reluctant to talk about this part too." Julia waited. "I understand—I promise I do—but we need to know what happened."

Evy was losing patience with the reluctant ghost. None of this was actual proof; it was ghostly hearsay, and she was worried about the cops nabbing Curtis for something she was convinced he didn't do.

"Chip called Bunny the night of the television appearance. He said he knew Baron wasn't Baron and asked Bunny what was going on. She should have played it off, but she was flustered and she thought he was a friend. She ended up telling him everything about Baron and the breeding contracts."

"But instead of being a friend," Vivian said, "he blackmailed you."

"Yes," Julia said. "He's the one who urged her to file an insurance claim, not just on Baron but on the Cartier. He said if she didn't, he'd tell everyone at the kennel club that she'd been passing off another dog as a champion."

"It would ruin her reputation," Evy said. "She'd never recover, and all of Baron and Zara's line might have been seen as suspicious too."

Vivian raised her eyebrows. "Know who that would have damaged? Stewart Barker. He's the one who has most of Baron and Zara's puppies."

Julia turned to Evy and Vivian with wide eyes. "Guys, I think Chip might have been the one holding the necklace." She looked back at the tree. "Bunny, did he? Did Chip have the necklace? Was he the one who was going to sell it in England?"

They waited for several long minutes, but Julia finally shook her head. "She's not saying anything. She's gone quiet again."

Vivian bit her lip. "I know this sounds bad, but I'm not sorry Chip is dead."

Chapter Twenty-Five

"I had to take him in," John said.

"You didn't. What did he do wrong?"

John seemed confused that Evy even asked the question. "*He took the dog.*"

"Because Bunny told him to!"

He didn't have a response for that.

"He'll answer questions," Evy said. "He answered everything I asked him, and I read him, John. He didn't have anything to do with the murder or the insurance fraud. This kid is trying to do the right thing."

"By passing off a no-name dog as a five-time champion?" John shook his head. "He was in this mess up to his neck."

"He's twenty-four and he followed the lead of a woman he knew and trusted who was his boss. There's nothing wrong with that. Bunny was in the wrong, Chip was in the wrong. Curtis was just trying to take care of the dogs." Evy sat back with a huff. "This is why I don't like cops."

"I have to follow the law!"

Evy pointed to the interview room where Curtis Weathers was innocently drinking a Pepsi. "Oh sure, you're all about following the very letter of the law when it comes to a twenty-four-year-old nobody with no money, but we're gonna walk on eggshells when Richard Putnam is accused of murder. We're going to tiptoe around the rich parents at the prep school when they murder their mom!"

"Hey!" He stood up and pointed at Curtis. "Do you see me putting the kid in cuffs, Evy? I'd like to think I've earned a little more trust than you automatically jumping to the wrong conclusion every single blasted time."

She spread her hands. "What's the wrong conclusion? The kid didn't do anything but babysit a dog, and you've got him in interrogation. What's his crime? Does he have a lawyer? Does he even know he needs one?"

"As a matter of fact—"

"Chief Marcos?" a voice from the lobby called out. "I'm Susan Crossman, attorney for Curtis Weathers. Is my client being detained?"

John eyed Evy, and she heard him clearly in her mind. *Did you call her?*

"I don't know lawyers," she hissed. "Maybe Richard or—"

"Stewart Barker hired me," Ms. Crossman said. "He'd like Curtis released unless he's being detained."

"Stewart wants the kid out?"

Susan Crossman motioned to the swinging door that separated the lobby from the main office area of the Palm Springs police department.

John waved her in, and Susan reached in her bag as she walked toward them.

"Strictly between us," Crossman said. "Mr. Barker is grateful that Curtis returned to Palm Springs and doesn't want the young man to sit in jail in relation to a crime that occurred when he was out of the state. Mr. Weathers was a loyal employee of Mr. Barker's ex-wife, and he doesn't want the young man held. If you have questions for my client, I want to consult with him first."

"There aren't any questions about Mrs. Barker's murder," John said. "But we have some questions about what Mr. Weathers knew about the fraud."

"What fraud?" Susan Crossman cocked her head. "Has anyone brought an allegation of fraud?"

John took his time answering. "Not yet."

"It's my understanding that the insurance investigator, Rafe Howell, hasn't even made a recommendation to his company yet." She glanced at Evy. "Has the insurance company filed fraud charges?"

John looked about ready to explode. "No."

"Then aren't you searching for clues to a crime you're not even sure has happened? Judges don't like fishing expeditions, Chief Marcos."

Evy made a note to get Susan Crossman's business card. She probably couldn't afford her, but she still wanted to have it.

"Fine," John said between gritted teeth. "I'd like Mr. Weathers's statement about the last time he saw Bunny and a timeline of events as relates to Chip Dunklin and Bunny Barker's interactions the week before their deaths."

Crossman nodded. "I'll speak to my client."

She started to walk away, but Evy called out, "Ms. Crossman?"

Susan Crossman turned. "And you are?"

"She's an investigative consultant." John jumped in with an answer before Evy could mention the word *psychic*.

"What he said." Evy continued, "Please ask Curtis when was the last time he saw the Cartier necklace? We think finding it may be the key to solving Bunny's murder, and he was one of the last people alive to see it."

She gave Evy a short nod. "I'll see what I can find out."

Evy felt her phone buzzing in her pocket. She took it out and saw Rafe's name on the screen. Evy smiled and answered. "Hey, stranger."

"I heard Curtis Weathers made it back to Palm Springs."

"Was that your doing?"

"I've been tracking his debit card and credit cards for a week now. He finally used one yesterday at a gas station in Kettleman City. He must have run out of the cash Bunny gave him."

"He was on his way home," Evy said. "Showed up last night at Bunny's place and wandered over to Richard's. It's a long story."

"Why don't we meet over at your place and talk about it? Two heads are better than one."

Evy could feel herself smiling. "That sounds good."

John Marcos cleared his throat and glared at her.

"Hey, Rafe, on second thought, why don't we meet with the whole gang over at Sergio's so we don't have to repeat ourselves too much? We can head over to my place after."

"Yeah, that's probably a good idea. I've been on the road a couple of days and I need a shower, so I'll head home. See you over at Dean and Sergio's."

"Sounds good."

John looked at her. "Do you even know if Dean and Sergio want everyone gathering at their house tonight?"

"Why wouldn't they?" Evy leaned back, buoyed by the thought of seeing Rafe. "I'm a fucking delight and so are my friends."

"Whatever, Landa. Just tell me when, and don't argue with me. This case is weird on a couple of levels, and we need all the brains we can get."

Vivian brought her white dry-erase markers to Sergio and Dean's to use the windows as a whiteboard, but by the time everyone had settled outside with tacos and drinks, Sergio had drawn an elaborate, swirling fractal design that stretched from the french doors across the kitchen windows.

He was staring at the hedge that surrounded the patio. "Dean, my love."

"No." Dean sat down and poured a glass of white wine from a clear gold bottle.

"You don't even know what I'm going to ask you!"

"Sergio, my husband of many years, I have learned that when you use that tone, you're trying to convince me to say yes to something when you know I would not normally say yes." He sipped his wine. "So I'm just skipping ahead."

Sergio pouted. "Topiary is an ancient art form."

"So it is." Dean looked at Evy. "How was your day, comedian lady?"

"Not bad, office-building man." She grinned at him. "I feel like we're finally making progress on this case. Some pieces are finally falling into place."

"Like?"

Rafe slipped into the seat beside her. "The dog is just fine."

"Oh, thank God!" Sergio yelled. "Where was he?"

"It's a little complicated," Julia said. "Which dog are we talking about?"

"Baron, of course." Sergio reached for a wineglass. "We're talking about Baron."

"So... little thing about Baron." Evy took a deep breath and blurted all of it out in one breath: "Baron Barker—the Baron you knew—has passed away, seemingly from natural causes, though a necropsy was never performed. And Curtis and Bunny kept up the appearance of Baron because of financial responsibilities, contracts she'd already signed, and Bunny's seeming inability to face the reality of losing a beloved pet."

Sergio and Dean were both staring. Dean was blinking rapidly, and Sergio murmured, "Who...?"

"Curtis took Baron II—you can call him Butch—to Oregon to stay with his brother last week so Baron II wouldn't be subjected to scrutiny by the judges during the dog show. But then, after

Chip's and my appearance on the *Desert Daily* morning show, Chip Dunklin realized that Baron wasn't Baron and he threatened to expose the whole scheme unless Bunny filed an insurance claim with Rafe's company and split the money with him."

Dean frowned, then nodded a little. "You know, that actually makes sense."

"But what about Coma Guy?" Sergio asked. "Why did he get beat up?"

"Stewart Barker maintains that Shawn Dumas—Coma Guy— reported to him Saturday afternoon, but then he didn't hear from him again. It's possible that while he was snooping around Bunny's house, he saw something he shouldn't have and Bunny's killer attacked him."

Richard said, "Whoever did it probably didn't think he'd be found."

"If Evy hadn't been over at Bunny's house, Dumas probably would have died right there," Vivian said. "He was pretty well hidden."

"There's something about this case that's bothering me," Rafe said. "I've worked a lot of insurance cases over the years, and unfortunately more than one of them wound up with someone—or multiple people—ending up dead."

"Greed makes people do stupid, risky things," John said quietly. "And some of those things are violent."

"Agreed," Rafe said. "It doesn't surprise me that with a motive of half a million dollars and social reputation on the line, three people in this case were killed. My problem is with the murders themselves."

Julia said, "I think we all have a problem with murder." She turned to Mick. "Wouldn't you say you had an aversion to murder?"

"Hell yeah, but think I know where Rafe might be going with this." Julia's boyfriend was still wearing his "set beard" and hadn't, as feared, brought home a street dog from Thailand. He did have

Paco hovering over his shoulder though. Paco loved tacos and white wine. "Think about these crimes as independent events," Mick said. "The narrative doesn't work."

"Coma Guy was beaten up first," Rafe said. "Which led to his death. It was a crime of passion, likely unplanned."

"Agreed," John Marcos said. "Shawn Dumas was snooping around the house and saw something that got him killed."

"It was sudden," Rafe continued. "And—not to be too grim—but it was an incomplete attack. The killer put him in a coma, but he didn't kill him."

"Yes," John said. "Similar to what happened to Bunny. Another beating, another vicious attack, but with Bunny he finished the job. The murderer didn't leave any loose ends this time; when Bunny was out cold from his attack, he smothered her with a pillow."

"But Bunny let him in," Evy said. "The dogs didn't bark. It was someone she knew and trusted."

"That fits with her ghost too," Julia said. "Why she still won't talk about her murder. If it was a friend, the betrayal would have traumatized her spirit even more than the physical attack."

Rafe leaned his elbows on the table. "I think Bunny's murder was a crime of passion too. Even though she knew her attacker, I don't think it was planned; I think it was a fight that got out of control."

"The evidence fits that idea," John said. "Better than anything else."

"Now let's think about the third murder," Rafe said.

Mick spoke again. "Completely different. Not a single thing the same. Like a totally different story."

"Chip's murderer used poison in his whiskey," Evy said. "That's what the report said."

John nodded. "We found strychnine in one glass, which is not easy to come by these days. It would have worked very quickly. It wasn't in the whiskey bottle, just the glass, and the other one had been carefully wiped. No evidence at all. No fingerprints, no hairs. Nothing."

"Which differs from the physical evidence at Bunny's house too," Rafe said. "Right? There's so much evidence there they're still organizing it."

"Bunny had a lot of company," Vivian said. "Especially in the month before the dog show. Had lots of people coming and going. Her housekeeper only came once a week. The physical evidence at her place is probably all over the place while Chip was staying in a hotel with housekeeping every day."

"Any mystery writer will tell you," Mick said, "poisoning is methodical, careful, and most of all *planned*. It's the opposite of a crime of passion; it's a crime of calculation."

John raised his eyebrows. "Mick's right. Different narrative."

Rafe narrowed his eyes. "If I examined these cases in isolation, no way would I link them together. At least not Bunny and Chip."

Evy blinked and realized what they were getting at. "You don't think it's the same guy."

Julia's eyes went wide. "You think there are *two* murderers that belong to the Desert Fancy Kennel Club?"

"Yep." Rafe nodded slowly. "Three murders. Two murderers."

Julia said, "So we've got two conspiracies? The fraud conspiracy and the murder conspiracy?" She shook her head. "Dog-show people really are crazy."

"They have to be linked," Evy said, "but we don't even know where to start."

"When it comes to insurance fraud, I always follow the money," Rafe said. "And this case isn't any different. Who would benefit from Bunny's death? Who would benefit from Chip's?"

"Bunny had secrets," Vivian said. "Chip was profiting from them. But in the end, they were working together, right? For the insurance?"

"So we start with Bunny," Evy said. "Who would want to kill Bunny? She had two big secrets: Baron and the missing Cartier necklace. She wasn't a hardened criminal, so whoever she trusted enough to help her get Baron II is probably the same person she'd go to if she needed to fence a stolen necklace."

"And who's that?" Julia asked.

Evy looked at John. "Time to go talk to Curtis Weathers again."

Chapter Twenty-Six

John and Evy questioned Curtis again the next morning, this time with his lawyer present, in the home of Stewart Barker, where Curtis and Baron II were staying.

"You okay over here?" Evy asked, glancing at Stewart, who was reading the paper in the breakfast nook.

"Oh yeah," Curtis said. "I probably should have told you yesterday that my dad works for Mr. Barker. That's how I got the job working for Bunny."

"It sounds like Mr. Barker is pretty loyal to his employees," John said. "Do you think it's strange that he didn't know Shawn Dumas had been beaten up?"

The lawyer asked, "How is that relevant? You said you wanted to ask Curtis about Baron II."

Curtis ignored the lawyer. "I mean, I didn't know Shawn Dumas either. I don't think he'd worked for Stew very long."

"Curtis." The lawyer's voice was soft. "Only answer questions about Baron II."

"Can I just call him Butch?" The young man looked at Evy. "It's less confusing."

Anything had to be less confusing than the muddle of voices in the room. Geoff couldn't seem to isolate Curtis's thoughts, maybe because he was so attached to his lawyer.

"So when Baron died, how long did it take to get Butch?"

"It was a week or so." He scrunched up his face. "Maybe more like two. I don't know where she got him; all she said was that she had a friend with a connection."

"No name?"

"No."

"Could it have been Chip Dunklin?" Evy asked.

"I don't think so," Curtis said. "I don't think she liked Chip much, and she definitely didn't trust him."

"Did she talk about paying anyone off?" John asked. "I looked at her banking records, and I didn't see any large withdrawals around that time. Do you know how she paid her friend?"

Curtis looked lost. "I guess I always assumed she paid them back with the dog show."

"What do you mean?" John asked. "'With the dog show?'"

"The international champions," Evy said. "One of the people she sponsored." She looked at Curtis. "Am I right?"

Curtis squirmed, and even though Evy couldn't grab on to an intelligible string of thoughts, he was clearly hiding something.

The lawyer must have sensed the same thing. "Curtis, why don't you—?"

"It's not illegal," Curtis blurted. "I didn't do anything illegal, and neither did Bunny."

John and the lawyer exchanged a look.

"If he didn't do anything," John said, "there's no danger in him telling me. But if there was a quid pro quo that might have led to Bunny's death..."

The lawyer looked at Curtis. "Okay, be careful. If you're not sure about something, shut up."

Curtis nodded.

Evy asked, "Did Bunny rig the judging?"

"No!" Curtis said. "Not... exactly."

"How would you rig dog-show judging?" John asked. "Bribes?"

"Nothing like that," Curtis said. "It doesn't... Bunny was the one to hire the judges for the show."

"So bribes?" Evy asked.

"So the dirty secret of dog shows is that you can kind of manipulate judging even without doing anything illegal," Curtis said. "Because at the end of the day, all of it is subjective."

Stewart must have been listening from across the room because he piped up. "That's all true. Dog-show judges are more like art critics than athletic referees."

John scooted forward and kept his eyes on Curtis. "Explain."

"So the breed standard is the breed standard," Curtis continued. "But if you want to invite a person and you know they're bringing a particular dog, then you can hire judges—and there're lots of them—who like the *type* of dog your people are bringing."

Evy sat back. "I still don't understand."

"Take Labrador retrievers," Curtis said. "Super popular dogs, right?"

"Yeah," John said. "Every other bird hunter in the desert has a Lab."

"Okay, so some judges like a blockier head and a shorter nose on Labradors. Others like more of a field dog with a longer nose and a slimmer build. Both of those things are within the breed standard, but some judges have certain preferences."

Evy nodded. "Gotcha. So if Bunny wanted to make sure Rania won the toy group—even though a Havanese had never won before—she'd need to find a judge who likes Havanese and the particular kind of Havanese that Rania was bringing."

"Exactly. Bunny has been showing dogs for so many years, but she knew that Lorain was trying to push her out. She knows judges all over the country; she knows the trends. She had friends, and she wanted to reward them. None of that is illegal. Technically."

John asked, "So who did she want to reward? Other than Rania al Ahmadi."

"I think all the people she sponsored, you know? The Lomaxes for sure. The Webers. Liam Davies—well, technically Liam's dad. Marina Wesley. She had her favorites."

Holy shit, Curtis had just named the majority of the group winners. "She arranged for all those people to win?" Evy asked.

"Not exactly." Curtis was squirming again. "Those dogs are all champions already. Let's just say she created the most... advantageous circumstances for her favorite dogs, okay? I mean, not all of them won!"

"And if someone found out that she manipulated the show to advantage her friends?" John said. "Would someone have killed her for that?"

"No!" Curtis was adamant. "This is a dog show. People don't kill people over dog shows!"

John looked at Stewart Barker. "Mr. Barker?"

The old man shrugged. "I'm as competitive as they get, but I have a hard time imagining it. You want a motive for all this? Follow the money."

"And the money goes back to Baron II and the necklace," Evy said. "Chances are good that one of the international champions was the one who supplied Bunny with Baron II."

"And it couldn't be Bunny buying the dog," Stewart said from across the living room. "Every poodle breeder in the United States and most of the ones in Europe know Bunny."

"*Knew* Bunny," Curtis whispered.

"So you needed someone more anonymous. Someone unknown in the poodle world for sure." Evy thought about the winners. There had been two relative newcomers to the Best in Show ring—Liam Davies and the Webers from Germany.

Then again, Rafe's mother could have bought a dog in Europe without attracting too much attention. After all, she'd lived in the US for decades. And the Lomaxes were known for their terrier breeding, not their poodles, but they seemed like the kind of people with connections all over.

"Let's bring them in," Evy said. "Just bring every single one of them in and let's question them all. They each knew Bunny, and she wanted them in the Best of Show ring. Let's find out why."

LIAM DAVIES BROUGHT BADGER THE CORGI TO THE police station that afternoon. It was hard to glower at a rosy-cheeked man in wire-rimmed glasses and a flamingo-print shirt even if he was a suspect in a murder/dognapping/fraud case. Especially when that rosy-cheeked man did silly voices for his corgi.

"We've just had the most lovely holiday, haven't we, Badger?" Liam changed his voice. "Oh yes, Liam, we saw the giant dinosaurs on the highway and the funny-looking Joshua trees. And I got to sniff so many lovely things and meet lots of new friends."

Evy scanned the man with ease. Geoffrey was right on top of it in the interview room, and Liam's thoughts beamed right through to Evy with clarity. The friendly Welshman's thoughts were nearly a direct reflection of his dialogue. The man hid nothing.

Evy looked at John, her eyes saying one thing.

If Liam Davies was a murderer, there's no hope for humanity.

"Mr. Davies," John said, "we understand that your father and Bunny Barker were great friends."

"Oh yes, I've known Bunny since I was a child. She was a good friend of my mother's first, but then Mum passed away from breast cancer when I was twenty." He shook his head. "Horrible. Dad never really recovered from it; that's why he mostly focuses on the corgis now. Doesn't travel much, but Bunny stayed in touch with Dad and me. Always there to answer a question for Dad or offer her support." Liam smiled. "She could be abrasive, Bunny could, but she was as loyal a friend as anyone could ask for." His expression fell a little. "My dad never much liked Chip, I'm sad to say. I don't want to speak ill of the dead, but my dad called him a pretentious wanker."

John flipped through a file that Evy knew was full of evidence from Bunny's crime scene. "Did you feel the same way about Chip?"

"Oh..." Liam lifted one shoulder. "I try to give people the benefit of the doubt. I thought Chip did a marvelous job with Miss Lane here." Liam grinned at Evy. "Wonderful commentary. And Chip knows his dogs, doesn't he?"

Evy nodded. Chip did know his dogs, and apparently that had been the problem. "What about you, Liam? How many dog shows have you exhibited at?"

"Well, you have to do your time on the local level, of course. Badger and I have driven all over Great Britain to dog shows in England and Scotland. Local shows too. This was my first dog show in the US though."

"What about poodles?" John said. "You know anything about poodles?"

Liam looked lost. "Poodles?"

"How about your dad?" Evy asked. "Does he know any poodle breeders?"

"Bunny," Liam said. "I think that was it. We know quite a few herding dog breeders, of course. Got your collies and shepherds. All quite popular in Wales. Standard poodles aren't as common."

"So if Bunny wanted to obtain new blood for her breeding program," John asked, "do you know who she might ask?"

"Oh, I've no idea," Liam said. "Maybe ask Juliet and Edgar. They're in London, so I imagine they're much better connected in the dog world than I am. Dad and I, we're farming people really."

Evy looked at John and nodded. Liam wasn't hiding anything. She kind of doubted that was possible.

EDGAR LOMAX SHOWED UP TO THE INTERVIEW WITH A lawyer and his handler, Kenzie.

"I've been advised that I shouldn't speak to you at all," Edgar said. "And according to my attorney, I am not obligated to do so."

"No, you're not, but thank you for coming in. The faster we can close the murders of Chip Dunklin and Bunny, the faster we can allow everyone to go home."

"I know," Edgar said. "That's why we're here."

John flipped a folder closed and clasped his hands on the desk. "Was Mrs. Lomax busy this morning?"

"She's not feeling well," Kenzie said. "She gets migraines, and she's currently trying to find someone who can refill her prescription. We were supposed to be home already, and she's out of her medication."

"I'm sorry to hear she's feeling ill, but we appreciate your help," John said. "And we understand it's an inconvenience, but three people are dead and it all seems to circle back to the dog show."

Kenzie exchanged a glance with Edgar and the lawyer, who nodded.

Evy scanned them both, but Geoffrey was focusing more on Kenzie than Edgar, and the young handler had very sturdy walls. Evy heard murmurs, but they came from a distance.

"I was the one who spent the most time at the show," Kenzie said. "What do you want to know?"

"How much do you know about poodles?"

Edgar frowned. "Poodles?"

Kenzie took the question in stride. "I have experience with a few of the non-sporting breeds. I handled a miniature poodle for a year or so before I moved to working with a bichon frise breeder. That's where Juliet met me and hired me."

"And standard poodles?" John asked. "What about them?"

Kenzie frowned. "I don't handle large dogs."

John turned his attention to Edgar. "Mr. Lomax, how about you?"

Evy felt Geoffrey's attention shift.

...what they want to know has to do with Bunny's death not much we can do just want to go home wonder if Jules has found some pills yet might call Dr. Bashir what time? Probably already out of the office blasted American health care so clumsy...

Edgar seemed preoccupied with his wife's illness, but at least that told Evy that Juliet Lomax truly was ill and not just making excuses.

"If you're asking about standard poodle breeders," Edgar Lomax began, "I know a few. Bunny, of course, and Juliet and I have dear friends in upstate New York who breed both standard poodles and miniature poodles, but they were not at this show. The Clements family. They mostly keep to the East Coast. I don't know any standard poodle breeders in the UK very well, but we do have a dear friend in Brittany who breeds poodles and Portuguese water dogs."

"And did Bunny know of any of these friends?"

"I'm sure she knew of the Clements, but I doubt she knew our friends in France. It's a small world in elite dog circles, but not *that* small."

Nothing in his internal thoughts contradicted what he was saying. Evy nodded at John.

"And what about Chip Dunklin?" John asked. "Did you know Chip well?"

Evy sensed a sudden spike from Edgar Lomax.

...incompetent, irresponsible grasper good thing he moved to the US never going to get near a dog in European breeding circles just a horrible shame not sure what this inspector thinks I didn't like him should I say so? Have to say so I think...

"I didn't like Chip," Edgar said. "Julia and Kenzie would probably be more charitable, but something about the man always put me off. He liked knowing secrets about people and then insinuating things to make them uncomfortable. He was a grasping kind of fellow, and his manners were absurd."

How much of that was genuinely Chip and how much was Edgar Lomax being a snob? It was hard to tell, but Evy didn't hear anything from Edgar's internal monologue that mentioned poison or getting rid of Chip. Did murderers think of their crimes later? That was something she was going to have to figure out.

"Do you think that others had the same opinion of Chip?" John asked. "Kenzie?"

"Hmm." She was a blank wall who chose her words carefully. "Let's just say that I got the same vibe from Chip that Edgar did. I think he liked gossip and he liked knowing people's secrets. He liked having leverage over people."

"What about other people in the Best in Show circle?" Evy asked. "Did any of them have a problem with Chip?"

Edgar closed his mouth, but Kenzie spoke. "I think most of them did. Well, maybe not Liam—he loves everyone." Kenzie smiled. "But I know Sergio thought he was an asshole." Kenzie glanced at Evy. "And the Webers didn't quite know what to do with him. They're new to this whole scene. Marina kind of let Chip charm her, but I think that was only out of self-interest. Chip had a lot of sway with the show's director."

"And what about Bunny's influence on the show?" John asked. "The judges she hired?"

Edgar and Kenzie frowned and looked at each other. "What about them?"

Damn. The question didn't produce a single sketchy thought. Both Edgar and Kenzie were truly and purely confused.

"What about the judges?" Edgar scooted forward and folded his hands on the table. "What are you trying to say?"

Chapter Twenty-Seven

Edgar Lomax and Kenzie had walked out of their interview looking and sounding truly confused about the thought of Bunny manipulating the judges, but when John brought the possibility up to Marc and Geerta Weber, they did not look confused at all.

"We have heard of such things happening," Marc said in a soft German accent. "We are quite new to the dog-showing world, so I do not think we can give you any information about how this is done, but we are happy to answer any questions you have."

Geerta Weber looked distinctly less cooperative than her husband. Evy turned her attention to the silent woman.

Unfortunately, all of Geerta Weber's internal monologue was in German.

"What do you know about Bunny's poodle?" Evy asked.

Marc frowned. "The missing dog? We have heard of it. We did not take it, of course." He laughed a little. "Where would we hide a poodle?"

"It was good she did not show him," Geerta said quietly.

John zeroed in on Geerta. "Why not?"

Geerta said nothing.

"Do you know something about Bunny's poodle, Mrs. Weber?"

She turned to Marc and said something low in German.

John Marcos added something in the same language.

Evy blinked. "You speak German?"

"I speak enough." John was glaring at Geerta. "Tell us what you know about the dog."

Geerta's face had gone pale, and Marc Weber looked thoroughly confused.

"Geerta?" he asked. "What is it? What is going on?"

"I met Juliet Lomax in Berlin at a show with Lulu two years ago. She saw Lulu's potential in the ring—she has an excellent eye. I came from a dog-breeding family; so did her husband. We exchanged information and kept in touch."

"Juliet Lomax?" John scooted forward.

"Edgar and Juliet Lomax are very wealthy," Marc said. "But they are not elitist and have been very welcoming. Our first show in the UK was a result of their invitation."

Geerta looked at Evy. "Three months ago, Juliet called me and asked me for a very... specific favor."

"She needed a dog."

Geerta nodded a little, then continued quietly. "The dogs my family breeds are standard poodles from very old lines. They live just outside Munich, and Juliet asked me to find a very specific dog. Seven to eight years old, pure black and in good health. Breeding quality, she specified. She sent me a picture of a dog and asked me if I could find one to match as closely as possible."

"Did you ask why?"

"I did, and she said it was a favor for a dear friend who had lost her companion and wanted a dog who looked like the dog she had lost." Geerta frowned. "I told her that I would inquire, but I will admit the breeding quality gave me... a little confusion. If this was a companion dog, why would it need to be intact?" She shrugged. "In the end, I found a poodle that matched her description quite quickly, so I did not think on it too much."

"Then what?"

"I called Juliet; she paid me far more than the couple was asking and requested I be discreet. Then I shipped the dog to the UK with an animal transporter she sent to Munich."

"And you didn't think anything else about it," John said. "Until you got to the US."

Marc said, "We received the invitation directly from Bunny Barker. She said she had heard about Lulu from Juliet and Edgar. We didn't question it. We were surprised she was so generous—"

"She paid for our plane tickets," Geerta said. "We paid for our lodging."

Marc nodded. "We assumed she wanted someone from the German show community and the Lomaxes had recommended us. Now are you saying the judging was manipulated?"

"No one cheated," John said. "Not exactly. It seems like Bunny wanted to... reward her friends."

"We did not know Bunny before this," Marc said. "We only know the Lomaxes."

"But... I think the poodle she was calling Baron was the dog I found for her," Geerta said quietly. "As soon as I saw him, I suspected. He was groomed differently, but I believe it was the same dog."

Evy said, "You'd be correct. Her handler already confessed that the original Baron died three months ago."

"And the dog that went missing? Has he been found?"

"He has, and he's perfectly healthy," John said. "He's staying with Stewart Barker and Bunny's handler Curtis."

Geerta said something in German that sounded relieved.

"I am so confused by all this," Marc said. "Are you saying that Bunny was doing us a kind of favor? Lulu is a champion dog; she does not need any favors or any cheating."

"We're not sure what her motive was," Evy said. "But she was losing control of the show. She might have been simply trying to do something good for everyone who'd done her favors."

"Or maybe," Geerta said, "she was trying to make us part of her plan. If we had success here, then said something about her dog, people would not see us as... impartial."

Marc looked disturbed by the idea and said something quietly in German.

Geerta said, "Bunny should not have been calling the dog Baron. If I knew she was going to do that, I would not have done Juliet this favor. And we would not have anything to do with this kennel club show."

John turned to Evy. "I think we need a meeting with Juliet Lomax. It seems like she has some explaining to do."

EVY WAS EATING A SANDWICH IN THE POLICE department break room when John walked in, looking stormy. "What's up?"

"US Customs is giving me the runaround. Then sent me to the USDA, who sent me to the CDC. And no one is answering my calls or emails. If Juliet Lomax shipped a dog to the United States three months ago, there has to be a record of it no matter how sneaky she was. You just don't bring a dog in without papers. But they're saying it's going to take days to process the request."

Her eyebrows went up. "Can you keep them that long?"

"I don't know. Plus, as of right now, all Juliet Lomax did was get a dog for a friend. We can't prove she had anything to do with the fraud."

"If she's the kind of friend Bunny trusted to get her a replacement for Baron, Bunny probably told her about the insurance scam. After all, Juliet knew Baron wasn't Baron, and she was likely the only person Bunny could trust that had the kind of connections to fence a Cartier necklace."

John sank into a seat across from Evy. "But how does any of that explain Bunny or Shawn Dumas's attacks? Juliet Lomax doesn't seem capable of that kind of physical attack. She's what? Seventy-something?"

"She could have hired someone," Evy said. "Maybe she and Bunny had a falling out over the necklace? Maybe she got angry and snapped."

"It's possible." John rubbed his jaw. His mouth said "possible," but his face said "not likely." "What are you going to do this afternoon?"

"Head home. Even if you have more questions for the Webers, I'm completely useless. They think in German."

"Yeah, I hadn't thought about that."

Evy's phone buzzed. She glanced down and saw Rafe had messaged her. "Maybe I'll hang out with Rafe."

"He still on the necklace?"

"That's his job. He's been poking around in Curtis's history, but so far he says the kid looks to be only interested in the dog. The necklace is still smoke."

"I don't think Stewart Barker is wrong. I think all this circles back to money. So if you and Rafe find that necklace, then we probably find the murderer. Well, *murderers*."

Two murderers, two different motives.

Something was tickling the back of Evy's brain. Something about this wasn't fitting together. At the end of the day, she still couldn't figure out why anyone would want to kill Bunny. Nothing in the insurance fraud worked unless Bunny was there to collect the money.

So why had all this happened?

John was staring out the window. "This is the weirdest fucking chain of events I've ever seen on a murder case."

It was a chain. Evy blinked. "Of course."

She stood up and tossed the rest of her sandwich in the trash. "I'll see you later. Let me know if customs gets back to you."

"Where are you going?"

She turned and the door and looked at him. "I have an idea."

John raised his eyebrows. "I'm paying you to consult, so consult, Landa."

"This idea requires... less of a cop and maybe just a little bit of a criminal."

He closed his eyes. "I don't want to know."

"No, you don't." She turned and walked out the door.

John yelled after her, "Say hi to Rafe."

THE FRONT ROOM OF THE LOMAXES' RENTAL WAS DIM, the lights lowered to keep Juliet Lomax comfortable. She sat on a couch in a loose, kaftan-like dress, her hair piled on top of her head in a tower of silver-threaded braids while her tiny miniature schnauzer, Jade, sat on her lap. The dog sat at attention, watching Rafe and Evy, who had been shown to two wingback chairs across from Juliet in the formal living room.

"Mrs. Lomax," Rafe began, "Curtis Weathers has confessed to us that the dog my employer insured, Baron, did die of natural causes three months ago. But since no payout happened from the insurance company, we are comfortable leaving the matter of a fraudulent claim alone so it won't affect Mrs. Barker's estate."

Juliet lifted her chin. "And what does this have to do with me?"

Rafe's smile was kind. "You know exactly what, Mrs. Lomax. You were the party who obtained a replacement dog for Mrs. Barker. You participated in the fraud."

"I don't know why you think that."

"Because three months ago, you entered the United States with a dog." He looked at the tiny schnauzer on Juliet's lap. "A dog that necessitated a large crate on an international flight. Surely you know those records can be easily obtained. It will take a few days for the police to get official confirmation from US Customs, but I had copies of the customs entry forms emailed to me this morning from our office in Flagstaff."

Juliet's mouth twitched. "And? My friend lost her dog and wanted another. I helped her find an appropriate replacement. Is that illegal?"

"No, but helping to pass that dog off as another animal is," Rafe said. "You went along with the charade, Mrs. Lomax."

"Bunny was a friend," Juliet said. "I am loyal to my friends. And as you said, the insurance never paid her for either the dog or the necklace, so I don't see why you are here, Mr. Bamford-Howell."

"Where is the necklace now?" Evy asked. "I suspect you took it from Chip Dunklin after you killed him, but I don't know what you were planning to do with it."

Juliet froze. "You're mad."

...found out what will they do God Edgar never going to find any proof the necklace turned in there won't be any reason for them to suspect...

Evy kept her eyes fixed on Juliet. "So you were planning to turn the necklace in? That's good."

"All I'm interested in is the return of the Cartier," Rafe said. "If it's turned in anonymously, I won't ask any questions."

The little dog on Juliet's lap stood and started barking at them.

"Juliet?" Kenzie walked in from the kitchen. "What's wrong? Do these people need to leave?"

She turned and handed the dog to Kenzie. "It's fine, dear. Could you get me a cup of tea please?"

"Of course." Kenzie looked at Evy and Rafe. "Why are the police here?"

"They're not the police; they work for the insurance company."

Kenzie pointed at Evy. "She works with the police. She was at the police station in the interview with Edgar and me."

Juliet turned and narrowed her eyes. "I'd like you to leave now."

"That's fine." Rafe said. "Please do remember what I've said, Mrs. Lomax. I am not the police, and I really am only interested in the necklace."

Her negative expression didn't change.

Rafe looked at Kenzie. "Before we leave, can I use your facilities?"

"I..." Kenzie seemed confused at first, but just like Evy, she fell for Rafe's accented charm. "Okay, sure."

Juliet looked like she wanted to object, but she kept her eyes on Evy. "Rafe, tell your mother I said hello."

"I will, Juliet."

Rafe wandered off down the hallway, leaving Evy in the living room with Juliet Lomax.

"I know you killed Chip," Evy said quietly. "You don't have to say anything. I'm a telepath, and I can read your mind."

Juliet's expression turned from irritated to amused. "Is that so?"

"Yep."

...ridiculous California nonsense cannot believe the police would give her a mote of attention wonder what Rafe wants looking at the house they won't find the necklace hope it's cool enough in London a coat in summer won't even glance at the stitching...

Evy took out her phone and texted Rafe: *It's in Juliet's coat. Check the seams.*

He sent her back a thumbs-up emoji.

"I'm really sorry about this." Evy tucked her phone away. "It took me a while to put it together because I couldn't figure out why Chip would want to kill Bunny. After all, he was only after her for the money and if she wasn't alive, how could he collect the money?"

Juliet looked at her and said nothing.

"Then I realized this wasn't a web of conspiracy. Not like you and Bunny replacing Baron." Evy laughed a little. "I mean, that was good. That was *organized*. No one would have ever known, and even if Geerta Weber guessed after she saw Baron II, she would have kept her mouth shut to everyone else because Bunny paying for her plane tickets and stuff to come here would have made it look like she was in on it. Did you suggest that part?"

Juliet smiled. "You're a ridiculous woman, and I have nothing to say to you."

"Okay, that's fine." How long was Rafe going to take? Dammit, she wished they could get a proper search warrant because this was nerve-racking. "It was just that when I realized this wasn't an organized conspiracy, it finally made sense." She looked at Juliet. "I mean, I'm not really the organized type, I'm more of the 'stumbling through life, putting out fires as they happen' type."

The Englishwoman pressed her fingers to her temple, but she said nothing.

"But that's when I realized how it happened," Evy said. "It *wasn't* planned. None of it was planned after Chip discovered the fraud. He busted into your neatly planned minor conspiracy, and then boom." Evy clapped her hands and Juliet flinched. "Chip figured it out. He realized who Baron was and proceeded to black-mail you and Bunny, forcing Bunny to file the claim for the neck-lace. Then Chip found Shawn Dumas on the property—probably thought he was snooping for Stewart—beat him up, and left him for dead. Did he tell Bunny? Maybe not. But not even that went to plan, because I came over and heard Dumas in the garden. He wasn't dead!"

Juliet was frozen.

"What happened then? See, I know Bunny wasn't a bad person. In fact, I think she was probably a really good person. I suspect that once she knew that Chip had put a man in the hospi-tal, she was ready to give all of it up and go to the police. Maybe you didn't agree. Maybe you didn't even know about it, but she made the mistake of telling Chip, didn't she?"

She heard Rafe coming back down the hall.

Juliet was starting to suspect that Evy was the real thing. At least that's what Evy assumed since the woman was humming Beatles lyrics in her head.

"That's why Chip killed Bunny, right?" Evy's voice got softer. "She wanted to go to the police, and he couldn't have that. He lost it, killed your friend, and stole the necklace."

Rafe sauntered out, and his usually genial expression was gone. He held up a glistening band of diamonds, onyx, and platinum. "Juliet, I'm sorry."

"You took it back though." Evy took a deep breath. "You took the necklace back from Chip when you killed him."

Chapter Twenty-Eight

Two days later, Evy sat across from Juliet Lomax in the interview room of the Palm Springs police department. Juliet's lawyer was next to her with a serious-looking briefcase on the table, but John Marcos had a fat file in front of him, and on top of that file was a picture of the Cartier necklace that Rafe Bamford-Howell had found sewn into Juliet Lomax's trench coat.

"Mrs. Lomax, I understand your lawyer has told you not to talk to us, but I just want you to know that we're searching your house thoroughly right now. There *will* be evidence tying you to Chip Dunklin's killing. There will be hair, fibers, the poison you used. There will be something."

"As I have advised my client not to speak," the lawyer started, "you may direct any questions you have toward me. My client maintains that Mr. Bamford-Howell planted the Cartier necklace at her home and she had no involvement with the theft from Mrs. Barker, whatever conspiracy Chip Dunklin or Bunny Barker might have been involved in, and no motive to kill anyone. You have no case against her. My client is an exemplary and respected citizen of the United Kingdom with no criminal record, and she will be going home soon."

Evy glanced between Juliet and her lawyer, knowing that the woman wanted to talk, wanted to explain herself. She also knew Juliet was too smart to give the police a single word.

Can you really hear me?

Evy cocked her head and her eyes turned to Juliet. She gave her a slight nod.

Then I will tell you because I know for a fact that nothing you say is admissible in court. That police chief next to you may believe. I may believe. But nothing you say is evidence. No judge would ever allow it.

Evy offered her a slight shrug.

Why tell you? Because I want you to know. Juliet's internal voice was acid. *I want you to know that I was the one to poison that little worm. I watched him die, and I smiled. It was painful, and he deserved it. He was a horrible, vile creature who killed Bunny, then played innocent to everyone with his crocodile tears.*

John Marcos was still speaking. "We have connected the evidence at Bunny Barker's crime scene with Chip Dunklin. We know he killed her, but we don't know why. Does your client have any insight to that?"

"My client has no statement to make at this time," the lawyer said.

John flipped open another file. "Evidence also connects Mr. Dunklin to the violent assault on Shawn Dumas, an employee of Stewart Barker's, who was found behind Bunny's house. We are still conducting inquiries into how Shawn Dumas died, but preliminary results indicate that it might not have only been the result of his injuries."

Evy moved her hands to the table and tapped one finger.

The first death?

Evy nodded.

Chip had come to Bunny. He didn't know that I knew about

257

Baron, but he told Bunny that unless she filed an insurance claim on the Cartier, he'd tell everyone in the club and the dog-show world. She would be ruined. Stewart and all his dogs would be ruined. No one would trust their breeding lines again.

Evy sighed and nodded a little.

I don't know if the Dumas man overheard something or if Chip ran into him while he was sneaking around, but he beat him. He told Bunny the man was dead and if she didn't do what he wanted, he'd do the same to her.

"Mr. Winthrop, we know your client and Mrs. Barker were close friends. If she has any information about Bunny's death—"

"As I've said before" —the lawyer stopped him— "we have no statement at this time, and my client is exercising her right to remain silent."

Evy tapped her second finger on the table.

Bunny was horrified. She called me and told me what had happened. I told her to go to the police. I told her not to even talk to Chip or reason with him. He had already beaten a man nearly to death. She could not risk it.

Evy shook her head.

Obviously she didn't listen. I suspect she tried to appeal to a sense of decency he didn't have. She was always too trusting. He assaulted her, an elderly woman, only this time he didn't take any chances. He bragged to me that he smothered my friend with a pillow.

John Marcos pretended he didn't notice that Evy and Juliet were communicating as he stalled the lawyer. "Mr. Winthrop, your client understands that while this investigation is ongoing, she will be required to surrender her passport?"

"She understands that you're going to make that request of a judge, and we are prepared to challenge it. My client had nothing to do with the death of Bunny Barker, Shawn Dumas, or Chip Dunklin. And again, she has no criminal record or history of violence."

Juliet stared at Evy, telepathically admitting to everything. *Chip told me that he knew Bunny had told me about the necklace. He wanted me to sell it for him. Can you believe his gall?*

That was pretty ballsy. Evy shook her head.

Juliet continued. *He told me I could get a better price for it than he could, and if I didn't go along with it—or if I went to the police— he'd expose Bunny's and my charade about Baron; he'd hurt my family, my dogs, and me. He told me he'd killed the man in the coma so no one could testify against him. He claimed that there was no evidence.*

Evy shook her head. There was plenty of evidence, but Juliet had no way of knowing that.

I didn't know if what he was saying was true, so I played along —that's why we met at his house after the reception at the country club. I brought the poison with me and dosed his whiskey glass.

Evy stared at Juliet's unrepentant expression.

He deserved to die.

"I can't argue with you," Evy said softly. The Chip she had known had only been a facade.

"What's that?" the lawyer asked.

"Nothing." She patted John's leg. "We clearly aren't going to be able to argue with him," she said. "I don't think there's anything you're going to learn from Mrs. Lomax today."

John nodded. "Fine." He turned to Juliet and her lawyer. "We'll see you in court about surrendering your passport."

The lawyer picked up his briefcase. "And Mrs. Lomax will look forward to returning home. Good day."

Evy and John watched them walk out of the interview room. Then John stood, gathered his files, and walked out. Evy followed him into his office, where he sank into his desk chair. She sat down on the other side of his desk.

John drummed his fingers on his desk. "She confessed everything to you, didn't she?"

"Yep."

"And she knows we can't use a single word."

"Yep."

"Dammit." He let out a frustrated breath. "She did it. She killed Chip Dunklin. And other than the necklace we found at her house, we have no evidence. I was bluffing. There were no fibers or hairs at Chip's murder scene."

"She wore opera gloves to the reception that night," Evy said. "It was black tie. Her hair was in a beautiful wrap."

"And Rafe isn't exactly the best witness," John said. "Her lawyer's right. A judge could easily doubt the word of an insurance investigator, plus she and Bunny were friends! She could claim that Bunny gave it to her to hold or something. It's iffy at best."

Evy stayed quiet for a moment, letting John stew in his anger and frustration. She knew he had an innate sense of justice that wouldn't allow him to see things the way she did, but she still tried to explain.

"John, she killed a two-time murderer," Evy said softly. "She killed the man who killed one of her best friends. And the man who killed Coma Guy in the hospital."

His eyebrows went up. "She told you that?"

"Chip told her that he did it. He said that if she didn't fence the necklace for him or if she went to the police, he'd hurt her family and her dogs." Evy crossed her hands in her lap. "I'm not saying she was right—"

"If she'd come to us, we could have arrested him. He wouldn't have been a threat to her or her family if he was under arrest."

"I know." Evy nodded. "I know. But do you really think she's a danger to anyone else?"

"She was a danger to Chip Dunklin."

"Who killed two people," Evy said. "Who blackmailed and assaulted people. Whatever Chip we thought we saw? He was someone else."

John stared out the window to where Juliet's lawyer was helping her into a black luxury car. "She's going to get away with it."

"Yeah." Evy nodded. "She probably is."

But Evy was having a hard time feeling bad about it.

S<small>HE AND</small> R<small>AFE WERE LYING IN BED.</small> "I <small>KNOW IT WASN'T</small> right, but—"

"Fuck that," Rafe said. "The woman is how old? She didn't go on a random killing spree, darling. She poisoned a murderer who beat two people to death and was blackmailing her." Rafe slapped his hands together in a brushing motion. "Good riddance to Chip Dunklin."

"You're just saying that because you got the necklace back."

"No..." He pursed his lips. "Partly. But only because now I am assured she's not going to profit from this. Juliet Lomax avenged a friend, and I can't find fault with it."

"I guess I can't either. I tried to imagine what I would do if someone killed Julia or Vivian..." Evy shuddered. "I might burn down the world."

"See?" He closed his eyes and pulled her closer. "I'm Team Juliet for this one." He peeked one eye open. "I do wonder what she would have done with the necklace if I hadn't found it."

"Probably have it returned anonymously or something. I don't think she wanted anything to do with it."

"I don't know—she had it sewn into that coat seam fairly securely." He ran a hand up and down Evy's bare back.

"It was Bunny's. Maybe she just wanted it to remember her friend."

"Or maybe the lure of the diamonds was too much."

"Either way." Evy shifted and laid her head on his bare chest. "Your job is done. Necklace recovered. Baron the poodle put to rest. Your mom left two days ago. How long are you sticking around?"

He sighed. "I probably shouldn't leave Harvey with my neighbors much longer or they'll never agree to watch him again. It's been two weeks."

"Poor Harvey."

He played with a strand of her hair, running it through his fingers and tickling her nose with the end. "Have you ever considered visiting Flagstaff, Miss Landa? It's only an hour's flight."

She focused her mental ears, but all she heard was:

Please please please please please please please.

She couldn't stop the laugh. "I hear the weather in Flagstaff is really nice in the summer."

Rafe nodded with enthusiasm. "Much cooler than here. Beautiful deserts, cool nights, glorious stars."

She smiled. "I might have to come check it out."

"Really?"

"But I don't like the cold." She stretched her arms over her head, and Rafe took the opportunity to run a hand over her naked belly. "You might have to come back to Palm Springs in the winter."

"I am very..." He put his mouth on one breast. "Mmm, yum. *Very* open to that idea."

"Good." She ran her hands through his hair as he tasted every inch of her bare torso. "You're not leaving right away though, right?"

"Oh no. I believe I have one or two... loose ends to tie up."

"Tie up?"

"Leashes, harnesses..." He scooted up and slapped her bare bottom. "I told you dog-show people are strange."

Evy laughed, and Rafe lifted her thigh, hiking it over his hips as he moved closer. She could feel his erection pressed against her and the electric heat of the friction between them.

It was delicious, ecstatic, and real. While she could sense Rafe's thoughts flutter against her mind like butterflies in the wind, her telepathy took a back seat to the intimate skin-to-skin contact and the overload of physical sensation.

She didn't hear; she felt. She didn't listen; she touched. Being with Rafe was pure pleasure compounded by the fact that he knew exactly what Evy could do and he wasn't afraid. He had nothing to hide.

Evy didn't need to read his mind to know that Rafe was with her, moving in sync, focused on her, exactly in the moment and nowhere else. It wasn't pure mental silence; it was much, much better.

Chapter Twenty-Nine

Evy adjusted her sunglasses as she, Vivian, and Julia watched the sunset from the backyard of Casa de Lirio. Sergio, Dean, Richard, and Mick were in the kitchen finishing dinner. Butch the standard poodle was romping in the backyard, bouncing from one palm tree to the other, his head darting around as Henry giggled madly from his exercise saucer on the edge of the patio.

Every few minutes Butch would bounce over, give Henry a sniff, then bounce away. And every time it made Henry erupt in laughter.

"Do you think dogs and babies can see ghosts?" Evy asked.

Julia said, "They appear to. At least the dog does."

Vivian turned. "Really? Interesting. Butch should be very happy here then. Lots of ghosts for his entertainment."

"I can't believe you convinced Richard to adopt a show poodle," Julia said. "Is he going to keep taking him to dog shows? Is he going to breed him?"

Evy smiled. "Is Richard going to turn into a dog-show person?"

Julia laughed. "I can't imagine it."

"No to *all* that." Vivian waved a hand. "Even if he wanted to show him, I don't think he could. His paperwork is a mess. He just liked the dog so much from when we thought it was Baron, he asked Stewart if he could buy it from him." She smiled as Henry erupted in giggles again. "He knows Henry loves him. Maddie does too."

"Awww!" Julia grinned. "Richard is such a good dad."

Vivian gave her side-eye but didn't say anything.

"Personally, I'm just relieved Butch has a good home," Evy said. "He and Henry and the ghosts seem to be the best of friends."

"Speaking of other types of grown-up friends." Julia wiggled her eyebrows. "Rafe is back in Flagstaff now. Any plans to go visit?"

"He's going to see what weekends he has free when he gets back in the office on Monday," Evy said. "Did you know it's only an hour to fly up there? Six hours driving, but only an hour to fly."

Vivian smiled as she kept her eyes on Henry. "I like him for you."

"I don't," Julia said. "I mean, don't get me wrong, Rafe is very nice and very cute, but I still think you and John have the most amazing chemistry."

"We would fight constantly," Evy said. "Drop it, Julia."

"Fine." Then she whispered, "*Maybe*. I'll think about it."

Vivian shook her head. "Well, I think you and Rafe are great. Hot-and-cold relationships are overrated. Maybe he's not the love of your life. Maybe he is. Anything's possible."

"He's not." Evy turned to Vivian and Julia. "You two are."

"Don't make me cry, Landa." Julia bit her lip. "I love you too."

"You're going to make me cry." Vivian cleared her throat. "Of course, everything makes me cry lately because I still have *so* many hormones."

"Seriously," Evy said. "I was listening to Juliet Lomax detail how she got revenge on the man who killed her friend and part of me was horrified. And the other part of me was just thinking...

yeah." She nodded. "If someone ever hurt one of you like that? I would probably poison them, put them in the trunk of my giant car, and dump their bodies in the desert to get eaten by coyotes."

Julia lifted her sunglasses. "That's a... fairly detailed scenario."

"Remember when you and Mick were fighting last year?"

"Please don't murder my boyfriend," Julia said.

Evy lifted her Paloma and toasted Julia. "As long as he keeps making you happy, he's safe."

"Joking aside," Vivian said, "if there's one thing we've discovered about murder, it's that things always fall apart in the end. Zero out of ten. Do not recommend."

"That said," Julia added, "I understand Juliet Lomax, and I'm kind of feeling the way Evy is. I can't hate her."

Vivian kept her eyes trained on her infant son, who was still laughing at the ridiculous dog that seemed to be performing for an audience of one. "I think when it comes to the people we love" — she turned to glance at Evy and Julia— "none of us knows quite how far we'd go."

None of them said anything for a while after that. They listened to the fountain and Henry's laughter. They watched the sun set over the mountains and smelled the scent of lemon blossoms from the tree near the kitchen door. Male laughter drifted through the windows, and the distant scent of grilled meat touched the air.

The evening was cool and the desert sky over Vista de Lirio shifted to a brilliant array of pink, gold, and blue as the sun sank lower behind the mountains.

Evy reached over and touched the edge of her cocktail glass to Julia's wineglass and Vivian's iced seltzer. "We're lucky to have each other. When I think about who I want around when my wrinkled old ass gets into trouble, it's you two."

Julia blew her a kiss and smiled. "Don't get maudlin, Landa. Your ass is pretty big; it's going to be a lot of years before it wrinkles."

Evy flipped her off as Julia laughed.

Vivian's shoulders were shaking with silent laughter. "But when your *beautifully* wrinkled ass does get into trouble, you know who you can call."

"Sergio," Evy said. "And Dean. They'll know the right lawyers."

"Us!" Julia threw a napkin at her. "Then *we'll* call Dean and Sergio."

"Or, depending on the situation, Richard," Vivian said. "Maybe Paco."

Evy shuddered. "The world's most judgmental alpaca."

"Just call your friends," Vivian said. "Whatever mess you get into, just call us and we'll be there."

"Hear, hear," Julia said.

Evy watched as the sun finally slipped below the horizon, cooler air nipped at her ears, and the wind carried to her the silent voices she loved the most.

Julia. Vivian. Henry.

Richard in the distance. Sergio and Dean. Even Julia's Mick. The air around Casa de Lirio was alive with the thoughts of friends who were really—more than anything—family.

And that was the sweetest sound of all.

The End

Thank you for visiting Vista de Lirio with me!
For more paranormal women's fiction, please visit the Glimmer Lake series or Moonstone Cove. For even more books from Elizabeth Hunter, please visit ElizabethHunterWrites.com.

Looking for more?

Whether you're a fan of contemporary fantasy, fantasy romance, or paranormal women's fiction, Elizabeth Hunter has a series for you!

The Elemental Mysteries

Discover the series that has millions of vampire fans raving! Immortal book dealer Giovanni Vecchio thought he'd left the bloody world of vampire politics behind when he retired as an assassin, but a chance meeting at a university pulls student librarian Beatrice De Novo into his orbit. Now temptation lurks behind every dark corner as Vecchio's growing attachment to Beatrice competes with a series of clues that could lead to a library lost in time, and a powerful secret that could reshape the immortal world.

Ebook/Audiobook/Paperback

The Cambio Springs Mysteries

Welcome to the desert town of Cambio Springs where the

water is cool, the summers sizzle, and all the residents wear fur, feathers, or snakeskin on full moon nights. In a world of cookie-cutter shifter romance, discover a series that has reviewers raving. Five friends find themselves at a crossroads in life; will the tangled ties of community and shared secrets be their salvation or their end?

Ebook/Audiobook/Paperback

THE IRIN CHRONICLES

"A brilliant and addictive romantic fantasy series." Hidden at the crossroads of the world, an ancient race battles to protect humanity, even as it dies from within. A photojournalist tumbles into a world of supernatural guardians protecting humanity from the predatory sons of fallen angels, but will Ava and Malachi's attraction to each other be their salvation or their undoing?

Ebook/Audiobook/Paperback

GLIMMER LAKE

Delightfully different paranormal women's fiction! Robin, Val, and Monica were average forty-something moms when a sudden accident leaves all three of them with psychic abilities they never could have predicted! Now all three are seeing things that belong in a fantasy novel, not their small mountain town. Ghosts, visions, omens of doom. These friends need to stick together if they're going to solve the mystery at the heart of Glimmer Lake.

Ebook/Audiobook/Paperback

And there's more! Please visit ElizabethHunterWrites.com to sign up for her newsletter or read more about her work.

Acknowledgments

As I'm writing this, I'm in my office at my house in Addis Ababa while my husband is resting from another day of wrestling me through Addis traffic so I could see an art exhibit on the other side of the city, my sister-in-law just made us a late lunch, and my brother-in-law is working on the water boiler.

Back in California, my sister is getting the email I sent her with the files she needs to use for graphics, my editor just confirmed my time slot for editing the next Ben and Tenzin book, my proofreader just sent me the final files of this book, my narrator is coordinating with my audio proofer for the audiobook of Martyr's Promise, and my public relations agent is sending out advance copies of Trouble Play.

Needless to say, there are so many people who make my work possible, and that goes double when you live in two places. So once again, I'd like to thank the incredible professionals who make all my books happen on a semi-regular basis:

Genevieve Johnson, assister extraordinaire and graphic design pro
Amy Cissell, content editor and cocktail connoisseur
Anne Victory, line editor and hunter of feral commas
Linda, she of the eagle eyes
The entire cast and crew of **Valentine PR** for all their dedicated work

And of course, my family here and in the USA for all the love, support, understanding, and coffee. A lot of thanks for the coffee.

As a creative person, we are inspired by many things. I want to offer a special nod to Christopher Guest for writing one of the finest and most hilarious movies in the entire world, BEST IN SHOW. If you felt like parts of TROUBLE PLAY were an homage to that cinematic work of genius, you would be correct. I'd also like to offer an enthusiastic ESPN Ocho shout-out to the makers of DODGEBALL: A TRUE UNDERDOG STORY and a tip of the feathered cap to the unique filmmakers behind the 2016 work of brilliance, CHICKEN PEOPLE.

Vision, you have it.

Take care, everyone. And don't forget to pet your dog.

About the Author

ELIZABETH HUNTER is a ten-time *USA Today* and international best-selling author of romance, contemporary fantasy, and paranormal mystery. Based in Central California and Addis Ababa, she travels extensively to write fantasy fiction exploring world mythologies, history, and the universal bonds of love, friendship, and family. She has published over forty works of fiction and sold over a million books worldwide. She is the author of the Glimmer Lake series, Love Stories on 7th and Main, the Elemental Legacy series, the Irin Chronicles, the Cambio Springs Mysteries, and other works of fiction.

She is also the proud servant of Charlie, the standard poodle, Chidi, the dog of mystery, and Simba, a mutt of unusual smallness. Their work as canine assistants to the author is unparalleled in literary history. At least, according to them.

facebook.com/elizabethhunterwrites

twitter.com/ehunterwrites

instagram.com/ehunterwrites

tiktok.com/@ehunterwrites

bookbub.com/profile/elizabeth-hunter

Also by Elizabeth Hunter

Vista de Lirio

Double Vision

Mirror Obscure

Trouble Play

Glimmer Lake

Suddenly Psychic

Semi-Psychic Life

Psychic Dreams

Moonstone Cove

Runaway Fate

Fate Actually

Fate Interrupted

The Cambio Springs Series

Long Ride Home

Shifting Dreams

Five Mornings

Desert Bound

Waking Hearts

The Elemental Mysteries

A Hidden Fire

This Same Earth

The Force of Wind

A Fall of Water

The Stars Afire

The Elemental World

Building From Ashes

Waterlocked

Blood and Sand

The Bronze Blade

The Scarlet Deep

A Very Proper Monster

A Stone-Kissed Sea

Valley of the Shadow

The Elemental Legacy

Shadows and Gold

Imitation and Alchemy

Omens and Artifacts

Obsidian's Edge (anthology)

Midnight Labyrinth

Blood Apprentice

The Devil and the Dancer

Night's Reckoning

Dawn Caravan

The Bone Scroll

Pearl Sky

The Elemental Covenant

Saint's Passage

Martyr's Promise

Paladin's Kiss

Bishop's Flight

(Summer 2023)

The Irin Chronicles

The Scribe

The Singer

The Secret

The Staff and the Blade

The Silent

The Storm

The Seeker

Linx & Bogie Mysteries

A Ghost in the Glamour

A Bogie in the Boat

Contemporary Romance

The Genius and the Muse

7th and Main

Ink

Hooked

Grit

Sweet

Made in United States
North Haven, CT
18 October 2022

25565777R00157